little black dress
· IT'S A GIRL THING ·

Dear Little Black Dress Reader,

Thanks for picking up this Little Black Dress book, one of the great new titles from our series of fun, page-turning romance novels. Lucky you — you're about to have a fantastic romantic read that we know you won't be able to put down!

Why don't you make your Little Black Dress experience even better by logging on to

www.littleblackdressbooks.com

where you can:

- ♥ Enter our **monthly competitions** to win **gorgeous** prizes
- ♥ Get **hot-off-the-press** news about our latest titles
- ♥ Read **exclusive** preview chapters both from your **favourite** authors and from brilliant new writing talent
- ♥ Buy **up-and-coming** books online
- ♥ Sign up for an essential slice of romance via our **fortnightly email** newsletter

We love nothing more than to curl up and indulge in an addictive romance, and so we're delighted to welcome you into the Little Black Dress club!

With love from,

The *little black dress* team

Five interesting things about Rachel Gibson:

1. Growing up, I didn't like to read. I liked to play tetherball and wanted to be a tetherball champion.

2. I have a deadly fear of grasshoppers.

3. I am a shoe-aholic. I think ugly shoes are an abomination of biblical proportion.

4. I love to read the tabloids. Especially the ones featuring stories such as Bat Boy and women having Big Foot's baby.

5. I write romance novels, but I hate overly sentimental movies and sappy love songs.

By Rachel Gibson

Daisy's Back in Town
Sex, Lies and Online Dating
I'm in No Mood for Love
The Trouble with Valentine's Day
Simply Irresistible
Tangled Up in You
It Must Be Love
True Confessions
Lola Carlyle Reveals All
Not Another Bad Date
Truly Madly Yours
See Jane Score

See Jane Score

Rachel Gibson

little
black
dress

First published in 2003 by
AVON BOOKS
An imprint of HARPERCOLLINS PUBLISHERS, USA

First published in Great Britain in 2009
by LITTLE BLACK DRESS
An imprint of HEADLINE PUBLISHING GROUP

A LITTLE BLACK DRESS paperback

1

ISBN 978 0 7553 4634 9

Typeset in Transit511BT by Avon DataSet Ltd,
Bidford-on-Avon, Warwickshire

Printed and bound in Great Britain by
Clays Ltd, St Ives plc

Headline's policy is to use papers that are natural, renewable and
recyclable products and made from wood grown in sustainable forests.
The logging and manufacturing processes are expected to conform to the
environmental regulations of the country of origin.

HEADLINE PUBLISHING GROUP
An Hachette UK Company
338 Euston Road
London NW1 3BH

www.littleblackdressbooks.com
www.headline.co.uk
www.hachettelivre.co.uk

With much gratitude
to the men and women
who play the coolest game on ice.
And, of course, to the Messiah.

Prologue

The Life of Honey Pie

Of all the smoky bars in Seattle, he had to walk into the Loose Screw, the dive where I worked five nights a week pulling beer and choking on secondhand smoke. A careless lock of black hair fell across his forehead as he tossed a pack of Camels and a Zippo onto the bar.

'Give me a Henry's,' he said, his voice as rough as velveteen, 'and put a hustle on it, babe. I don't have all day.'

I've always been a sucker for dark men with bad attitudes. One look and I knew this man was as dark and as bad as a thunderstorm. 'Bottle or draft?' I asked.

He lit a cigarette and looked at me through a cloud of smoke. His heavenly blue eyes were packed with sin as his gaze lowered to the front of my tank top. One corner of his mouth kicked up in appreciation of my thirty-four D's. 'Bottle,' he answered.

I grabbed a Henry's from the cooler, popped the cap, and slid it across the bar. 'Three-fifty.'

He grasped the bottle in one big hand and raised it to his lips, those eyes watching me as he took several long pulls. Foam rose to the top when he lowered it, and he licked a drop of beer from his bottom lip. I felt it in the backs of my knees.

'What's your name?' he asked and reached into the back pocket of his worn Levi's to pull out his wallet.

'Honey,' I answered. 'Honey Pie.'

The other corner of his full mouth lifted as he handed me a five. 'Are you a stripper?'

I get that a lot. 'That depends.'

'On what?'

I handed him his change and let the tips of my fingers brush his warm palm. A shiver tickled the pulse at my wrist and I smiled. I let my eyes wander up his big arms and chest to his wide shoulders. Anyone who knew me knew I had very few rules when it came to men. I liked them big and bad, and they had to have clean teeth and hands. That was about it. Oh, yeah, I preferred a dirty little mind, although it wasn't absolutely necessary, since my mind has always been dirty enough for two. Even as a kid, my mind had revolved around sex. While other girls' Barbies played school, my Barbie played doctor. The kind where Dr. Barbie checked out Ken's package, then humped him into a sweaty coma.

Now, at the age of twenty-eight, while other women took up golf or ceramics, men were my hobby and I collected them like cheap Elvis memorabilia. As I looked into the sexy blue eyes of Mr. Bad Attitude, I checked my rapid pulse and the *ache between my thighs and figured I just might collect him too. I just might take him home. Or in the back of my car, or a stall in the ladies' bathroom.*

'On what you have in mind,' I finally answered, then folded my arms on the bar and leaned forward, giving him a nice view of my perfect breasts.

He lifted his gaze from my cleavage, his eyes hot and hungry. Then he flipped open his wallet and showed me his badge. 'I'm looking for Eddie Cordova. I hear you know him.'

Just my luck. A cop. 'Yeah, I know Eddie.' I'd dated him once, if you could call what we did dating. The last time I'd seen Eddie, he'd been comatose in the bathroom at Jimmy Woo's. I'd had to step on his wrist to get him to let go of my ankle.

'Do you know where I can find him?'

Eddie was a small-time thief, and worse, he'd been a lousy lay, and I didn't feel a twinge of guilt when I said, 'I might.' Yeah, I might help this guy out, and the way he was looking at me, I could tell he wanted more than

The telephone next to Jane Alcott's computer rang, pulling her attention away from the screen and out of the latest installment of *The Life of Honey Pie*.

'Damn,' she swore. She pushed her fingers beneath her glasses and scrubbed her tired eyes. From between her fingers she glanced at the caller ID and picked up.

'Jane,' the managing editor at the *Seattle Times*, Leonard Callaway, began without bothering to say hello, 'Virgil Duffy is talking to the coaches and general manager tonight. The job is officially yours.'

Virgil Duffy's corporation was a member of the Fortune 500 and he was the owner of the Seattle Chinooks hockey team. 'When do I start?' Jane asked and rose to her feet. She reached for her coffee and spilled a drop on her old flannel pajamas as she brought the cup to her lips.

'The first.'

January first gave her only two weeks to prepare. Two days ago, Jane had been approached by Leonard and asked if she was interested in covering for sports-beat reporter Chris Evans while he underwent treatment for non-Hodgkin's lymphoma. The prognosis for Chris was good, but his leave of absence left the paper in need of someone to cover the Seattle Chinooks hockey team. Jane never dreamed that someone would be her.

Among other things, she was a feature writer for the *Seattle Times* and was known for her monthly *Single Girl in the City* columns. She didn't know a thing about hockey.

'You'll hit the road with them on the second,' Leonard continued. 'Virgil wants to smooth over the details with the coaches, then he'll introduce you to the team the Monday before you leave.'

When she'd first been offered the job last week, she'd been shocked and more than a little puzzled. Surely Mr. Duffy would want another sports reporter to cover the games. But as it turned out, the offer had been the team owner's idea.

'What will the coaches think?' She set the mug on her desk, next to an open day planner with various colors of sticky notes stuck all over it.

'Doesn't really matter. Ever since John Kowalsky and

Hugh Miner retired, that arena hasn't seen a capacity crowd. Duffy needs to pay for that hotshot goalie he bought last year. Virgil loves hockey, but he's a businessman first and foremost. He'll do what it takes to get the fans in those seats. Which is why he thought of you in the first place. He wants to attract more female fans to the game.'

What Leonard Callaway didn't say was that Duffy had thought of her because he thought she wrote fluff for women. Which was okay with Jane; fluff helped pay her bills and was wildly popular with women who read the *Seattle Times*. But fluff didn't pay all the bills. Not even close. Porn payed most of them. And the porn serials, *The Life of Honey Pie*, she wrote for *Him* magazine were wildly popular with males.

As Leonard talked about Duffy and his hockey team, Jane picked up a pen and wrote on a pink sticky note: *Buy books on hockey*. She tore the note from the top of the block, flipped a page, and stuck it in her day planner beneath several other strips of paper.

'. . . and you have to remember you're dealing with hockey players. You know they can be real superstitious. If the Chinooks start losing games, you'll get blamed and sent packing.'

Great. Her job was in the hands of superstitious jocks. She tore an old note marked *Honey deadline* from the planner and tossed it in the trash.

After a few more minutes of conversation, she hung up the telephone and picked up her coffee. Like most Seattlites, she couldn't help but know the names and some of the faces of the hockey players. The season was long and hockey was mentioned on *King-5 News* most nights, but she'd actually only met one of the Chinooks, the goaltender Leonard had mentioned, Luc Martineau.

She'd been introduced to the man with the thirty-three-million-dollar contract at a Press Club party just after his trade to the Chinooks last summer. He'd stood in the middle of the room looking healthy and fit, like a king holding court. Considering Luc's legendary reputation both on and off the ice, he was shorter than Jane had imagined. About five-eleven, but he was pure muscle. His dark blond hair covered his ears and the collar of his shirt, slightly windblown and finger-combed.

He had a small white scar on his left cheekbone and another on his chin. Neither did a thing to detract from the sheer impact of him. In fact they made him appear so bad there hadn't been a woman in the room who didn't wonder just how bad the bad boy got.

Between the lapels of his subdued charcoal suit, he'd worn a silky red tie. A gold Rolex had circled his wrist, and an overblown blonde had been bonded to his side like a suction cup.

The man clearly liked to accessorize.

Jane and the goalie had exchanged hellos and a handshake. His blue eyes had hardly fallen on her before he'd moved on with the blonde. In less than a second, she'd been found lacking and dismissed. But she was used to it. Men like Luc usually didn't pay much attention to women like Jane. Barely an inch over five feet, with dark brown hair, green eyes, and an A-cup. They didn't stick around to hear if she had anything interesting to say.

If the other Chinooks dismissed her as quickly as Luc Martineau had, she was in for an aggravating few months, but traveling with the team was too good an opportunity to pass up. She would write her articles about the sport from a woman's point of view. She would report on the highlights of the game as expected, but she would pay more attention to what happened in the locker room. Not penis size or sexual hang-ups – she didn't care about that stuff. She wanted to know if women still encountered discrimination in the twenty-first century.

Jane returned to the chair in front of her laptop and got back to work on the *Honey Pie* installment that was due to her editor tomorrow and would appear in the magazine in February. While a lot of men considered her *Single Girl* column fluff and didn't admit to reading it, a lot of those same men did read and love Jane's *Honey Pie* serial. No one but Eddie Goldman, the magazine's editor, and her best friend since the third grade, Caroline Mason, knew that she wrote the lucrative monthly articles. And she wanted it to stay that way.

Honey was Jane's alter ego. Gorgeous. Uninhibited. Every man's dream. A hedonist who left men in sweaty comas throughout Seattle, wrung out and incapable of speech, yet somehow able to beg for more. Honey had a huge fan club, and there were also half a dozen fan sites on the Internet devoted to her. Some of them were sad, others funny. On one of the sites, there was speculation that the author of *Honey Pie* was actually a man.

Jane liked that rumor best. A smile touched her lips as she read the last line she'd written before Leonard had called. Then she got back to the business of making men beg.

The Shave: Rookie Initiation

The locker room was thick with trash talk as Luc 'Lucky' Martineau tucked himself into his cup and strapped on his gear. Most of his teammates stood around Daniel Holstrom, the rookie Swede, giving Daniel his choice of initiations. He could either let the guys shave his hair into a Mohawk or take the whole team out to dinner. Since rookie dinners cost between ten and twelve thousand dollars, Luc figured the young winger was going to end up looking like a punker for a while.

Daniel's wide blue eyes searched the locker room for a sign that the guys were kidding him. He found none. They'd all been rookies once, and every one of them had endured hazing of some sort. In Luc's rookie season, the laces in his skates disappeared on more than one occasion, and the sheets in his hotel room were often shorted.

Luc grabbed his stick and headed into the tunnel. He passed some of the guys working with blowtorches on the blades of their sticks. Near the front of the tunnel Coach

Larry Nystrom and General Manager Clark Gamache stood talking to a short woman dressed completely in black. Both men had their arms folded across their chests, and they scowled down at the woman as she spoke to them. Her dark hair was scraped to the back of her head and held in one of those scrunchie things like his sister wore.

Beyond mild curiosity, Luc paid her little attention and forgot her completely as he hit the ice for practice. He listened for the crisp *shhh-shhh* that he'd come to expect from spending an hour honing the edges of his skates. Through the cage of his mask, cool air brushed his cheeks and filled his lungs as he made several warm-up laps.

Like all goalies, he was a member of the team, yet set apart by the solitary nature of his job. There was no covering for men like Luc. When they let a puck in, lights flashed like a big neon fuck-up sign, and it took more than intense determination and guts to face the pipes game after game. It took a man who was competitive and arrogant enough to believe himself invincible.

The goalie coach, Don Boclair, pushed a basket of pucks onto the ice while Luc performed the same ritual he'd been performing for the past eleven years, be it game night or practice. He circled the net clockwise three times, then he skated counterclockwise once. He took his place between the pipes and whacked his goalie stick on the poles to his left and right. Then he crossed himself like a priest as he locked his gaze on Don, who was standing at the blue line, and for the next thirty minutes the coach skated around him, shooting like a sniper at all seven holes and firing from the point.

At the age of thirty-two, Luc felt good. Good about the

game, and good about his physical condition. Relatively pain-free now, he took no drugs stronger than Advil. He was having the best season of his career, and heading into the conference finals, his body was in excellent condition. His professional life couldn't be any better.

Too bad his personal life sucked.

The goalie coach fired a puck top shelf, and with a heavy *thwack*, Luc caught it in his glove. Through the thick padding, the half pound of vulcanized rubber stung his palm. He dropped to his knees on the ice as another puck flew for his five hole and slammed into his pads. He felt the familiar stitch of pain in his tendons and ligaments, but it was nothing he couldn't handle. Nothing he *wouldn't* handle, and nothing he'd ever admit to feeling out loud.

There were those who'd written him off. Put a period on his career. Two years ago while playing for the Red Wings, he'd blown out both knees. After several major reconstructive surgeries, countless hours of rehab, a stint at Betty Ford to get off pain medication, and a trade to the Seattle Chinooks, Luc was back and playing better than ever.

This season he had something to prove. To himself. To those who'd crossed him off. He'd recaptured the qualities that had always made him one of the best. Luc had an uncanny puck sense and could see a play a second before it happened, and if he couldn't stop it with his quick hands, he always had brute strength and a mean hook in reserve.

After he finished practice, Luc changed into shorts and a T-shirt and moved to the training room. He did forty-five minutes on the exercise bike before switching to the free weights. For an hour and a half, he worked his arms, chest, and abdomen. The muscles of his legs and back burned and sweat rolled down his temples as he breathed through the pain.

He took a long shower, wrapped a towel around his waist, then headed to the locker room. The rest of the guys were there, sprawled out on chairs and benches, listening to something Gamache was saying. Virgil Duffy was in the middle of the room too, and began talking about ticket sales. Luc figured ticket sales weren't his job. His concern was to make saves and win games. So far, he was doing his job.

Luc leaned one bare shoulder into the doorframe. He crossed his arms over his chest, and his gaze lowered to the short woman he'd seen earlier. She stood next to Duffy, and Luc studied her. She was one of those natural women who didn't wear a touch of makeup. The two slashes of her black brows were the only color on her pale face. Her black jacket and pants were shapeless, hiding even a hint of curves. On one shoulder hung a leather briefcase, and in her hand she held a to-go cup of Starbucks.

She wasn't ugly – just plain. Some men liked those natural kind of women. Not Luc. He liked women who wore red lipstick, smelled like powder, and shaved their legs. He liked women who made an effort to look good. This woman clearly made no effort at all.

'I'm sure you're all aware that reporter Chris Evans has taken a medical leave of absence. In his place, Jane Alcott will be covering our home games,' the owner explained. 'And traveling on the road with us for the rest of the season.'

The players sat in stunned silence. No one said a word, but Luc knew what they were thinking. The same thing he was thinking, that he'd rather get puck-shot than have a reporter, let alone a woman, traveling with the team.

The players looked at the team captain, Mark 'the Hitman' Bressler, then they turned their attention to the coaches, who also sat in stony silence. Waiting for someone to say something. To rescue them from the short, dark-haired nightmare about to be foisted on them.

'Well, I don't believe this is a good idea,' the Hitman began, but one look of Virgil Duffy's frosty gray eyes silenced the captain. No one dared speak out again.

No one but Luc Martineau. He respected Virgil. He even liked him a little. But Luc was having the best season of his life. The Chinooks had a real good shot at the Cup, and he'd be damned if he'd let some journalist ruin it for them. For him. This had disaster written all over it.

'With all due respect, Mr. Duffy, have you lost your friggin' mind?' he asked and pushed himself away from the wall. There were certain things that happened on the road that you just didn't want the rest of the country to read about over a bowl of Wheaties. Luc was more discreet than some of his teammates, but the last thing they needed was a reporter traveling with them.

And there was always the jinx factor to consider. Anything out of the norm could turn their good luck bad. And a woman traveling with them was definitely out of the norm.

'We understand you boys' concerns,' Virgil Duffy continued. 'But after a great deal of thought and the assurance of both the *Times* and Ms. Alcott, we can guarantee you all your privacy. The reporting in no way will infringe on your personal lives.'

Bullshit, Luc thought, but he didn't waste his breath arguing further. Seeing the determination on the owner's face, Luc knew it was pointless. Virgil Duffy paid the bills. But that didn't mean Luc had to like it.

'Well, you better prepare her for some real crude language,' he warned.

Ms. Alcott turned her attention to Luc. Her gaze was direct and unwavering. One corner of her mouth lifted as if she were slightly amused. 'I'm a journalist, Mr. Martineau,' she said, her voice more subtle than her gaze, a surprising mix of soft femininity and edgy determination. 'Your language won't shock me.'

He gave her a wanna-bet smile and made his way to his stall at the back of the room.

'Iz she woman who write columnz about finding date?' asked Vlad 'the Impaler' Fetisov.

'I write the *Single Girl in the City* column for the *Times*,' she answered.

'I thought that woman was Oriental,' Bruce Fish commented.

'No, just bad eyeliner,' Ms. Alcott explained.

Christ, she wasn't even a real sports reporter. Luc had read her column a few times, or at least he'd attempted to read it. She was the woman who wrote about her and her friends' trouble with men. She was one of those women who liked to talk about 'relationships and issues,' as if everything needed to be analyzed to death. As if most problems between men and women weren't the direct invention of females anyway.

'Who's she gonna room with on the road?' someone asked from the left, and laughter eased the tension somewhat. The conversation moved from Ms. Alcott to the upcoming four games in an eight-day grind.

Luc dropped his towel to the floor and dug into his duffel bag. Virgil Duffy had gone senile, Luc thought, as he tossed his white briefs and T-shirt on the bench. That or the divorce he was going through was making him crazy. This woman probably didn't know a thing about hockey. She'd probably want to talk feelings and dating troubles. Well, she could ask him questions until she turned blue and passed out, he wasn't going to answer a damn thing. After his troubles of the last few years, Luc no longer spoke to reporters. *Ever*. Having one travel with them wasn't going to change that.

He pulled his briefs up over his behind, then glanced over his shoulder at Ms. Alcott before he slipped his T-shirt over his head. He caught her staring at her shoes. Women sports reporters were nothing new in the locker room. If a woman didn't mind seeing a room full of bare-assed men, as far as he could tell they were treated pretty much as their male counterparts. But Ms. Alcott looked as uptight as an old virgin aunt. Not that he would know anything about virgins.

He finished dressing in a pair of faded Levi's and a blue ribbed sweater. Then he shoved his feet into his black boots and strapped his gold Rolex onto his wrist. The watch had been given to him as a signing gift from Virgil Duffy. A little flash to seal the deal.

Luc grabbed his leather bomber jacket and duffel bag, then made his way to the front office. He picked up the itinerary for the next eight days and spoke with the business office to make sure they remembered that he roomed alone. Last time there'd been a mix-up in Toronto, and they'd stuck Rob Sutter in his room. Usually, Luc could fall asleep within seconds of lying down, but Rob snored like a buzz saw.

It was just after noon when Luc left the building, the thud of his boot heels echoing off the concrete walls as he made his way to the exit. As he stepped outside, a gray mist touched his face and slid down the collar of his jacket. It was the kind of haze that didn't actually rain, but was gloomy as hell. The kind he had yet to get used to living in Seattle. It was one of the reasons he liked to travel out of the city, but it wasn't the biggest reason. The biggest reason was the peace he found on the road. But he had a real bad feeling that his peace was about to be shattered by the woman standing a few feet away, digging around in the briefcase hanging from her shoulder.

Ms. Alcott had wrapped herself up in some sort of slick raincoat that tied around the waist. It was long and black and the wind from the bay filled out the bottom and made her look as if she were carrying ballast in her rear end. In one hand, she still held her to-go cup of Starbucks.

'That six a.m. flight to Phoenix is a killer,' he said as he walked toward her on his way to the parking garage. 'Don't be late. It'd be a shame if you missed it.'

'I'll be there,' she assured him as he moved past her. 'You don't want me traveling with the team. Is it because I'm a woman?'

He stopped and turned to face her. A crisp breeze tugged at the lapels of her coat and blew several strands from her ponytail across her pink cheeks. On closer inspection, she really didn't improve all that much. 'No. I don't like reporters.'

'That's understandable given your history, I suppose.' She'd clearly read up on him.

'What history?' He wondered if she'd read that piece-of-shit book *The Bad Boys of Hockey*, which had devoted five chapters to him, complete with pictures. About half of what the author claimed in that book was pure gossip and absolute fabrication. And the only reason Luc hadn't sued was because he didn't want the added media attention.

'Your history with the press.' She took a drink of her coffee and shrugged. 'The ubiquitous coverage of your problems with drugs and women.'

Yep, she'd read it. And who the hell used words like *ubiquitous*? Reporters, that's who. 'For the record, I've never had problems with women. Ubiquitous or otherwise. You should know better than to believe everything you read.'

At least not anything criminal. And his addiction to painkillers was in the past. Where he intended for it to stay.

He ran his gaze from her slicked-back hair, across the flawless skin of her face, and down the rest of her wrapped up in that awful coat. Maybe if she loosened up her hair she wouldn't look like such a tight ass. 'I've read your column in the paper,' he said and glanced up into her green eyes. 'You're the single girl who bitches about commitment and can't find a man.' Her dark brows slashed lower and her gaze turned hard. 'Meeting you, I can see your problem.' He'd hit a nerve. Good. Maybe she'd stay away from him.

'Are you still clean and sober?' she asked.

He figured if he didn't answer, she'd make up something. They always did. 'Absolutely.'

'Really?' Her lowered brows rose in perfect arches as if she didn't really believe him.

He took a step closer. 'Want me to piss in your cup, sweetheart?' he asked the hard-eyed, uptight, probably-hadn't-had-sex-in-five-years woman in front of him.

'No, thanks, I take my coffee black.'

He might have taken a moment to appreciate her comeback if she wasn't a reporter and if it didn't feel as if she were being forced on him, like it or not. 'If you change your mind about that, let me know. And don't think that Duffy shoving you down the guys' throats is going to make your job easy.'

'Meaning?'

'Meaning whatever you think it means,' he said and walked away.

He walked the short distance to the parking garage and found his gray Ducati leaning on its stand next to the handicapped slot. The color of the motorcycle perfectly matched the thick clouds hanging over the city and the gloomy garage. He strapped his duffel on the back of the Duke and straddled the black seat. With the heel of his boot, he kicked up the stand and fired the twin-cylinder engine. He didn't spare Ms. Alcott another thought as he sped from the parking lot, the muffled bark of the engine trailing behind him. He made his way past Tini Bigs bar and up Broad to Second Avenue, and within a few short blocks he pulled into the common garage of his condominium complex and parked the motorcycle next to his Land Cruiser.

Luc hooked two fingers beneath the cuff of his jacket and glanced at his watch. Grabbing his duffel, he figured he had three more hours of quiet. He thought he might put in a game tape and relax in front of his big-screen television. Maybe call a friend and have her over for lunch. A certain leggy redhead came to mind.

Luc stepped out of the elevator onto the nineteenth floor and moved down the hall to the northeast corner condo. He'd bought it shortly after his trade to the Chinooks last summer. He wasn't crazy about the interior – which reminded him of the old cartoon *The Jetsons* with its chrome and stone and rounded corners – but the view . . . the view kicked ass.

He opened the door, and his plans for the day collapsed as he tripped over a blue North Face backpack thrown on the beige carpet. A red snowboard coat was tossed on the navy leather sofa, and rings and bracelets were piled in a heap on one of the wrought-iron-and-glass end tables. Rap music blared through his stereo system, and Shaggy did the bump and grind on Luc's big-screen television, which was tuned in to MTV.

Marie. Marie was home early.

Luc tossed the backpack and his duffel on the sofa as he moved down the hall. He knocked on the first of the three bedroom doors, then he cracked it open. Marie lay on her bed, her short dark hair pulled up on top of her head like a stunted black feather duster. Mascara pooled beneath her eyes and her cheeks were pale. She held a ragged blue Care Bear to her chest.

'What are you doing home?' he asked.

'The school tried to call you. I don't feel well.'

Luc moved into the room for a closer look at his

sixteen-year-old sister all curled up on her lace duvet. He figured she was probably crying about her mother again. It had only been a month since her funeral, and he thought he ought to say something to console Marie, but he really didn't know what to say and he always seemed to make everything worse when he tried.

'Do you have the flu?' he asked instead. She looked so much like her mother it was spooky. Or what he remembered her mother looked like.

'No.'

'Coming down with a cold?'

'No.'

'What's wrong?'

'I just feel sick.'

Luc had been sixteen himself when his sister had been born to his father and his father's fourth wife. Other than a few holiday visits, Luc had never been around Marie. He'd been so much older. They'd lived in Los Angeles; he'd lived across the country. He'd been busy with his own life, and until she'd come to live with him last month, he hadn't seen her since their father's funeral ten years ago. Now he found himself suddenly responsible for a sister he didn't even know. He was her only living relative under retirement age. He was a hockey player. A bachelor. A guy. And he didn't have a clue what in the hell to do with her.

'Do you want some soup?' he asked.

She shrugged as more water filled her eyes. 'I guess so,' she sniffed.

Relieved, Luc quickly left the room and headed for the kitchen. He pulled a big can of chicken noodle from the cupboard and shoved it beneath the can opener sitting on the black marble countertop. He knew she was having a difficult time, but Jesus, she was driving him crazy. If she wasn't crying, she was sulking. If she wasn't sulking, she was rolling her big blue eyes at him as if he were a moron.

Luc poured the soup into two bowls and added water. He'd tried to send her to counseling, but she'd been through counseling during her mother's illness and she was adamant that she'd had enough.

He shoved his and Marie's lunch into the microwave and set the time. Besides making him crazy, having a moody teenage girl in his house seriously cut into his social life. Lately, the only time he had to himself was on the road. Something had to change. This situation wasn't working out for either of them. He'd had to hire a responsible woman to come and stay with Marie and live in his condo when he was out of town. Her name was Gloria Jackson and she was probably in her sixties. Marie didn't like her, but Marie didn't seem to like anyone.

The best thing to do would be to find Marie a good boarding school. She'd be happier there, living with girls her own age who knew about hair and makeup and *liked* listening to rap. He felt a twinge of guilt. His reasons for sending her to boarding school weren't totally altruistic. He wanted his old life back. That might make him a selfish bastard, but he'd worked hard to reclaim that life. To climb out of the chaos and into relative calm.

'I need some money.'

Luc turned from his observation of the soup spinning around in the microwave to his sister standing in the doorway of the kitchen. They'd already talked about a special account for her. 'After we sell your mother's house and your Social Security starts to kick in, you'll—'

'I need some today,' she interrupted him. 'Right now.'

He reached for the wallet in his back pocket. 'How much do you need?'

A wrinkle appeared across her brow. 'I think seven or eight dollars.'

'You don't know?'

'Ten to be on the safe side.'

Curious and because he thought he should ask, he said, 'What do you need the money for?'

Her cheeks flushed. 'I don't have the flu.'

'What do you have?'

'I have cramps and I don't have anything.' Her gaze lowered to her stocking-covered feet. 'I don't know any girls at school to ask, and by the time I got to the nurse, it was too late. That's why I had to come home from school.'

'Too late for what? What are you talking about?'

'I have cramps and I don't have any . . .' Her face turned red and she blurted, 'Tampons. I looked in your bathroom 'cause I thought maybe one of your girlfriends might have left some. But you don't have any.'

The microwave dinged at the same moment Luc finally understood Marie's problem. He opened the door and burned his thumbs as he set the soup on the counter. 'Oh.' He pulled two spoons from a drawer, and because he didn't know what to say, he asked, 'Do you want crackers?'

'Yes.'

Somehow, she didn't seem old enough. Did girls start their periods at sixteen? He guessed so, but he'd never thought about it. He'd been raised an only child, and his thoughts had always revolved around playing hockey.

'Do you want some aspirin?' One of his old girlfriends had taken his painkillers when she'd had cramps. When he thought back on it, his money and their addiction had been the only thing they'd had in common.

'No.'

'After lunch we'll go to the store,' he said. 'I could use some deodorant.'

She finally glanced up, but she didn't move.

'Do you need to go now?'

'Yes.'

He looked at her standing there, embarrassed and as uncomfortable as he was. The guilt he'd experienced a moment ago eased. Sending her to live with girls her own age was definitely the right move. A girls' boarding school would know about cramps and other female things.

'I'll get my keys,' he said. Now he just had to find a way to break it to her that wouldn't make it sound as if he were trying to get rid of her.

Exchanging Pleasantries: A Fight

'Say that again?' Caroline Mason's fork paused halfway to her mouth, a piece of lettuce and chicken suspended in midair.

'I'm covering the Chinooks games and traveling with them on the road,' Jane repeated for the benefit of her childhood friend.

'The hockey team?' Caroline worked at Nordstrom's selling her favorite addiction – shoes. In appearance, she and Jane were on opposite ends of the spectrum. She was tall, blonde, and blue-eyed, a walking advertisement of beauty and good taste. And their temperaments weren't much closer. Jane was introverted, while Caroline didn't have a thought or emotion that wasn't expressed. Jane shopped from catalogues. Caroline considered catalogues a Tool of Satan.

'Yep, that's what I'm doing on this side of town. I just came from a meeting with the owner and the team.' The two friends were fire and ice, night and day, but they shared a common background and history that bonded them like Super Glue.

Caroline's mother had run off with a trucker and had drifted in and out of her life. Jane had grown up without a mother at all. They'd lived next to each other in Tacoma, on the same desolate block. Poor. The have-nots. They both knew what it was like to go to school wearing canvas sneakers when most everyone else wore leather.

Grown up now, they each dealt with the past in their own ways. Jane socked away money as if each paycheck were her last, while Caroline blew outrageous sums on designer shoes like she was Imelda Marcos.

Caroline set her fork on the side of her plate and placed a hand on her chest. 'You get to travel with the Chinooks and interview them while they're naked?'

Jane nodded and dug into the lunch special, macaroni and cheese with smoked ham chunks and crushed croutons baked on top. With the weather outside, it was definitely a mac-and-cheese day. 'Hopefully, they'll keep their pants up until I leave the locker room.'

'You're kidding, right? What reason, other than seeing buff men, is there for walking into a smelly locker room?'

'Interviewing them for the paper.' Now that she'd seen all of them this morning, she was beginning to feel a bit apprehensive. Next to her five foot stature, they were huge.

'Do you think they'd notice if you snapped some pictures?'

'They might.' Jane laughed. 'They didn't seem as dumb as you'd expect.'

'Bummer. I wouldn't mind seeing some naked hockey players.'

And now that she'd seen them all, seeing them naked was one aspect of the job that worried her. She had to travel with these men. Sit with them on the airplane. She didn't want to know what they looked like without their clothes. The only time she wanted to be near a naked man was when she was naked herself. And while she wrote explicit sexual fantasies for a living, in her real life she wasn't all that comfortable with blatant nudity. She was not like the woman who wrote about dating and relationships in the column for the *Times*. And she was absolutely nothing like Honey Pie.

Jane Alcott was a fraud.

'If you can't take pictures,' Caroline said as she reached for her fork once more and picked the chicken from her Oriental salad, 'take notes for me.'

'That's unethical on a lot of different levels,' she informed her friend. Then she thought about Luc Martineau's offer to 'piss' in her coffee, and she figured she could bend ethics in his case. 'I did see Luc Martineau's butt.'

'*Au naturel?*'

'As the day he was born.'

Caroline leaned forward. 'How was it?'

'Good.' She pictured Luc's sculpted shoulders and back, the indent of his spine, and his towel sliding down his perfect round cheeks. 'Really fine.' No denying it, Luc was a beautiful man; too bad his personality sucked.

'God,' Caroline sighed, 'why didn't I finish college and get a job like yours?'

'Too many parties.'

'Oh, yeah.' Caroline paused a moment, then smiled. 'You need an assistant. Take me.'

'The paper won't pay for an assistant.'

'Bummer.' Her smile fell and her gaze lowered to Jane's blazer. 'You should get new clothes.'

'I have new clothes,' Jane said around a bite of ham and cheese.

'I mean new, as in attractive. You wear too much black and gray. People will begin to wonder if you're depressed.'

'I'm not depressed.'

'Maybe not, but you should wear color. Reds and greens especially. You're going to be traveling with big, strong, testosterone-infused men all season. It's the perfect opportunity to get a guy interested in you.'

Jane was traveling with the team on business. She didn't want to catch the interest of a man. Especially a hockey player. Especially if they were all like Luc Martineau. When she'd declined his offer concerning the coffee, he'd almost smiled. Almost. Instead he'd said, *If you change your mind about that, let me know.* Only he hadn't said *about.* He'd said *aboot.* He was a jerk who hadn't completely lost his Canadian accent. The last thing she wanted or needed was to attract attention from men like him. She glanced down at her black blazer and pants, and her gray blouse. She thought she looked okay. 'It's J. Crew.'

Caroline narrowed her blue eyes and Jane knew what was coming. J. Crew was *not* Donna Karan. 'Exactly. From the catalogue?'

'Of course.'

'And black.'

'You know I'm color blind.'

'You're not color blind. You just can't tell when things clash.'

'True.' That's why she liked black. She looked good in black. She couldn't make a fashion faux pas in black.

'You've got a nice little body, Jane. You should work it, show it off. Come back to Nordy's with me, and I'll help you pick out some nice things.'

'No way. The last time I let you pick out my clothes, I looked like Greg Brady. Only not as groovy.'

'That was in the sixth grade and we had to go to Goodwill to do our shopping. We're older and have more money. At least you do.'

Yes, and she planned to keep it that way too. She had plans for her nest egg. Plans that included buying a house, not designer clothes. 'I like the way I dress,' she said as if they hadn't had the same conversation a thousand times in the past.

Caroline rolled her eyes and changed the subject. 'I met a guy.'

Of course she had. Since they'd both turned thirty last spring, Caroline's biological clock had started ticking and all she'd been able to think about were her eggs shriveling up. She'd decided it was time to get married, and since she didn't want to leave Jane out of the fun, she'd decided it was time they *both* got married. But there was a problem with Caroline's plan. Jane had pretty much decided she was a magnet for men who would break her heart and treat her bad, and since jerks seemed to be the only type of man who made her go all weak and sweaty, she'd been thinking about getting a cat and staying home. But she was stuck in a catch-22. If she stayed home, she wouldn't discover new material for her *Single Girl* column.

'He has a friend.'

'The last "friend" you set me up with drove a serial killer van with a couch in the back.'

'I know, and he wasn't real pleased to read about himself in your *Times* column.'

'Too bad. He was one of those guys who assumes I'm desperate and horny because of the column.'

'This time will be different.'

'No.'

'You might like him.'

'That's the problem. If I like him, I know he'll treat me like crap, then dump me.'

'Jane, you rarely give anyone the chance to dump you. You always keep one foot out the door, waiting for an excuse.'

Caroline didn't have a lot of room to talk. She dumped guys for being too perfect. 'You haven't had a boyfriend since Vinny,' Caroline said.

'Yeah, and look how that turned out.' He'd borrowed money from her to buy other women presents. As far as she could tell, he'd bought mostly cheap lingerie. Jane hated cheap lingerie.

'Look on the bright side. After you had to dump him, you were so upset you regrouted your bathroom.'

It was a sad fact of Jane's life that when she was brokenhearted and depressed, she cleaned with a vengeance. When she was happy, she tended to overlook towels falling out of the closet onto her head.

After lunch, Jane dropped Caroline off at Nordstrom's, then drove to the *Seattle Times*. Because she wrote a monthly column, she didn't have a desk at the paper. In fact, she'd hardly ever ventured into the building.

She met with the sports editor, Kirk Thornton, and he didn't have to tell her he was less than thrilled to have her covering for Chris. His reception of her was so cold, he could have chilled a glass on his forehead. He introduced her to the three other sports reporters, and their welcome wasn't much warmer than Kirk's. Except for Jeff Noonan's.

Even though Jane was hardly ever in the *Seattle Times* building, she'd heard about Jeff Noonan. He was known by the female staff as the Nooner and was a sexual harassment lawsuit just waiting to happen. Not only did he believe a woman's place was in the kitchen, he believed it was on her back on the kitchen table. The look he gave her told her he was thinking about her naked, and he smiled like she should be flattered or something.

The look she returned told him she'd rather eat rat poison.

The BAC-111 lifted off from SeaTac at six twenty-three a.m. Within minutes, the jet broke through the cloud cover and banked left. The morning sun shot through the oval windows like spotlights. Almost as one, the shades were slammed shut against the brutal glare, and a good number of hockey players put their seats back and sacked out for the four-hour flight. A mix of aftershave and cologne filled the cabin as the jet finished its ascent and evened out.

Without taking her eyes from the itinerary in her lap, Jane reached over her head and adjusted the air. She turned its full force on her face as she looked over the team schedule. She noticed that some of their flights left right after a game while others left the next morning. But except for the flight times, the schedule was always the same. The team practiced the day before each game and had a 'light' run-through the day of the game. It never varied.

She set aside the itinerary and picked up a copy of the *Hockey News*. The morning light broke over the NHL team reports, and she paused to read a column concerning the Chinooks. The subhead read, 'Chinooks' Goaltending Key to Success.'

For the past few weeks, Jane had crammed her head with NHL stats. She'd familiarized herself with the names of the Chinooks and the positions they played. She'd read as many newspaper articles on the team as she could find, but she still didn't have a firm grasp on the game or its players. She was going to have to fly by the seat of her pants and hope she didn't crash and burn. She needed the respect and trust of these men. She wanted them to treat her as they did other sports journalists.

In her briefcase, she'd stashed two invaluable books: *Hockey for Dummies* and *The Bad Boys of Hockey*. The first gave her the rudiments and the how-tos, while the second told the dark side of the game and the men who played it.

Without lifting her face, she glanced across the aisle and down a row. Her gaze followed the emergency lights running down the dark blue carpeting and stopped on Luc Martineau's polished loafers and charcoal trousers. Since their conversation at the Key Arena, she'd done more research on him than the other players.

He'd been born and raised in Edmonton, Alberta, Canada. His father was French-Canadian and divorced his mother when Luc had been just five years old. Luc had been drafted sixth overall into the NHL at the age of nineteen by the Oilers. He'd been traded to Detroit and finally Seattle. The most interesting reading had come from *The Bad Boys of Hockey*, which had devoted an entire five chapters to Luc. The book had gone into detail about the bad-boy goalie, claiming he had the quickest hands on and off the ice. The photos had shown a string of actresses and models on his arm, and while none of them had come right out and claimed they'd slept with him, they hadn't denied it either.

Her gaze rose to his big hand and long fingers tapping the arm of his seat. A sliver of his gold Rolex showed from beneath the cuff of his white-and-blue-striped shirt. She took in his shoulder and the profile of his high cheekbones and straight nose. His hair was cut short like a gladiator ready to do battle. Assuming half the juicy details of the bad-boy book were true, Luc Martineau had a woman stashed in each city the team visited. Jane was surprised he wasn't terminally exhausted.

Like all of the other players, this morning Luc looked more like a businessman or an investment banker than a hockey player. Earlier at the airport, Jane had been surprised to see the whole team show up in suits and ties as if they were on their way to the office.

Her view suddenly blocked, Jane glanced up into the battered face of enforcer Rob 'the Hammer' Sutter. Bent over to accommodate the low ceiling, he appeared scarier than usual. She didn't have the faces of all the Chinooks memorized yet, but Rob was one of those guys who was easy to remember. He was six foot three, two hundred and fifty pounds of intimidating muscle. At the moment, he sported a fuzzy goatee on his chin and a brilliant shiner beneath one of his green eyes. He'd taken off his suit jacket, rolled up his sleeves, and loosened his tie. His brown hair needed cutting and he had a piece of white tape across the bridge of his nose. He glanced at the briefcase on the seat next to her.

'Do you mind if I sit down for a few?'

Jane hated to admit it, but she'd always been a bit unnerved by big guys. They took up so much space and made her feel small and a little vulnerable. 'Ahh, no.' She grabbed the leather handles and shoved the briefcase on the floor by her feet.

Rob crammed his big body in the seat next to her and pointed to the newspaper in her hands. 'Did you read the article I wrote? It's on page six.'

'Not yet.' Feeling a bit boxed in, Jane thumbed to page six and looked at a game photo of Rob Sutter. He had some guy in a headlock and was punching his face.

'That's me feeding Rasmussen his lunch in his rookie season.'

She glanced sideways at Rob, taking in his black eye and broken nose. 'Why?'

'Scored a hat trick.'

'Isn't that his job?'

'Sure, but it's *my* job to make things rough for him.' Rob shrugged. 'Make him a little nervous when he sees me coming.'

Jane thought it prudent to keep her opinion of his job to herself. 'What happened to your nose?'

'Got too close to a stick.' He pointed to the paper. 'What do you think?'

She skimmed the article, which seemed to be well enough written.

'Do you think I hooked the reader in the first graph?'

'Graph?'

'That's journalist talk for paragraph.'

She knew what *graph* meant. '"I am more than a punching bag,"' she read out loud. 'That got my attention.'

Rob smiled, showing a row of beautiful white teeth. Jane wondered how many times they'd been knocked out and replaced. 'I had a lot of fun writing that,' he said. 'When I retire, I'm thinking maybe I'll write articles full-time. Maybe you could give me some pointers.'

Getting a foot in the door was a lot easier said than done. Her own résumé was less than stellar, but she didn't want to rain on Rob's parade by telling him the truth. 'I'll help you, if I can.'

'Thanks.' He half rose and pulled a wallet from his back pocket. When he sat down again, he flipped it open and pulled out a photograph. 'This is Amelia,' he said as he handed her a picture of a baby girl resting on his chest.

'She's so tiny. How old is she?'

'One month. Isn't she the prettiest thing you've ever seen?'

Jane wasn't about to argue with the Hammer. 'She's gorgeous.'

'Are we showing baby pictures again?'

Jane looked up and into a pair of brown eyes watching her over the seat in front of them. The man handed back a photo. 'That's Taylor Lee,' he said. 'She's two.'

Jane looked at the photo of a toddler as bald as the guy who'd handed it over, and she wondered what it was about people assuming everyone wanted to see their baby's pictures. She didn't recognize the eyes staring at her over the seat until Rob gave her a clue.

'She's awfully bald, Fishy. When she gonna get some hair?'

Bruce Fish, second-string winger, half rose and took back his photograph. The light shone on his bald scalp while a scruffy beard covered the lower half of his face. 'I was bald until I was five, and I turned out cute.'

Jane managed to keep a straight face. Bruce Fish might be a skilled puck handler, but he was not an attractive man.

'Do you have any kids?' he asked her.

'No, I've never been married,' she answered, and the conversation turned to which Chinook was married and who had how many children. Not exactly stimulating conversation, but it alleviated her worry that the players would shut her out.

She handed Rob his photograph and decided to get down to business. To dazzle them with her research, or to at least show them that she wasn't completely clueless. 'Given the age and lack of franchise players, the Coyotes are playing better than expected this year,' she said, reciting what she'd just read. 'What are your biggest concerns going into Wednesday's game?'

They both stared at her as if she'd just spoken a language they didn't understand. Latin, perhaps.

Bruce Fish turned around and disappeared behind his seat. Rob shoved the baby photo in his wallet. 'Here comes breakfast,' he said as he stood. The Hammer quickly departed, making it quite clear that while she was good enough to talk with about journalism and babies, he wasn't going to talk with her about hockey. And as the flight progressed, it became even more clear to Jane that the players were ignoring her now. Except for her brief conversation with Bruce and Rob, no one spoke to her. Well, they couldn't ignore her forever. They had to allow her locker room access and answer her questions. They had to talk to her then or face a discrimination lawsuit.

She refused a muffin and orange juice and raised the arm between the chairs. She scooted to the aisle seat, spread out her articles and books, then took off her gray wool blazer. She got down to the business of trying to figure out what points were as opposed to goals. What penalty was awarded for which infraction, and the ever-confusing icing call. She grabbed a brick of Post-its out of her briefcase, scribbled notes, and stuck them inside the book.

Keeping track of her work and life via sticky notes wasn't the most efficient way to run things, and she had tried more organized methods. She'd tried a software program on her laptop, but she'd ended up scribbling notes about what to write in it. She'd bought the day planner she currently used, but only to stick notes on the calendar pages. Last year, she'd bought a Palm Pilot, but she'd never gotten comfortable with it. Without her sticky notes she'd had an anxiety attack and had ended up selling the handheld device to a friend.

She scribbled notes about hockey terminology she didn't know, stuck them in the book, then glanced down a row at Luc. His hand rested beside a glass of orange juice on the tray table. His long fingers tore at a cocktail napkin, and he rubbed bits of paper between his fingers and thumb.

Someone called Luc's name and he leaned forward and glanced toward the back. His blue gaze landed somewhere behind Jane, and he laughed at some joke she didn't get. His teeth were white and straight, and he had a smile that could make a woman think of hot sinful things. Then he lowered his gaze to her and she forgot about his teeth. He simply looked at her as if he couldn't quite figure out how she'd gotten there – like a spot on his tie – then his scrutiny slid down her face and neck to the middle of her plain white blouse. For some disturbing reason, her breath caught in her chest, right where his gaze rested. The moment became suspended. Prolonged. Hanging between them until his brows pulled into a straight line. Then, without looking up, he turned away. She finally let out her breath, and once again she had the feeling she'd been judged and found lacking by Luc Martineau.

By the time the aircraft touched down in Phoenix, the weather was fifty-three degrees and sunny. The hockey players straightened their ties, put on their jackets, and filed out toward the bus. Luc waited until Jane Alcott passed before he stepped into the aisle behind her. While shrugging into his Hugo Boss jacket, he studied her from behind.

She'd hung a wool blazer over the same arm that held a big briefcase crammed full of books and newspapers. Her hair was pulled back again into a tight ponytail, and the ends curled and brushed her shoulders as they moved forward. She was so short, the top of her head reached to just below his chin, and through the haze of cologne and aftershave he smelled a hint of something flowery.

The edge of her briefcase caught the back of a seat and she stumbled. Luc grasped her arm to steady her as newspapers, books, and multiple notes fell to the cabin floor. He let go of her arm, then knelt beside her in the cramped aisle. He picked up a book on the official NHL rules and *Hockey For Dummies*.

'Don't know much about the game, huh?' he said as he passed her the books. The tips of his fingers brushed hers and she glanced up at him.

With her face a few inches from his, he took the opportunity to study her. Her skin was flawless and there was a slight pink flush to her smooth cheeks. Her eyes were the color of summer grass, and he could make out the faint lines of contact lenses on the edges of her irises. If she wasn't a reporter and hadn't already asked him if he was still drug-free the first time they'd met, maybe he'd think she wasn't all that bad-looking. Maybe he'd even think she was kind of cute. Maybe.

'I know plenty,' she said as she pulled her hand away and stuffed the books into the front pouch.

'Sure you do, Ace.' He tore a sticky note from the knee of his pants. On it was written: *What the heck is a body check?* He grabbed her wrist and slapped the note in her palm. 'Looks like you know squat.'

They stood and he took the briefcase from her.

'I can carry that,' she protested as she shoved the note into her pants pocket.

'Let me.'

'If you're trying to be nice, it's too late.'

'I'm not being nice. I'd like to get out of here before the bus leaves.'

'Oh.' She opened her mouth to say more but closed it again. They proceeded down the aisle; the swing of her ponytail told him of her agitation. Once inside the bus, she sat next to the general manager, and Luc dumped the briefcase into her lap and walked to the back.

Rob Sutter leaned forward as Luc dropped into a seat in front of the enforcer. 'Hey, Lucky,' Rob said. 'Don't you think she's kinda cute?'

Luc glanced several rows up at the back of Jane's head and the curls of her tight ponytail. She wasn't bad-looking, but she wasn't his type. He liked Barbie Doll women. Long legs and big breasts. Big hair and red lips. Women who liked to please men and didn't expect anything but pleasure in return. He knew what that said about him, and he didn't particularly care. Jane had nice skin and her hair might be okay if she didn't pull it back so tight, but her breasts were small.

A picture of the front of her blouse flashed across his brain. He'd turned to answer something Vlad Fetisov had asked him, and he'd noticed her for the first time since takeoff. Then he'd noticed the two distinct points in the front of her silky blouse. For a brief moment, he'd wondered if she was cold or turned on.

'Not especially,' he answered Rob.

'Do you think it's true that she slept with Duffy to get this assignment?'

'Is that what the guys are saying?'

'Either him or his friend at the *Seattle Times*.'

The thought of a young woman like Jane getting it on with two old geezers to get a job turned Luc's stomach.

He didn't know why it should bother him one way or the other, and with a shrug he dismissed Jane and whom she may or may not be sleeping with from his mind.

He was expecting an important call from his business manager, Howie. Howie lived in LA and sent all three of his children to boarding school in southern California. The more Luc had thought about it, the more he'd convinced himself that boarding school in California was the perfect solution for Marie. Marie had lived in southern California for most of her life. It would be like going back home for her. She'd be happier and he'd get his life back. An all-round win situation for everyone.

The Chinooks checked into the hotel by eleven, had a quick lunch, and were on the ice by two for their scheduled practice at the America West Arena. The team hadn't lost a game in two weeks, and Luc had put up five shutouts already this season. The team hadn't been a real threat since their former captain, John Kowalsky, retired. This year was different. This year they were hot.

By four, the Chinooks were back at the hotel and Luc rode the elevator to his room and placed a phone call to a friend. Two hours later, he stepped back off the elevator, ready to live his life while he could.

He'd first met Jenny Davis on a United flight to Denver. She'd served him a soda water and lime, a bag of nuts, and a cocktail napkin with her name and telephone number written on it. That was three years ago, and they got together when he was in Phoenix or she happened to be in Seattle. The situation was mutually satisfying. He satisfied her. She satisfied him.

Tonight he met Jenny in the lobby and together they

drove to Durant's, where Luc ate his night-before-the-game meal of lamb chops, Caesar salad, and wild rice.

After dinner, Jenny took him to her home in Scottsdale, where she fed him his dessert. She had him back at the hotel by curfew; he loved his life on the road. Walking back into the hotel, he was completely calm, relaxed, and ready to take on the Coyotes tomorrow night.

He talked for a few minutes with his teammates in the lobby bar, then made his way up to his room. His right knee bothered him a little, and he grabbed the empty ice bucket from atop the television, then walked down the hall to the ice machine. He almost turned back when he saw Jane Alcott standing in front of the vending machine feeding it change. Her hair was pulled on top of her head and fell in a tangle of loose curls. She stepped forward and pushed the button to her selection, and a bag of Peanut M&M's dropped to the bottom of the machine.

She bent over, and that's when he noticed her nicely rounded butt with cows on it. In fact, she had cows all over her blue flannel pajamas. The thing was one piece, and from the back looked like long johns. She turned and he was confronted by a horror worse than those pajamas. A pair of black-rimmed glasses sat on her face. The lenses were small and square, and he supposed they were in style with militant women's groups. They were just plain ugly.

Seeing him, her eyes widened and she sucked in a startled breath. 'I thought you guys were supposed to be in bed by now,' she said.

Damn, he didn't think a woman could look any more

sexless. 'What is this?' he asked and pointed the bucket at her. 'The I-don't-ever-want-to-get-laid-again look?'

She frowned. 'This may shock you, but I'm here to do a job. Not to get laid.'

'Good thing.' He thought of his conversation with Sutter and wondered if she'd slept with old Virgil Duffy to get her job. He'd heard the stories of Virgil's fondness for women young enough to be his granddaughter. In fact, when Luc had first moved to Seattle, Sutter told him that in 1998 Virgil had been set to marry a young woman, but the woman had come to her senses and had left him at the altar. Luc didn't listen to gossip and didn't know how much of it was true. He just couldn't picture Virgil in the role of a hound, though. 'I doubt you'll find any action in that getup.'

Jane ripped open her bag of candy. 'You don't seem to have a problem with finding action, *Lucky*.' Luc didn't like the way she said *Lucky* and he didn't ask her to elaborate. She did anyway. 'I saw you leave with the blonde. If I had to guess, I'd say she was a stewardess. She had that come-fly-me look about her.'

Luc moved to the ice machine and lifted the lid. 'She was my cousin, twice removed.' She didn't look like she believed him, but he really didn't care. She'd believe what she wanted and write what sold papers.

'What's with the ice? Your knees bothering you?'

'Nope.' She was too damn smart for her own good.

'Who's Gump Worsley?' she asked.

Gump was a hockey great who'd played more games than any goalie in history. Luc admired his record and his dedication. Years ago, he'd taken Gump's number for luck. It was no big deal. No big secret either.

'Have you been reading up on me again?' he asked as he scooped ice with his bucket. 'I'm flattered,' he said, but he didn't bother to make it sound convincing.

'Don't be. It's my job.' She popped an M&M into her mouth, and when he didn't say anything she lifted a brow. 'You're not going to answer my question?'

'Nope.' She'd soon learn that none of the guys were going to cooperate either. They'd all talked about it and come up with a plan to confuse and bug the hell out of her. Maybe get her to go home. Outside the locker room, they'd show her baby pictures and talk about anything other than what she was dying to talk about. Hockey. Inside the locker room they'd cooperate just enough to avoid a discrimination suit, but that was it. Luc didn't think much of the scheme. Sure it would bug her, but not enough to make her go home. No, after talking to her a few times, he figured there wasn't much that could knock Ms. Alcott off her pumps.

'Tell you what, though.' Luc shut the lid to the ice machine and said close to her ear as he walked past, 'Keep digging, 'cause that Gump thing's a real interesting story.'

'Digging is also my job, but don't worry, I'm not interested in your dirty little secrets,' she called after him.

Luc didn't have any dirty secrets. Not anymore. There were parts of his personal life he'd rather not read about in the papers, though. He'd rather it wasn't known that he had several different women friends in several different cities, although that piece of information in itself wouldn't make banner headlines. Most people wouldn't care. He wasn't married and neither were his friends.

He opened the door to his room and shut himself

inside. There was only one secret he didn't want anyone to know. One secret that woke him up in a cold sweat.

Each time he played, he played with the possibility that one good hit would cripple him for life, and worse, end his career.

Luc dumped the ice into a hand towel and stripped to his white boxers. He scratched his belly, then sat on the bed with his knee elevated over a pillow, the ice packed around it.

His whole life, all he'd ever wanted was to play hockey and win the Stanley Cup. He'd lived and breathed it for so long, that's all he knew. Unlike some guys who got drafted out of college, he'd been drafted into the NHL at the age of nineteen, a bright future ahead of him.

For a while, his future had gotten off track. He'd slid into a vicious cycle of pain and addiction and prescription drugs. Of recovery and hard work. And now finally a chance to return to the game that made him feel alive. But the sport that had given him a Conn Smythe the year before his injury now looked at him sideways and wondered if he still had what it took. There were those, some within the Chinook management, who wondered if they'd payed too much for their premier goalie, if Luc could still deliver on his once-promising career.

Whatever it took, no matter how much pain he had to play through, he'd be damned if he'd let anything stand between him and his shot at the cup.

Right now, he was hot. Saw every play, got a piece of every puck. He was in his zone, but he knew how fast his hot streak could turn cold and unforgiving. He could lose focus. Let in a few soft goals. Misjudge the speed of the puck, let too many get past, and get pulled from the net.

Having an off night and getting yanked from the pipes happened to all goalies, but that didn't make it any less appalling.

A bad game didn't mean a bad season. Most of the time. But Luc could not afford most of the time.

Paraphernalia:
Between a Player's Legs

The telephone next to Jane's laptop rang and she stared at it for a moment before she picked up.

'Hello.' But there was no one on the other end. There hadn't been the last seven times it had rung either. She dialed the front desk and was told they didn't know where the calls originated. Jane had a pretty good idea the calls were coming from men with fish on their jerseys.

She left the receiver off the hook and glanced at the clock on the bedside stand. She had five hours before the game. Five hours to finish her *Single Girl in the City* column. She should have started her column for the *Times* last night, but she'd been exhausted and jet-lagged and all she'd wanted was to lie in bed, read her research books, and eat chocolate. If Luc hadn't snuck up on her at the vending machine the night before, she would have bought a Milky Way too. Having been caught in her cow

PJs had been bad enough. She hadn't wanted him to think her a pig, but really, why should she care what he thought of her?

She didn't know, except she supposed it was in a woman's genetic makeup to care what handsome men thought. If Luc was ugly, she probably wouldn't have cared. If he didn't have those clear blue eyes, long lashes, and a body to make a nun weep, she would have grabbed that Milky Way and maybe chased it with a Hershey's Big Block. If it weren't for his evil grin that had her thinking sinful thoughts and remembering the sight of his naked butt, she might not have heard herself babbling about stewardesses like a jealous puck bunny.

She could not afford for any of the players to see her as anything other than a professional. Their reception of her had warmed little since they'd arrived. They spoke to her about recipes and babies, as if by virtue of having a uterus she was naturally interested. But if she brought up hockey, their mouths shut tight as clams.

Jane reread the first part of her column and made a few changes:

Single Girl in the City

Tired of talking about hair care products and men with commitment issues, I tuned out my friends and concentrated on my margarita and corn chips. As I sat looking around at the parrot and sombrero decor, I wondered if men were the only ones with commitment phobias. I mean, here we sat, four thirty-year-old women who'd never been married, and except for Tina's one attempt at living with her ex-boss, none of

48

us had ever had a real committed relationship. So was it them, or was it us?

There is a saying that goes something like, 'If you put two neurotics in a room of one hundred people, they'd find each other.' So was there something else? Something deeper than a lack of available men without issues?

Had the four of us 'found' each other? Were we friends because we truly enjoyed each other's company? Or were we all neurotic?

Five hours and fifteen minutes after she'd started her column, she finally pushed send on her laptop. She shoved her notebook into her big purse, then raced to the door. She ran down the hall to the elevators and practically had to wrestle an elderly couple from a cab. When she walked into the America West Arena, the Phoenix Coyotes were just being introduced. The crowd went crazy cheering for their team.

She'd been given a pass to the press box, but Jane wanted to be as close as possible to the action. She'd finagled a seat three rows up from the boards, wanting to see and feel as much as she could of her first hockey game. She really didn't know what to expect, she just hoped to God the Chinooks didn't lose and blame it on her.

She found her place behind the goalie cage just as the Chinooks stepped onto the ice. Boos filled the arena, and Jane glanced around at the ill-behaved Coyotes fans. She'd been to a Mariners game once, but she didn't remember the fans being so rude.

She turned her attention back to the ice and watched Luc Martineau skate toward her, geared up and ready for battle. She'd done more research on Luc than on the other players, and she knew that everything he wore was custom-made. The arena lights shone off his dark green helmet. His name was sewn across the shoulders of his jersey in dark green above the number of the legendary Gump Worsley. *Why* Mr. Worsley was legendary, Jane had yet to discover.

Luc circled the goal twice, turned, and circled it in the opposite direction. He stopped within the crease, slapped his stick on the posts, and crossed himself. Jane took out her notebook, a pen, and her Post-its. On the top note she wrote: *Superstitions and rituals?*

The puck dropped, and all at once the sounds of the game rushed at her, the clash of sticks, scraping of skates on ice, and the puck slamming into the boards. The fans screamed and cheered and the smells of pizza and Budweiser soon hung in the air.

In preparation, Jane had viewed many game tapes. While she knew the game to be fast-paced, the tapes had not conveyed the frenetic energy or the way that energy infected the crowd. When play stopped, infractions were announced from the sound system and music blared until the puck was once more dropped and the team centers hacked it out.

As Jane took note of everything around her, she discovered what the tapes, and even televison, did not show. The action wasn't always where the puck was being played. A lot of the activity took place in the corners with punches and blows while the puck was at center ice. On several occasions she watched Luc whack the ankles of a Phoenix player unfortunate enough to stand within whacking distance. He seemed very good at hooking

Coyote skates with his stick, and when he stuck out his arm and clotheslined Coyote Claude Lemieux, two men behind Jane jumped up and yelled, 'You play like a girly man, Martineau!'

Whistles blew, the play stopped, and as Claude Lemieux picked himself up off the ice, the penalty was announced. 'Martineau, roughing, two minutes.'

Because a goalie could not do time in the sin bin, Bruce Fish took his place. As Fish skated to the penalty box, Luc simply picked up his water bottle from the top of the net, shot a stream through the cage into his mouth, then spit it out. He shrugged, rolled his head from side to side, and tossed the bottle back onto the net.

Game on.

The pace fluctuated from wild to almost orderly. *Almost.* Just when Jane thought both teams had decided to play nice, the scrum for the puck turned physical. And nothing brought the crowd to their feet like the sight of players throwing their gloves and mixing it up in the corner. She couldn't actually hear what the players were saying to each other, but she didn't need to. She could clearly read their lips. The F-word seemed a real favorite. Even by the coaches who stood behind the bench in mild-mannered suits and ties. And when the players on the bench weren't swearing, they were spitting. She'd never seen men spit so much.

Jane noticed that the heckling from the crowd was not limited to the Chinooks' goalie. Anytime a Seattle player came within hollering distance, the men behind Jane yelled, 'You suck!' After several Budweisers, they got more creative: 'You suck, eighty-nine,' or thirty-nine, or whatever the player's number.

Fifteen minutes into the first period, Rob Sutter checked a Coyote into the boards, and the Plexiglas shook so hard Jane thought it would crack. The player slid to the ice and the whistles blew.

'You suck, Hammer,' the men behind Jane yelled, and she wondered if the players could hear the fans over the collective noise. She knew she'd have to drink a lot of alcohol before she had the courage to tell the Hammer he sucked. She'd be too afraid he'd meet her in the parking lot later and 'feed her lunch.'

After the first two periods, the score remained zero–zero, mostly due to some amazing saves by both goaltenders. But the Coyotes came out strong in the third. The team's captain broke through the Chinook defense and sped down the ice toward the Chinooks' goal. Luc came out of the crease to meet him, but the captain snipered a shot past his left shoulder. Luc got a piece of it with his stick, but the puck waffled and sailed into the net.

The crowd jumped to their feet as Luc skated to the goal. He calmly placed his stick and blocker on top of the net. As the blinking blue light announced the goal, he pushed his mask to the top of his head, picked up his water bottle, and shot water into his mouth. From where Jane sat, she watched him in profile. His cheek was slightly flushed, his damp hair stuck to his temple. A stream of water ran from the corner of his mouth, down his chin and neck, and wet the collar of his jersey. He lowered the bottle, tossed it on the cage, and shoved his hand into his blocker.

'Eat me, Martineau!' one of the men behind her yelled. 'Eat me!'

Luc glanced up and one of Jane's questions was answered. He'd clearly heard the men behind her. Without expression of any sort, he simply looked at them. He picked up his stick and lowered his gaze until it landed on Jane. He stared at her for several long seconds before he turned and skated to the Chinooks' bench. Jane couldn't tell what he thought of the two men, but she had bigger concerns than Luc's feelings. She crossed her fingers and hoped like hell the Chinooks made a goal within the next fifteen minutes.

We have to remember we're dealing with hockey players. You know they can be real superstitious, Leonard had warned. *If the Chinooks start losing games, you'll get blamed and sent packing.* After the way they were already treating her, Jane figured they didn't need much of an excuse.

It took them fourteen minutes and twenty seconds, but they finally scored on a power play. When the last buzzer sounded, the score was tied, and Jane let out a relieved breath.

Game over, or so she thought. Instead five more minutes were put on the clock, while four skaters and the goaltenders battled it out in overtime. Neither team scored and the game went into the record book as a tie.

Now Jane could breathe easy. They couldn't blame her for their loss and send her packing.

She gathered her purse and shoved her notebook and pen inside. She headed to the Chinooks' locker room, flashing her press pass. Her stomach twisted into knots as she moved down the hall. She was a professional. She could do this. No problem.

Keep your gaze pinned to their eyes, she reminded

herself as she took out her small tape recorder. She entered the room and stopped as if the bottoms of her Doc Martens were suddenly glued to the floor. Men in various degrees of undress stood in front of benches and open stalls, peeling off their clothes. Hard muscles and sweat. Bare chests and backs. A flash of a naked stomach and butt, and . . .

Good Lord! Her cheeks burned and her eyes about jumped from her skull as she couldn't help but stare at Vlad 'the Impaler' Fetisov's Russian-sized package. Jane jerked her gaze up, but not before she discovered that what she'd heard about European men was true. Vlad wasn't circumcised, and that was just a little more info than she wanted. For one brief second she thought she should mumble an apology, but of course she couldn't apologize, because that would be admitting that she'd seen something. She glanced at the other male reporters and they weren't apologizing. So why did she feel like she was in high school peeking in the boys' locker room?

You've seen a penis before, Jane. No big deal. If you've seen one penis, you've seen them all . . . Well, okay, that's not true. Some penises are better than others. Stop! Stop thinking about penises! she chastened herself. *You're not here to stare. You're here to do a job, and you have just as much right to be here as male reporters do. It's the law, and you're a professional.* Yeah, that's what she told herself as she wove her way through players and other journalists, careful to keep her gaze above the shoulders, but she was the only female in a room filled with big, rugged, *naked* hockey players. She couldn't help but feel very much out of place.

She kept her eyes up as she joined the reporters

interviewing Jack Lynch, the right winger who'd made the Chinooks' only goal. She dug out her notebook as he dropped his shorts. She was almost certain he was wearing long underwear, but she wasn't about to check it out. *Don't look, Jane. Whatever you do, don't look down.*

She turned on her tape recorder and interrupted one of her male counterparts. 'After your injury last month,' she began, 'there was some speculation that you might not be able to finish the season as strong as you'd started. I think that goal put the rumors to bed.'

Jack planted a foot on the bench in front of him and glanced across his shoulder at her. His cheek had an angry red welt, and an old scar creased his top lip. He unwound the tape from the top of his socks and took so long to respond that Jane began to fear he didn't plan to answer at all.

'I hope so,' he finally spoke. Three words. That was it.

'How do you feel about the tie?' asked a reporter next to her.

'The Coyotes played a tough game tonight. Naturally we wanted the win, but we'll take a tie.'

When she tried to ask more questions, she was talked over and shut out. She soon felt as if she were being conspired against. She tried to tell herself that she was probably being paranoid, but when she moved to the small group interviewing the captain of the Chinooks, Mark Bressler, he looked right through her and answered the questions put to him by other reporters.

She talked to a rookie with a blond Mohawk, figuring he'd be grateful for any exposure, but his English was so poor, she didn't understand more than two words. She walked toward the Hammer, but he dropped his cup and she kept going. While she could tell herself that she was a professional and this was a job, she couldn't bring herself to walk up to a totally naked man. Not on the first night.

Soon it became obvious to her that some of the other reporters resented her too, and the players were not going to answer any more of her questions. She wasn't all that surprised by the male journalists' attitudes. The sports-beat reporters at the *Times* hadn't treated her any better.

Fine, she could write the column with what she already had, she thought as she made her way to the team's goalie. Luc sat on a bench in the corner of the room, a big duffel on the floor by his feet. He'd removed everything but his thermal underwear bottoms and socks. He was bare from the waist up, and he'd wrapped a towel around his neck. The ends hung halfway down his chest, and as he watched her approach, he shot water from a plastic bottle into his mouth. A bead of moisture dripped from his bottom lip, slipped down his chin, and dropped to his sternum. Leaving a trail of moisture, it descended the defined planes of his chest and hard stomach and dipped into his navel. He had a black horseshoe tattooed on his lower belly. The shadowing of the groove and nail holes gave depth and dimension to his flesh, and the heels curved upward on each side of his belly button. The bottom of the tattoo disappeared beneath the waistband of his underwear, and Jane doubted he needed the luck of a horseshoe tattooed above his goods.

'I don't give interviews,' he said before she could ask him a question. 'With all that research you've done on me, I'd have thought you'd know that.'

She did, but she wasn't feeling particularly amiable. The boys' club had shoved her out, and she felt like shoving back. She turned on her recorder. 'How do you feel about tonight's game?'

She didn't expect him to answer and he didn't.

'It looked like you got your stick on that puck right before it went into the net.'

The scar on his chin appeared especially white, but his face remained expressionless. Jane only dug in her heels.

'Isn't it hard to concentrate when fans are yelling at you?'

With the edge of the towel, he wiped his face. But he didn't respond.

'If it were me, I think I'd have a hard time ignoring those nasty insults.'

His blue eyes continued to stare into hers, but one corner of his mouth turned down as if he found her very annoying.

'Until tonight, I had no idea hockey fans were so rude. Those men behind me were drunk and disgusting. I can't imagine standing up and yelling, "Eat me," in a crowd like they did.'

He pulled the towel from around his neck and finally said, 'Ace, if you'd stood up and yelled, "Eat me," I doubt you'd be standing here right now bugging the hell out of me.'

'Why's that?'

'Because I imagine, you'd have gotten a taker or two.'

It took a few moments for his meaning to become clear, and when it did, shocked laughter spilled from her lips. 'I guess it's not the same thing, is it?'

'Not quite.'

He stood and hooked his thumbs beneath the elastic of his underwear. 'Now run along and harass somebody else.' When she didn't move, he added, 'Unless you want to embarrass yourself some more.'

'I'm not embarrassed.'

'You keep blushing like your face is on fire.'

'It's very hot in here,' she lied. Was he the only one who'd noticed? Probably not. 'Very hot.'

'It's about to get hotter.' He'd said *aboot* again. 'Stick around and you're going to get an eyeful of the good wood.'

She turned and beat a hasty retreat. Not because he told her to or because of the threat of *getting an eyeful of the good wood*, but because she had a deadline. Yeah, she had a deadline, she told herself as she walked from the locker room, careful to keep her gaze from falling on any more naked parts.

By the time she made it back to the hotel, it was ten o'clock. She had a column to write and a deadline to meet, all before she could put herself to bed. She plugged in her laptop and got to work on her first sports column. She knew the beat reporters at the *Times* would tear it apart and look for flaws, and she was determined that they would find none. She was determined to write better than a man.

Chinooks Tie Coyotes; Lynch Makes Only Goal, she wrote, but she quickly discovered that writing sports copy wasn't as easy as she'd anticipated. It was *boring*. After several hours of struggling to get the words just right and answering repeated nuisance phone calls, she took the receiver off the hook, pressed delete, and began again.

From the second the puck dropped in the America West Arena tonight, the Chinooks and Coyotes treated fans to a wild roller-coaster ride of hard hits and white-knuckle suspense. Both teams kept up the frenetic pace until the very end, when Chinooks goalie Luc Martineau denied the Coyotes a smoker from the blue line. When the final buzzer sounded in overtime, the score remained tied at one with . . .

Along with Luc's many saves, she wrote about Lynch's goal and the hard hits on the Hammer. It didn't occur to her until after she'd sent the article early the next morning that Luc had been watching her in the locker room. As she'd been bouncing around like a pinball, not *everyone* had been ignoring her. Again she felt a disturbing catch in her chest and alarm bells rang in her head, signaling trouble. Big bad trouble with baby-blue eyes and legendary fast hands.

It was a good thing he didn't like her. And she most definitely didn't like anything about him.

Well, except his tattoo. The tattoo rocked.

Early the next morning, the Chinooks dressed in their suits, ties, and battle scars, and headed for the airport. A half-hour into the flight heading for Dallas, Luc loosened his tie and broke out a deck of cards. Two of his teammates and the goalie coach, Don Boclair, joined him in a game of poker. Playing poker on long flights was one of the only times that Luc truly felt a part of the team.

As he dealt, Luc gazed across the aisle of the BAC-111, at the heavy soles of a pair of small boots. Jane had pushed up the armrest between the seats and was sound asleep. She lay on her side, and for once her hair wasn't scraped back from her face. Soft brown curls fell across her cheek and the corner of her parted lips. One hand was folded beneath her chin.

'Do you think we were too rough on her last night?'

Luc looked up at Bressler, leaning over the back of his seat. 'Nah.' He shook his head, then laid the deck on the tray table in front of him. He glanced over his cards and bet on a pair of eights while the guy in the seat next to him, Nick 'the Bear' Grizzell, folded. 'She doesn't belong here,' Luc added. 'If Duffy was going to force a reporter on us, he could have at least picked someone who knows something about hockey.'

'Did you see the way she kept blushing last night?'

They all chuckled as the remaining players discarded.

'She got an eyeful of Vlad's dick.' Bressler threw down his cards. 'One.'

'She saw the Impaler?'

'Uh-huh.'

'Her eyes about bugged out of her head.' Luc dealt Don Boclair two cards while he took three. 'I don't think she'll ever be the same,' he said. It was a well-known fact within the team that Vlad had an ugly dick. The only man who didn't think so was Vlad himself, but everyone also knew that the Russian had taken a lot of hits to the head.

Luc bet on three eights and his win was recorded in Don's book. 'How long did you keep her up with calls to her room?' Luc asked.

'She finally took the phone off the hook around midnight.'

'That first night I felt a little bad when we all went out

and she was sitting by herself in the lobby bar,' Don confessed.

They all looked at him as if he were nuts. The last thing any of them wanted was a reporter – especially a woman – hanging around when they relaxed and cut loose. Be it relaxing in a strip club or nothing more than discussing an opposing team in the hotel bar, everything stayed within the team.

'Well,' Donny backpedaled as he dealt, 'I hate to see any woman sitting alone.'

'It was kind of pathetic,' Grizzell added.

Luc looked over his cards and placed his bet. 'Don't tell me you feel bad too, Bear?'

'Hell, no. She's got to go.' He threw down his cards. 'I'm out for good.'

'Too rich for your blood?'

'Nah, I'm going to kick back and read for the rest of the flight.' Everyone knew that the Bear didn't read anything that didn't have pictures. 'Reading is fundamental.'

'You got a *Playboy*?' Don asked.

'I picked up a *Him* last night after the game, but I haven't been able to get it away from the Stromster,' he said, referring to the rookie Daniel Holstrom. 'He's learning English by reading *The Life of Honey Pie*.'

They all laughed as Don recorded Bressler's win in the book. Living in Seattle especially, a lot of them were fans of Honey Pie. They read her column each month to see who she was screwing into a coma and where she'd left the body.

Luc shuffled the cards and glanced over at Jane sleeping peacefully. No doubt she was the kind of woman who'd get her panties in a twist if she saw one of the guys reading porn.

The talk around him turned to the previous night's game. No one was satisfied with the tie, least of all Luc. Phoenix had made twenty-two scoring attempts, and he'd made twenty-one saves. Not a bad night at the office, but out of all the shots on goal that night, he'd love to have that one back. Not necessarily because it went into the net, but because the goal had been more a fluke than a skilled shot. While Luc was intensely competitive and hated to lose, he really hated to lose on a fluke rather than a contest of skills.

Luc glanced again across the aisle to the woman sleeping like the dead. Her chest moved as her softly parted lips drew breath. Was last night's tie a fluke? A loss in the normal course of the season? Probably, but Luc had a lot on his mind these days, and that goal had come a bit too easy. Was his personal life affecting his game? He had yet to hear anything from his personal manager, and the Marie situation was still unresolved.

In her sleep, Jane pushed her hair from her face. Or was this the beginning of the curse of the woman reporter? Of course, one tie didn't a curse make. But it might be the beginning if they lost this Friday night in Dallas.

As if Bressler had read Luc's thoughts, he said, 'Did you know that it was considered bad luck for a woman to board a pirate ship?'

Luc hadn't known that, but it made perfect sense to him. There was nothing that could mess up a man's life quicker than an unwanted female.

*

Friday night the Chinooks lost in a four–three nail-biter with Dallas. Saturday morning while Luc waited outside for the bus to take them back to DFW, he read the sports section of the *Dallas Morning News*.

The headline read, 'Chinooks Spill Blood and Guts,' and that pretty much summed up the game after Chinooks rookie Daniel Holstrom took a puck to his cheek early in the second frame. The puck that dropped Holstrom like a rock had come from a Dallas stick. Holstrom had been helped off the ice and hadn't returned. Tempers flared, retaliation was sought. The Hammer mixed it up with the Dallas offense, grabbing a winger in the third period and giving him a glove rub in the alley.

After that, things got ugly, and while the Chinooks may have won the battles in the corners, they'd ultimately lost the war. Dallas's deep offensive lines had taken advantage of every power play and peppered Luc with thirty-two shots on goal.

This morning no one was saying much. Especially after the ass-ream they'd been given in the locker room by Coach Nystrom. The coach had closed the door on reporters and had proceeded to shake the cinder-block walls with his loud tirade. But he'd said nothing they hadn't deserved. They'd drawn stupid penalties and paid the price.

Luc folded the paper and stuck it beneath one arm. He unbuttoned his blazer as Ms. Alcott stepped from the revolving door to his left. The Texas sun bathed her in bright morning light, and a slight breeze played with the ends of her ponytail. She wore a black skirt down to her knees, a black blazer, and turtleneck. Her shoes were flat, and she carried that big briefcase of hers and a to-go coffee. She added to the visual assault by wearing an ugly pair of sunglasses on the bridge of her nose. They were round and green like a fly. Damn, but she was into looking sexless.

'Interesting game last night.' She set her briefcase on the ground between them and looked up into his face.

'You liked that?'

'Like I said, it was interesting. What was the team's motto? "If you can't beat 'em, beat 'em up?"'

'Something like that,' he said with a laugh. 'What's with all the gray and black you always wear?'

She glanced down at herself. 'I look good in black.'

'No, sweetheart, you look like the archangel of doom.'

She took a sip of her coffee and said totally urbanely, as if he hadn't hit a nerve, 'I could live the rest of my life without fashion commentary according to Lucky Luc.'

Or at least she tried for urbane. The bloom in her cheeks and her narrowed gaze behind those ugly glasses gave her away. 'Okay, but . . .' He stopped and shook his head. He looked up at the sky and waited for her to take the bait.

He did not wait long. 'I know I'm going to regret this,' she sighed, 'but what?'

'Well, I just think that a woman who has trouble getting a man might have better luck if she dressed up the package a little. Didn't wear ugly sunglasses.'

'My sunglasses aren't ugly, and my packaging is none of your business,' she said as she raised her coffee to her lips. 'So only my business is open for discussion? Your business is off limits?'

'That's right.'

'You little hypocrite.'

'Yeah, sue me.' He glanced down into her face and asked, 'How's the coffee this morning?'

'It's fine.'

'Still taking it black?'

She looked up at him out of the corner of her eye and placed a hand over the lid. 'Yes.'

Good Wood: Jabbing with the Butt End of a Stick

J ane was almost afraid to glance around her. This morning, looking at some of the Chinooks was kind of like looking at a train wreck. Horrifying, but she was unable to turn away. She sat near the front of the plane across the aisle from Assistant General Manager Darby Hogue, a copy of the *Dallas Morning News* opened to the sports page in her lap. She'd sent off her report of the previous night's bloodletting, but she was interested in what the Dallas reporters had to say about it.

Last night, she and the area sports reporters had gathered in the media room to wait for their chance to enter the Chinooks' locker room. They'd drunk coffee and cola and eaten some sort of enchilada concoction, but when Coach Nystrom had eventually come out, he'd informed them all there were to be no postgame interviews.

During the wait, the Dallas journalists had joked with

her and shared war stories. They'd even told her which athletes gave them a break and always answered their questions. They also told her which players never answered questions. Luc Martineau topped the arrogant-pain-in-the-ass list.

Jane folded the paper and stuck it in her briefcase. Perhaps the Dallas reporters had been nice because they hadn't seen her as a threat and weren't intimidated by a woman. Maybe they would have treated her differently if they'd been in the locker room competing for an interview. She didn't know and really didn't care. It was just nice to discover that not all male reporters resented her. She was relieved to know that when she wrote one last column about her experiences, she could report that some men had evolved and not everyone viewed her as an assault to their egos.

She'd sent off two columns to the *Seattle Times* now. And she hadn't heard a word from her editor. Not a word of praise or criticism, which she was trying to take as a good sign. She'd seen her first article passed around among the players, but none of them had commented either.

'I read your first column,' Darby Hogue said from across the aisle. In his bare feet, Jane estimated Darby Hogue to be five foot six. Five-nine in his cowboy boots. By the cut of his navy-blue suit, she'd guess it was custom-made and would probably cost most people a month's salary. His spiky gelled hair was the color of carrots and his complexion was even whiter than hers. Although she knew he was twenty-eight, he looked about seventeen. His brown eyes were intelligent and shrewd, and he had long, sweeping red lashes. 'You did a good job,' he added.

Finally, someone commented on her article. 'Thank you.'

He leaned across the aisle to give her some pointers. 'Next time you might want to mention our goal attempts.' Darby was the youngest assistant GM in the NHL, and Jane had read in his bio that he was a member of Mensa. She didn't doubt it. Although he appeared to have taken great pains to shake his nerddom, he hadn't quite been able to give up the pocket protector stuck in his white linen shirt.

'I'll tell you what, Mr. Hogue,' she said through what she hoped was a charming smile, 'I won't tell you how to do your job, if you don't tell me how to do mine.'

He blinked. 'That's fair.'

'Yes, I think so.'

He straightened and placed a leather briefcase on his lap. 'You usually sit in the back with the players.'

She'd always sat in back because by the time she'd boarded, the seats up front had been taken by coaches and management. 'Well, I'm beginning to feel persona non grata back there,' she confessed. The incident of the previous night had made their feelings for her perfectly clear.

He returned his gaze to hers. 'Has something happened that I should know about?'

Beyond the nuisance calls, she'd found a dead mouse outside her door last night. It had been very dehydrated as if it had been dead awhile. Obviously someone had found it somewhere and left it for her. Not exactly a horse's head in her bed, but she didn't think it was a coincidence either. But the last thing she needed was for the players to think she was running to management telling tales. 'Nothing I can't handle.'

'Have dinner with me tonight and we can talk about it.'

She stared across the aisle at him. For a second she wondered if he was one of those short guys who just naturally assumed she'd go out with him because she was short too. Her last boyfriend had been five-seven and had had the mother of all Napoleon complexes, which had butted heads with her own Napoleon complex. The very last thing she needed was a short guy asking her out. Especially a short guy who was also Chinooks management. 'I don't think that's a good idea.'

'Why?'

'Because I don't want the players to think you and I are involved.'

'I have dinner with male sports reporters all the time. Chris Evans, in fact.'

It wasn't the same. She had to be completely beyond gossip. More professional than men. Even though women had been allowed in the locker room for almost three decades now, speculation over women sleeping with their sources was still an issue. She didn't think her credibility or acceptance with the players could sink lower, but she really didn't want to find out.

'I just thought you might be tired of eating alone,' Darby added.

She *was* tired of eating alone. She was tired of staring at the walls of a hotel room or the inside of the team's jet. Maybe someplace very public would be okay. 'Just business?'

'Absolutely.'

'Why don't we meet in the hotel restaurant?' she proposed.

'Seven sound okay?'

'Seven is perfect.' She dug around in the front pocket of her briefcase and pulled out the itinerary. 'Where are we staying tonight?'

'LAX Doubletree,' Darby answered. 'The hotel shakes every time one of those airbuses takes off.'

'Marvelous.'

'Welcome to the glamorous life of an athlete,' he said and leaned his head back.

Jane had pretty much already figured out that a four-game grind was just that: a grind. Although she'd already studied it dozens of times, her gaze scanned the itinerary. LA, then San Jose. Just a little over halfway into the road trip and she was looking forward to going home. She wanted to sleep in her own bed, drive her own car instead of ride a bus, and even open her own refrigerator instead of a hotel minibar. The Chinooks had four more days on the road before they returned to Seattle for a four-game, eight-day stretch. Then it was off again for Denver and Minnesota. More hotels and meals by herself.

Maybe having dinner with Darby Hogue was not such a bad idea. It could be enlightening and break the monotony.

At seven o'clock, Jane stepped off the elevators and made her way to the Seasons Restaurant. She'd left her hair down and it fell in soft curls to her shoulders. She wore her black wool pants and gray sweater. The sweater opened on the side of her neck and had flared sleeves, and until Luc had made that comment about her looking like the archangel of doom, she'd really liked it.

Now she wondered if there was some hidden reason beyond her fear of clashing colors that made her gravitate to dark colors. Was she depressed and didn't know it, as Caroline had suggested? Have some undiagnosed mental disorder? Was she really an archangel of doom, or was Caroline delusional and Luc an arrogant A-hole? She liked to think the latter.

Darby waited for her at the entrance of the restaurant, looking very young in a pair of khakis, red and orange Hawaiian print shirt, and a new dose of gel in his hair. They were shown to a table near the windows and Jane ordered a lemon-drop martini to chase away her fatigue, if only for a few hours. Darby ordered a Beck's and was asked for his ID.

'What? I'm twenty-eight,' he complained.

Jane laughed and opened the dinner menu. 'People are going to mistake you for my son,' she kidded him.

The corners of his mouth turned downward and he pulled out his wallet. 'You look younger than I do,' he grumbled as he showed the waiter his identification.

When their drinks arrived, Jane ordered salmon and wild rice while Darby chose beef and a baked potato.

'How's your room?' he asked.

It was like every other room. 'It's fine.'

'Good.' He took a drink of his beer. 'Any problems with the players?'

'No, they all pretty much avoid me.'

'They don't want you here.'

'Yes, I know.' She took a sip of her martini. The sugar around the top of the glass, the floating lemon slice, and the perfect mix of Absolut Citron vodka and Triple Sec almost had her sighing like a seasoned alcoholic. But becoming an alcoholic was one thing that Jane didn't have to worry about, for two reasons. Her hangovers were too painful to ever allow her to turn pro, and when she got tanked her judgment went out the window, sometimes along with her panties.

Jane and Darby's conversation turned from hockey to other interests. She learned that he had graduated summa cum laude with an MBA from Harvard at the age of twenty-three. He mentioned his membership in Mensa three times, and that he owned a five-thousand-square-foot home on Mercer Island, a thirty-foot sailboat, and drove a cherry-red Porsche.

No doubt about it, Darby was a geek. Not that that was necessarily bad; besides being a fraud, she sometimes felt like a geek herself. To keep up her end of the conversation, she mentioned her undergraduate degrees in journalism and English. Darby didn't seem all that impressed.

Their food arrived and he looked up from putting butter on his baked potato. 'Am I going to end up in your *Single Girl* column?'

Jane paused in the act of placing her napkin on her lap. Most men feared showing up in the column. 'Would you mind?'

His eyes lit up. 'Hell, no.' He thought a moment. 'But it has to be good. I mean, I wouldn't want anyone to think I was a bad date.'

'I don't think I can lie,' she lied. Half the stuff in her column was made up.

'I'd make it worth your while.'

If he wanted to wheel and deal, the least she could do was listen. 'How?'

'I could tell the guys on the team that I don't think you're here to report on the size of their johnsons or strange sexual habits,' he said, which immediately made her wonder exactly who had strange sexual habits. Maybe Vlad the Impaler. 'And I could assure them you haven't slept with Mr. Duffy to get this job.'

Complete horror dropped her jaw, and she raised a hand to her mouth. She'd figured that there might be some small minds in the news-room who'd assumed she'd exchanged sexual favors with Leonard Callaway, because, after all, he was the managing editor and she was just that woman who wrote that silly column about being single in the city. She wasn't a *real* journalist.

But it had never entered her head that anyone would think she'd slept with Virgil Duffy. Good God, the man was old enough to be her grandfather. Sure, he had a reputation for dogging younger women, and there had been a time in her life when her standards had hit a real low patch and she'd had sex with some men she'd rather forget about, but she'd never dated anyone forty years older than herself.

Darby laughed and dug into his beef. 'I can see by the look on your face that the speculation isn't true.'

'Of course not.' She reached for her martini and polished it off. The vodka and Triple Sec warmed a path to her stomach. 'I'd never even met Mr. Duffy before that first day in the locker room.' The unfairness of it hit her and she signaled for another martini. Usually Jane hated to cry 'no fair.' She believed that life wasn't fair, and that crying about it only made things worse. She was a get-over-it-and-get-on-with-your-life type of girl, but in this case it really wasn't fair because there was nothing she could do about it. If she made a fuss and denied it, she doubted anyone would believe her.

'If you write about me in your column, make me sound good, I'll make things easier for you.'

She picked up her fork and took a bite of her wild rice. 'What, are you having trouble finding a date?' She'd been joking, but by the brilliant blush to his cheek, she could tell she'd hit a nerve.

'When women first meet me, they think I'm a dork.'

'Hmm, I didn't think so,' she lied, risking the bad karma.

He smiled, and the risk was worth it. 'They never give me a chance.'

'Well, maybe if you didn't talk about Mensa and about your advanced degrees, you'd have better luck.'

'Think so?'

'Yep.' She was halfway through her salmon when her second drink arrived.

'Maybe you could give me some pointers.'

Right, like she was an expert. 'Maybe.'

His shrewd gaze bored into her as he took a bite of potato. 'I could make it worth your while,' he said again.

'I'm getting nuisance calls. Make them stop.'

He didn't appear surprised. 'I'll see what I can do about that.'

'Good, because it's harassment.'

'Look at it more as initiation.'

Uh-huh. 'There was a dead mouse outside my door last night.'

He took a swig of his beer. 'It could have crawled there by itself.'

Sure. 'I want an interview with Luc Martineau.'

'You're not the only one. Luc is a very private guy.'

'Ask him.'

'I'm not the best person to ask him. He doesn't like me.'

She raised her lemon drop to her lips. Luc didn't like her either. 'Why?'

'He knows I advised against trading for him. I was fairly adamant about it.'

That was a surprise. 'Why?'

'Well, it's old news, but he was injured when he was with Detroit. I'm not convinced a player his age can come back from major ACT surgery on both knees. At one time Martineau was good, maybe one of the best, but eleven million a year is a lot to gamble on a thirty-two-year-old man with bad knees. We traded a first-round draft pick, a heavy-hitting defender, and a pair of bookend wings. That left us weak on the right side. I'm not sure Martineau was worth it.'

'He's having a good season,' she pointed out.

'So far. What happens if he's reinjured? You can't build a team around one player.'

Jane didn't know a lot about hockey, and she wondered if Darby was right. Had the team been built around their elite goalie? And did Luc, who appeared so cool and calm, feel the tremendous pressure of what was expected of him?

It took a frantic call from Mrs. Jackson for Luc to learn that Marie hadn't been to school since Luc had left Seattle. Mrs. Jackson told him she'd dropped Marie off every morning, and Marie had walked into the building.

What he also discovered was that she'd then gone straight out the back.

When he'd asked Marie where she'd been spending her time, she'd answered, 'The mall.' When he'd asked her why, she'd said, 'Everyone at that school hates me. I don't have any friends. They're all stupid.'

'Come on, now,' he'd said, 'you'll make friends and then everything will be okay.'

She'd started to cry, and like always, he felt bad and totally inadequate. 'I miss my mom. I want to go home.'

After he'd hung up with Marie and Mrs. Jackson, he'd called his personal manager, Howie Stiller. When Luc returned home Tuesday night, several brochures from private schools would be waiting for him in a FedEx mailer.

Now the music from the piano drifted to where Luc sat in the corner of the lobby bar. He lifted a bottle of Molson's to his mouth and took a long drink. For Marie, going home wasn't an option. Her home was with him now, but she obviously didn't like living with him.

He set the bottle on the table and relaxed in the wing chair. He had to talk to Marie about boarding school, and he hadn't a clue how she'd respond. He wasn't certain she'd like the idea or see the logic and benefit in it. He just hoped she didn't get hysterical.

The day of her mother's funeral, she'd been beyond hysterical, and Luc hadn't known what to do for her. He'd hugged her awkwardly and told her he'd always take care of her. And he would. He would see that she always had everything she needed, but he was a piss-poor substitute for her mother.

How had his life become so complicated? He rubbed his face with his hands, and when he lowered them, he saw Jane Alcott walking toward him. It was probably too much to hope that she'd walk on by.

'Waiting for a friend?' she asked as she came to stand beside the chair opposite him.

He had been, but he'd just called and canceled. After his conversation with Marie, he wasn't in the mood for one-on-one time. He was thinking that he might catch up with some of his teammates at a sports bar downtown. He reached for the bottle and looked at her over the top as he took a swig. He watched her watching him, and he wondered if she was assuming – wrongly – that because he'd been addicted to pain medication he was just as naturally an alcoholic. In his case, one didn't have anything to do with the other.

'Nope. Just sitting here alone,' he answered as he lowered the bottle. Something was different about her tonight. Despite the dark clothing, she looked softer, less uptight. Kind of cute. Her hair, usually held back in a controlled ponytail, fell in a tangle of unruly curls to her shoulder. Her green eyes were kind of dewy like wet leaves, and her bottom lip appeared fuller and the corners of her mouth were turned up.

'I just finished a dinner meeting with Darby Hogue,' she provided as if he'd asked.

'Where?' In his suite? That would explain the hair, the eyes, and the smile. Luc never would have guessed Darby even knew what to do with a woman, much less put that soft dewy look on her face. And he never would have thought Jane Alcott, the archangel of gloom and doom, could look so warm and sexy. Damn.

'In the hotel restaurant, of course.' Her smile fell. 'Where did you think?'

'The hotel restaurant,' he lied.

She wasn't buying it, and as he'd come to expect in the short time he'd known her, she wasn't going to let it go either. 'Don't tell me you're one of the guys who think I slept with Virgil Duffy to get this job.'

'No, not me,' he lied some more. They'd all wondered, but he didn't know how many actually believed it.

'Great, and now I'm sleeping with Darby Hogue.'

He held up a hand. 'None of my business.'

As the last strains of the piano died, Jane slid into the chair opposite him and blew out a breath. Damn, so much for a little peace.

'Why do women have to put up with this crap?' she said. 'If I were a man, no one would accuse me of exchanging sex for a promotion. If I were a man, no one would think I had to sleep with my sources just to get the story. They'd just slap me on the back and give me high fives and say . . .' She paused in her rant long enough to lower her voice and her brows at the same time. '"Good piece of investigative journalism. You're the man. You're the stud."' She ran her fingers though the sides of her hair and pushed it from her face. Her sleeves fell back and exposed the thin blue veins of her slim wrist, and the material of her sweater pulled across her small breasts. 'No one accused *you* of sleeping with Virgil to get *your* job.'

He lifted his gaze to her face. 'That's because *I'm* the stud.' They all had their crosses to bear, and after the day he'd had, he didn't have the energy to pretend sympathy and understanding. Luc Martineau didn't have the time or inclination to worry about a pain-in-the-ass reporter. He had his own damn problems, and one of them was her.

Jane looked over the table at Luc and crossed her arms over her chest. The light overhead picked out the blond in his short hair and settled on the broad shoulders of his blue chambray shirt. The color of his shirt brought out the blue of his eyes. After the two martinis she'd had during dinner, everything was surrounded by a nice cheery glow. Or at least it had been until Luc insinuated that she and Darby were sleeping together.

'If I had a penis,' she said, 'no one would think I was having sex with Darby.'

'Don't be too sure about that. We're not altogether sure of the little weasel's sexual orientation.' Luc reached for his beer and Jane's lungs squeezed a little. He'd left the top two buttons of his shirt undone and the soft material fell away from his chest, exposing his clavicle and the top of his muscular shoulder and neck.

She could set Luc straight on that score, but she didn't bother to inform him that Darby had wanted dating tips over dinner. 'How're your knees?' she asked as she rested her forearms on the table.

He raised the Molson's to his mouth and said, 'One hundred percent.'

'Completely pain-free?'

He lowered the bottle and sucked a drop of beer from his bottom lip. 'What? You don't know? I thought you made digging into my past your calling in life.'

His conceit was outrageous and a little too close to the truth. For some reason she could not even explain to herself, Luc intrigued her more than the other Chinooks. 'Do you really think that I don't have anything better to do than to spend my time thinking about you? Digging up a little of the goods on Luc Martineau?'

Fine lines appeared at the corners of his eyes and he laughed. 'Sweetheart, there is nothing little about Luc's goods.'

The Jane who wrote the *Single Girl* column would have a sophisticated comeback and dazzle him with her wit. Honey Pie would take him by his hand and lead him to a linen closet. She'd unbutton the rest of his shirt and place her mouth on his warm chest. Breathe heavily the scent of his skin and melt into his hot hard body. She would see for herself if he told the truth *aboot* those goods. But Jane was neither of those women. The real Jane was too inhibited and self-conscious, and she hated that a man who made her catch her breath was the same man who looked through her and found her so lacking.

'Jane?'

She blinked. 'What?'

He reached across the table and the tips of his long fingers brushed hers. 'Are you all right?'

'Yes.' It was the slightest of touches, maybe not even quite a touch, but she felt the tingles from it travel through her palm and up her wrist. She stood so quickly the table rocked. 'No. I'm going to my room.'

The combination of alcohol, Luc's molten mojo, and the grind of the last five days sloshed about in her brain as she looked around for the bank of elevators. For a few seconds she was disoriented. Three different hotels in five days, and suddenly she couldn't remember where the elevators were. She glanced toward the registration counter and spied them off to the right. Without a word, she walked from the lobby bar. This was not good, she told herself as she moved across the hotel lobby. He was so big and overtly male, he made her wrist tingle and her brain go numb. She stopped in front of the elevator doors, her cheeks hot. Why him? She didn't like him. Yes, he intrigued her, but that wasn't the same as liking him.

Luc reached around her from behind and pressed the elevator button. 'Going up?' he asked next to her ear.

'Oh, yeah.' She wondered how long she would have stood there like a fool before she realized that she hadn't pressed a button.

'Have you been drinking?'

'Why?'

'You smell like vodka.'

'I had a couple martinis with dinner.'

'Ah,' he said as the doors opened and they stepped into the empty elevator. 'Which floor?'

'Three.' Jane looked down at the toes of her boots, then moved her gaze to his blue and gray running shoes. As the doors closed, he leaned against the back panel and crossed one foot over the other. The hem of his Levi's brushed the white laces. She lifted her gaze up his long legs and thighs, up the bulge of his fly and the buttons of his shirt to his face. Within the cramped confines of the elevator, his blue eyes stared back at her.

'I like your hair down.'

She pushed one side behind her ear. 'I hate my hair. I can't ever do anything with it and it's always in my face.'

'It's not bad.'

Not bad? As compliments went, it ranked right up there with, 'Your butt's not *that* big.' So why did a tingle in her wrist travel to her stomach? The doors opened, saving her a response. She stepped out first and he followed.

'Where's your room?'

'Three-twenty-five. Where's yours?'

'I'm on the fifth floor.'

She stopped. 'You got off on the wrong floor.'

'No, I didn't.' He took her elbow in his big hand and moved with her down the hall. Through the material of her sweater, she felt the warmth of his palm. 'When you stood up in the lobby, you looked like you were about to fall over.'

'I haven't had *that* much to drink.' She would have stopped again if he hadn't kept moving her along the blue and yellow carpet. 'Are you escorting me to my room?'

'Yep.'

She thought of the first morning when he'd carried her briefcase, then told her that he wasn't trying to be nice. 'Are you trying to be nice this time?'

'No, I'm meeting the guys in a few and I don't want to have to wonder if you made it to your room without passing out on the way.'

'And that would ruin your fun?'

'No, but for a few seconds it might take my attention off Candy Peeks and her naughty cheerleader routine. Candy's worked real hard on her pom-poms, and it would be a shame if I couldn't give her my undivided attention.'

'A stripper?'

'They prefer to be called dancers.'

'Ahh.'

He squeezed her arm. 'Are you going to print that in the paper?'

'No, I don't care about your personal life.' She pulled her plastic room key from her pocket. Luc took it from her and opened the door before she could object.

'Good, because I'm yanking your chain. I'm really meeting the guys at a sports bar that's not too far away.'

She looked up into the shadows of his face created by her darkened room. She didn't know which story to believe. 'Why the BS?'

'To see that little wrinkle between your brows.'

She shook her head as he handed her the key.

'See ya, Ace,' he said and turned away.

Jane watched the back of his head and his wide shoulders as he walked down the hall. 'See ya tomorrow night, Martineau.'

He stopped and looked back over his shoulder. 'Are you planning on going into the locker room?'

'Of course. I'm a sports reporter and it's part of my job. Just as if I were a man.'

'But you're not a man.'

'I expect to be treated like a man.'

'Then take my advice and keep your gaze up,' he said as he turned once more and walked away. 'That way you won't blush and your jaw won't hit the floor like a woman.'

The next night Jane sat in the press box and watched the Chinooks battle it out with the Los Angeles Kings. The Chinooks came out strong and put three goals on the board in the first two periods. It appeared Luc would have his sixth shutout of the season until a freak shot glanced off defenseman Jack Lynch's glove and flipped behind Luc into the net. At the end of the third frame the score was three–one, and Jane breathed a sigh of relief. The Chinooks had won. She wasn't a jinx. At least not today. She would have a job when she woke in the morning.

She remembered in horrid Technicolor detail the first time she walked into the Chinooks' locker room, and her stomach twisted into a big knot as she passed through the doorway. The other reporters were already there questioning the team's captain, Mark Bressler, who stood in front of his stall taking questions.

'We played well in our own end,' he said as he pulled his jersey over his head. 'We took advantage of power plays and put the puck in the net. The ice was soft out there tonight, but we didn't let it affect our play. We came out knowing what we had to do and we did it.'

Keeping her gaze on his face, Jane felt around in her purse for her tape recorder. She brought the notes she'd been taking throughout the game up to eye level. 'Your defense allowed thirty-two shots on goal,' she managed between the other questions. 'Are the Chinooks looking to acquire a veteran defenseman before the March nineteenth trade deadline?' She thought the question was quite brilliant, if she did say so herself. Informed and knowledgeable.

Mark looked through the other reporters at her and said, 'That's a question only Coach Nystrom can answer.'

So much for her brilliance.

'You scored your three hundred and ninety-eighth career goal tonight. How does it feel?' she asked. The only reason she knew about the goal was because she'd heard the television reporters talking about it in the press box. She figured a bit of flattery would get a quote out of the captain.

'Good.'

So much for a quote.

She turned and headed down the row of towering men, moving toward Nick Grizzell, the forward who'd scored the first goal. Long johns fell and jocks snapped as if on cue when she walked past. She kept her eyes up and her gaze forward as she clicked on her tape recorder and let it record questions asked by other reporters. Her editor at the *Times* wouldn't know that she hadn't asked the questions. But she knew, and the players knew it too.

Grizzell had just returned the week before from the injured list and she asked him, 'How does it feel to be back in the game and scoring the first goal?'

He looked across his shoulder at her and dropped his jockstrap. 'Fine.'

Jane had had about enough of this crap. 'Great,' she said. 'I'll quote you on that.'

She glanced at the stall several feet away and saw Luc Martineau laughing at her. There was no way she would walk over there and ask him what he was laughing about.

She just didn't want to know.

Ringing the Berries: When the Puck Hits a Player's Cup

J ane leaned back against her seat, pushed up her glasses, and studied the laptop resting on her tray table. She read what she'd written so far:

Seattle Checkmates Kings

The Seattle Chinooks crowned all six Los Angeles power-play chances and Goalie Luc Martineau blocked twenty-three shots on goal in a 3–1 victory over the Los Angeles Kings. The Kings put a goal on the board in the last few seconds of the game when a freak shot glanced off Seattle player Jack Lynch's glove and flipped into the Chinooks' net.

On the ice, the Chinooks play a fast, fearless game, aggravating the opposition with skill and brute strength. Inside the locker room they seem to love to aggravate journalists by dropping their pants. I know of at least one reporter who would love to put 'the big hurt' on them.

She reached forward and deleted the last paragraph. It had only been six days, she reminded herself. The players were leery and superstitious. They felt she had been forced on them, and they were right: she had been. Now it was time for them to get over it so she could do her job.

She glanced at the snoring players sacked out in the team jet. How could she earn their trust or their respect if they wouldn't speak to her? How to resolve this issue so her job and her life were easier?

The answer came in the form of Darby Hogue. The night they arrived in San Jose, he phoned her room to tell her that some of the players were getting together at a bar somewhere downtown.

'Why don't you come?' he said.

'With you?'

'Yeah, and maybe wear something girly. That way the players might forget you're a reporter.'

She hadn't packed anything girly, and even if she had, she didn't want the players to see her as a girly girl. While she needed them to know she respected them and their privacy, they needed to respect her as they would any professional journalist. 'Give me about fifteen minutes and I'll meet you in the lobby,' she said, figuring interaction with the players away from the game might help and couldn't hurt.

Jane dressed in stretch wool pants that had two rows of buttons up the front like a sailor, a merino sweater set, and boots. All in black. She liked black.

She moved into the bathroom and gathered her hair at the back of her head. She didn't like it hanging in her face, and she didn't want Luc to think his opinion mattered. She looked in the mirror and dropped her hand to the counter. Her hair fell to her shoulders in dark shiny waves and curls.

He'd walked her to her hotel room. He'd thought she was sick or drunk, and he'd walked her back to make sure she got there safely. His one act of unexpected kindness affected her more than it should, especially since he'd only walked her to her door so he could thoroughly enjoy himself at a nudie bar. Or to yank her chain. That one simple gesture slid within her chest and warmed her heart, no matter if she wanted to be warmed or not. And she didn't.

Even if she were stupid enough to fall for a man like Luc, with all of the emotional and professional ramifications, he would never fall for a woman like Jane. And it wasn't because she thought herself unattractive or uninteresting. She didn't. No, she was a realist. Ken hooked up with Barbie. Brad married Jennifer and Mick dated supermodels. That was life. *Real* life, and she'd never been one to purposely set herself up for heartache. She never wanted to be the one left behind when the relationship was over. She always got out first. It hurt less that way. Maybe Caroline was right about her. She thought about it a moment and shook her head. Caroline watched too much Dr. Phil.

Jane reached for the brush once more and pulled her hair back. She smeared Chap Stick on her lips, grabbed her purse, and met Darby in the lobby. Upon seeing him, she almost ran the other way. Jane knew that she herself was not a fashion goddess, and she didn't try. Darby, on the other hand, wasn't a fashion god, but he *did* try. Only the results were unfortunate.

This evening he wore black leather pants and a silk

shirt with red flames and purple skulls on it. Leather pants on any man but Lenny Kravitz was a huge mistake, but she doubted even Lenny could pull off the shirt. Looking at him, Jane understood why the Chinooks might question Darby's sexual orientation.

They took a taxi from the hotel to Big Buddy's, a little bar more on the outskirts of the downtown area. The sun was just setting on a cloudless night, and the wind carried a hint of rain and dust. A crisp breeze brushed Jane's cheeks as she and Darby exited the taxi. A faded sign above the door read, 'Voted Best Ribs.' She almost tripped on the uneven sidewalk and wondered why the Chinooks had chosen such a dive.

Inside the building, several television sets hung suspended in the corners, while behind the bar a red and blue Budweiser sign glowed. A string of lights left over from Christmas was still taped to the mirror. It smelled of smoke and booze, barbeque sauce and roasted meat. If Jane hadn't already eaten, her stomach would have growled.

Jane knew that by being seen with Darby, she ran the risk of adding fuel to the rumor that they were lovers, but she also figured that there was nothing she could do about it. And she wondered which was worse, being seen as the lover of a man who dressed like a pimp, or as the mistress of Virgil Duffy, a man old enough to be her grandfather.

Pinball machines pinged and flashed and she recognized two Chinooks playing air hockey in the corner. About five Seattle players sat at the bar, watching the Rangers battle it out with the Devils. Another half dozen sat at a table with a pitcher of beer, empty tubs of coleslaw, and Fred Flintstone-sized piles of stripped rib bones.

'Hey, guys,' Darby called out. At the sound of his voice, they turned their attention toward Darby and Jane. The hockey players looked like cavemen after feasting on a woolly mammoth, all full and content and sluggish, but they didn't look too happy to see Darby, and even less happy to see her.

'Jane and I felt like a beer,' he continued as if he didn't notice. He pulled out a chair for her, and she sat next to Bruce Fish and across from the rookie with the blond Mohawk. Darby sat to her left at the head of the table. The red flames and purple skulls on his shirt were subdued somewhat by the dim lighting.

A waitress with a tight Big Buddy's T-shirt set two cocktail napkins on the table and took Darby's order. As soon as he uttered the word *Corona*, he was instantly carded. A scowl drew his red brows together as he flashed his identification.

'That's fake,' someone down the table said. 'He's only twelve.'

'I'm older than you, Peluso,' Darby grumbled and shoved his driver's license back into his wallet.

The waitress turned her attention to Jane.

'Bet she orders a margarita,' Fishy said out of the corner of his mouth.

'Or one of those wine spritzers,' someone else added.

'Something fruity.'

Jane looked up into the shadowy face of the waitress. 'Do you have Bombay Sapphire gin?'

'Sure do.'

'Fabulous. I'd like a dirty martini with three olives,

please.' She glanced at the stunned faces around her and smiled. 'A girl's gotta get her daily allowance of green veggies.'

Bruce Fish laughed. 'Maybe you should order a Bloody Mary for the celery.'

Jane grimaced and shook her head. 'I don't like tomato juice.' She looked across the table at Daniel Holstrom. The lights from the bar cast a reddish-pink glow in his white-blond Mohawk. She wondered if the young rookie was twenty-one yet. She had her doubts.

Two more waitresses in Big Buddy's T-shirts appeared and cleared and cleaned the table. Jane half expected flirting and a proposition or two – jocks were notorious for rude behavior toward women – but nothing happened besides a few polite thank yous. Conversation took place over and around Jane and involved nothing more important or more pressing than the latest movie they'd seen and the weather. She wondered if they were trying to bore her to death. She suspected that might be the case, and she could honestly say the most interesting thing going on was the flash of lights on Daniel's scalp.

Bruce must have noticed her attention to the Swede's head because he asked, 'What do you think of the Stromster's hair?'

She thought she detected a blush on Daniel's cheeks to match the pink tint of his hair. 'I like a man who is so secure in his own masculinity that he can dare to be different.'

'He didn't have much of a choice,' Darby explained as his beer and Jane's martini arrived. 'He's new to the team this year, and anyone new has to go through initiation.'

The Stromster nodded as if this made perfect sense.

'My first year,' Darby continued, 'they emptied their dirty laundry in my car.'

The guys around the table laughed, deep ha-ha-ha-has.

'My first season was with the Rangers and they shaved my head *and* buried my cup in the ice machine,' Peter Peluso confessed.

Bruce sucked in his breath, and she suspected he might have put a protective hand over his crotch if she hadn't been sitting next to him. 'That's harsh,' he said. 'My rookie season was spent in Toronto, and I got thrown outside in my underwear a lot. Talk about colder than a well digger's ass.' He shivered to prove his point.

'Wow,' Jane said and took a sip of her drink. 'Now I feel lucky that you boys just left me a dead mouse and call me all night.'

Several pairs of guilty eyes looked at her, then slid away.

'How's Taylor Lee?' she asked Fishy, deciding to let them all off the hook – for now. Just as she suspected he would, he launched into his daughter's most recent accomplishments, which began with toilet training and ended with a repeat of the telephone conversation he'd had with his two-year-old earlier that evening.

Since she'd met Bruce that first morning, she'd done a little reading on him. She'd discovered that he was going through a real messy divorce, and she wasn't all that surprised. Now that she'd lived a small sample of their lives, she imagined it would be difficult to keep a family together while on the road so much. Especially given the rink bunnies that hung out in the lobby bars.

At first Jane hadn't noticed them, but it hadn't taken

her long to pick up on who they were, and now she spotted them easily. They dressed in tight clothes, their bodies on display, and they all had that man-eater look in their eyes.

'Anyone want to play darts?' Rob Sutter asked as he approached the table.

Before anyone could speak, Jane was on her feet. 'I do,' she said, and by the scowl on the Hammer's face, it was clear he'd meant anyone *but* her.

'Just don't expect me to let you win,' he said.

Hustling darts had helped Jane put herself through college. She didn't expect anyone to *let* her win. She made her eyes go wide as she reached for her drink. 'Aren't you going to go easy on me because I'm a girl?'

'I don't give quarter to girls.'

With her free hand, she took the extra set of darts and headed across the bar. The top of her head didn't even reach his shoulder. The Hammer didn't know it, but he was about to get the big hurt he so richly deserved. 'Will you at least tell me the rules?'

He quickly explained how to play 501, which, of course, she already knew. But she asked questions like she'd never played before, and he was magnanimous enough to let her go first.

'Thanks,' she said as she put her martini on a nearby table and took her place at the taped toe line. Nailed to the wall a little over seven feet away, the board was lit from above. She rolled the shaft of the cheap house dart between her fingers, testing the weight. She preferred a ninety-eight percent tungsten dart with an aluminum shaft and Ribtex flights. Like the set she owned. The difference between the brass darts she held in her hands and the darts resting in their custom-made box at home was the difference between a Ford Taurus and a Ferrari.

She leaned way over the line, held the dart wrong, and glanced down the shaft as if she were sighting in a rifle. At the last second before release, she stopped. 'Don't you guys usually bet or something?'

'Yeah, but I don't want to take your money.' He looked at her and smiled as if he'd thought up something really funny. 'But we could play for drinks. Whoever loses has to buy all the guys a beer.'

She contrived to look worried. 'Oh. Hmm. Well, I've only got a fifty. Do you think that will cover it?'

'That ought to be enough,' he said, with all the arrogance of a man assured of his own success. And for the next half-hour, Jane let him think he was winning too. Some of the other players gathered around to watch and heckle, but once she was behind by two hundred points and Rob was beginning to feel sorry for her, she got to work and beat him in four turns at the board. Darts were serious business, and she took serious pleasure in trouncing the Hammer.

'Where did you learn to play like that?' he asked.

'Beginner's luck.' She downed the last of her drink. 'Who's next?'

'I'll take you on.' Luc Martineau stepped out of the darkness and took the darts from Rob. The light from the bar chased varying degrees of shadows across his broad shoulders and the side of his face. Raindrops shone in his hair and the scent of the cool night breeze clung to him.

'Watch out, Luc, she's a hustler,' Rob warned.

'Is that right?' One corner of Luc's mouth lifted. 'Are you a hustler, Ace?'

'Just because I beat the Hammer, I'm automatically a hustler?'

'No. You let poor Rob think he was winning and then you coldcocked him. That makes you a hustler.'

She tried not to smile, but she failed. 'Are you scared?'

'Not hardly.' He shook his head and a short lock of dark blond hair fell across his forehead. 'Ready to play?'

'I don't know,' she said. 'You're a really bad sport.'

'Me?' He placed a big hand on the front of his ribbed navy sweater, drawing her attention to his wide chest.

'I've seen you whack the goalposts when a puck gets by you.'

'I'm competitive.' His hand fell to his side. 'Not a bad sport.'

'Right.' She tilted her head and looked into his eyes, the light blue barely discernible within the dark bar. 'Do you think you can stand to lose?'

'I don't plan to lose.' He motioned toward the tape line. 'Ladies first.'

When it came to darts, she took no prisoners and was both competitive and a bad sport. If he wanted her to go first, she wasn't going to argue. 'How much money are you willing to bet?'

'I'll put my fifty against your fifty.'

'You're on.' Jane doubled on with her first throw and scored sixty points by the time she was through.

Luc's first throw bounced back and he didn't double on until his third dart. 'That sucked.' With his brows drawn together, he walked to the board and retrieved the darts. Standing within the pool of light, he studied the tips and flights. 'These are dull,' he said, then looked across his shoulder at her. 'Let me see yours.'

She doubted hers were sharper and moved next to him. He took them from her open palm and, with his head bent over hers, tested the points with his thumb. 'Yours aren't as dull as mine.'

He was so close, if she leaned forward just a little, her forehead would touch his. 'Fine,' she said, managing to sound halfway normal, as if the clean scent of him didn't make her breath catch in her throat. 'Pick whichever three you want, and I'll take the others.'

'No. We'll use the same darts.' He lifted his gaze to hers. 'That way, when I beat you, you can't cry.'

She looked into his eyes, so close to hers, and her heart thumped in her chest. 'I'm not the one who threw a bounce-back on the very first throw, then blamed the darts.' And while her heart was thumping, he appeared totally unaffected. She took a step back and put distance between him and her silly reaction. 'Now, are you going to talk all night, Martineau, or are we going to get busy so I can kick your butt?'

'You're cocky for such a short little thing,' he said and slapped the three darts he'd deemed the sharpest into her hand. 'I think you have one of those short-girl syndromes,' he added, then joined some of his teammates who'd moved to the table several feet away.

She shrugged as if to say, *Yeah, so?* and walked to the line. With her weight perfectly balanced on both feet, her wrist loose and relaxed, she shot a double, a triple, and a single bull. Luc strode to the toe line as she retrieved the darts from the board. 'You're right,' she said as she walked toward him, 'these are much better.' She placed all three in his outstretched hand. 'Thanks.'

His hand closed over hers, pressing the darts into her palm. 'Where did you learn to shoot like that?'

'At a little bar near the University of Washington.' The heat of his hand warmed hers. 'I worked there nights to put myself through school.' She tried to pull away, but his grasp tightened and the shafts dug into her flesh.

'Isn't Hooters around there?' He finally let go of her hand and she took a step back.

'No, it's across the lake from the university,' she answered, even though she figured he knew exactly where Hooters was located. His car could probably get there on its own. He was just trying to rattle her.

It wasn't working until he took a step toward her and said next to her ear, 'Were you a Hooters girl?'

Despite the heat creeping up her neck, she managed a cool and collected, if not quite a Honey Pie, response. 'I think it's pretty safe to say I'm not Hooters material.'

He lowered his voice, his warm breath touching her cheek as he asked, 'Why's that?'

'We both know why.'

He stepped back and looked at her mouth before slowly raising his gaze to her eyes. 'Tank top the wrong color?'

'No.'

'You don't like the shorts?'

'I'm not the kind of girl they're looking for.'

'I don't think that's true. I know for a fact they hire short girls. I've seen them in there.' He paused a moment, then added, 'Of course, that was in Singapore.'

They both knew they weren't talking about her height. 'You're trying to rattle me so you'll win, aren't you?'

Tiny creases appeared in the corners of his blue eyes. 'Is it working?'

'No,' she lied and moved to the sideline where the Chinooks stood. 'Did you come through with those beers, Rob?'

He patted her on the top of her head. 'Sure did, Sharky.'

Sharky? Well, she'd earned a nickname, and it was better than what she was sure they called her when she wasn't around. And he'd patted her head as if she were a dog. Progress, she thought as she watched Luc raise his hand, snap it forward, and bury the dart in the bull's-eye.

'Luc hates to lose more than anyone I've known,' Bruce told her.

'Maybe you shouldn't beat him,' Peter warned. 'It might snakebite his game.'

'Forget it, guys.' She shook her head as Luc buried the second dart in the out area and swore like a hockey player. 'I'm not going to let anyone win.'

'Losing might make him play with a real mad-on at the Compac Center tomorrow night.'

'Yeah, remember when he lost at bowling by one pin and the next night he duked it out with Roy?' Darby reminded everyone.

'That probably had more to do with Luc and Patrick's trash-talking than a bowling score.'

'Goalie grudge match.'

'They played old-time hockey that night.'

'Whatever the reason, they mixed it up at center ice, and man, it was beautiful.'

'When was that?' Jane wanted to know.

'Last month.'

Last month, and he still had more than half the season to go. For several long moments, Luc stood at the toe line, staring the board down as if he were in a contest of wills. A trail of light poured across the cheap red carpet and lit up his leather shoes and black pants to his knees. Then, as if he were launching a missile, he buried the dart deep in the double twenty for a total of sixty-five points. The scowl pulling at his brow as he strode to her and handed her the darts told her he wasn't satisfied with trailing behind by seventy-five points.

'If they gave points for burying the dart *through* the board, you'd stand a chance of winning,' she said. 'Next time you might want to use finesse rather than muscle.'

'I'm not a finesse kind of guy.'

No kidding. She moved into position, and just as she was about to release the dart, Luc spoke from the sidelines. 'How do you get your hair pulled back that tight?' The other Chinooks laughed as if Luc were real funny.

She lowered her arm and looked over at him. 'This isn't hockey. There's no trash-talking in darts.'

He flashed her a smile. 'There is now.'

Fine. She'd still beat him. While he continued to heckle from the sidelines, her three throws equaled an even fifty. Her lowest score so far. 'You're behind by a hundred and sixteen,' she reminded him.

'Not for long,' he boasted, then walked up to the toe line and threw a double bull and a single twenty.

Dang. Time for a little trash talk of her own. 'Hey, Martineau, is that a pumpkin on your shoulders or is that your vacuous head?'

He glanced at her. 'Is that the best you can do?'

The rest of the Chinooks seemed equally unimpressed.

Darby leaned toward her and whispered, 'That was kind of lame.'

'What the hell is vacuous?' Rob asked.

Darby answered for her. 'It means empty or hollow.'

'Why didn't you just say that, Sharky?'

'Yeah, you can't trash talk using words like that.'

Jane frowned and folded her arms across her chest. *Vacuous* was a perfectly good word. 'You guys don't like it because it doesn't start with an *F*.'

Luc threw his third dart and scored a total of eighty points. Time to quit playing around and get serious. She walked to the line, raised her arm, and waited for the heckling to begin. But Luc remained silent, unnerving her more than his insults. She managed to shoot a triple twenty, but when she took aim again, Luc said, 'Do you ever wear anything besides black and gray?'

'Of course,' she said without looking at him.

'That's right.' Then, just as she was about to shoot again, he added, 'Your cow pajamas are blue.'

'How do you know about her cow pajamas?' one of the guys asked.

Mr. Information failed to answer and she looked over at him, surrounded by his teammates, his hands on his hips and a smile on his lips.

'The other night I left my room to buy some M&M's,' she told them. 'I thought you guys would all be in bed, so I wore my PJs. Luc snuck up on me.'

'I didn't sneak.'

'Sure.' She lined up her shot and threw a double ten. Then he waited until the exact moment she released her third dart to say, 'She wears lesbian glasses.' She missed the board completely. That hadn't happened in years.

'I don't either!' Only after she denied it did she fear she may have objected a bit too vehemently.

Luc laughed. 'They're horrible little black squares like all those NOW girls wear.'

The rest of the Chinooks laughed too, and even Darby said, 'Oh, yeah, lesbian, all right.'

Jane pulled the darts from the board. 'They're not. They're perfectly heterosexual.' Geez, what was she talking about? Heterosexual eyeglasses? These guys were all making her crazy. She took a calming breath and handed the darts to Luc. She would not let these dumb jocks rattle her. 'I am not gay. Although there is certainly nothing wrong with it. If I were gay, I'd be out and proud.'

'That would explain the shoes,' Rob joined in.

Jane looked down at her boots. 'What's wrong with my Docs?'

For the first time that night, the Stromster decided to speak. 'Maahhn shuz,' he said.

'Man shoes?' She looked into his young face. 'Since I defended your Mohawk earlier, I expected better of you, Daniel.' His gaze slid away and he took sudden interest in something across the room.

Luc moved to the line and scored forty-eight points. When it was her turn again, all the guys on the sidelines took turns heckling her. The conversation turned severely politically incorrect when they decided that the reason she wore dark colors had to be because she was *depressed* about being gay.

'I'm *not* gay,' she insisted. She was an only child and hadn't been raised around boys, except her father, of course, but he didn't count. Her father was a serious man who never joked at all. She had no experience with this sort of teasing.

'It's okay, sweetheart,' Luc reassured her. 'If I were a girl, I'd be a lesbian too.'

Jane figured she had two choices. Get upset and indignant, or relax. She was a journalist, a professional woman. She wasn't traveling with the team to become buddies, and certainly not to be teased like they were all back in high school. But the professional approach hadn't worked so far, and she had to admit that she liked the teasing better than being ignored. Besides, these guys probably razzed male reporters also. 'Luc, you're already a prima donna,' she said.

Luc chuckled and she finally got a laugh out of the others. For the rest of the game, she tried to give as good as she got, but these guys were much better at it than she and had had years of practice. In the end, she beat Luc by almost two hundred points, but she lost in the war of words.

Somehow, during all the teasing and trash-talking, she'd moved up a few notches in their esteem. She probably could have done without their opinions on her clothes, shoes, and hair, but at least they weren't talking about the weather, giving her one-word answers, or ignoring her altogether. Yes, this was definitely progress.

After the game tomorrow night, they might actually speak to her. She didn't expect for them all to become good pals, but perhaps now they wouldn't give her such a hard time in the locker room. Perhaps they'd give her an interview and a break and keep their jockstraps up as she walked by.

*

Behind the wire cage of his mask, Luc watched the puck drop and spin on its side. Bressler muscled the puck out of the play-off circle, and the battle between Seattle and San Jose began.

Luc crossed himself for luck, but ten minutes into the first frame, his luck completely deserted him. Sharks right winger Teemu Selanne chipped the puck and it bounced into the net. It was an easy goal. One Luc should have stopped, and it seemed to trigger a complete blowout. Not only for Luc, but the entire team.

When the first period ended, two Chinooks players required stitches, and Luc had given up four goals. At two minutes into the second frame, Grizzell got brutally cross-checked at center ice. He went down hard and didn't get back up. He had to be carried from the ice, and ten minutes later Luc misplaced a puck in his glove hand and the fifth Sharks goal went up on the board. Coach Nystrom gave the signal, yanked Luc from the net, and replaced him with the second-string goalie.

The skate from the pipes to the bench is the longest of any netminder's life. Every goalie who ever played the game had an off night, but for Luc Martineau, it was more than that. He'd been through it too many times during his last season with Detroit not to feel it looming overhead now like an executioner's ax. He'd lost focus out there, felt out of sync. Instead of seeing the play before it happened, he was one second behind it. Was this it? The first bad game in a downhill slide? A fluke or a trend? The beginning of the end?

Apprehension and a real fear he didn't even want to admit feeling squeezed his chest and bit the back of his neck. He felt it as he sat on the bench, watching the rest of the game from the pines.

'Everyone has an off night,' Coach Nystrom told him in the locker room. 'Roy got pulled last month. Don't worry about it, Luc.'

'None of us played worth a shit tonight,' Sutter told him.

'We should have played better in front of you,' Bressler added. 'When you're in the goal, we sometimes forget to step in the crease and protect you.'

Luc didn't let himself off quite so easy. He'd never been one to blame others and was ultimately responsible for his own play.

As the jet took off from San Francisco, he sat in the dark cabin reliving his past, and not the good stuff. The horrible hit to his knees, the surgeries and months of physical rehabilitation. His addiction to painkillers, and the horrible body aches and nausea that rolled through him if he didn't feed it. And ultimately his inability to play the game he loved.

Failure whispered in his ear as he headed home, telling him he'd lost his edge. The glow of Jane Alcott's laptop screen and the *click-click* of her keyboard assured him that everyone else would know it too. In the sports section of the paper, he would read her report of that night's disaster.

At the airport in Seattle, Luc headed to long-term parking and caught a glimpse of Jane cramming her stuff into a Honda Prelude. She looked up as he passed, but neither of them spoke. She looked like she didn't need his help with her suitcase, and he didn't have anything to say to the archangel of gloom and doom.

A sprinkling of rain wet the windshield of his Land Cruiser as he made the forty-minute drive into downtown Seattle. He couldn't remember a time when he'd been so glad to be home.

Moonlight spilled through the eight-foot windows in the living room as he moved through his dark apartment. The light above the stove had been left on, illuminating the FedEx envelope on the counter. He walked into his bedroom and flipped on the light. He left the door partway open and tossed his duffel on the floor by his bed. Shrugging out of his blazer, he hung it next to his garment bag in his closet. He'd unpack tomorrow. Right now he was tired and relieved to be home, and he wanted nothing more than to fall face first into bed.

He loosened the knot of his tie as Marie knocked on his door, pushing it open the rest of the way. She wore a pair of flannel drawstring pajama bottoms and a Britney Spears T-shirt. She looked about ten years old.

'Guess what, Luc?'

'Hey, there.' He glanced at his watch. It was past midnight; whatever she wanted, she obviously didn't feel it could wait until morning. He wondered if she'd managed to get kicked out of school since he'd spoken to her last. He was almost afraid to ask. 'What's up?'

Her big blue eyes lit up and she smiled. 'I got asked to the dance.'

'What dance?'

'The dance at my school.'

He pulled the knot of his tie, and thought of the FedEx envelope sitting in the kitchen. He'd deal with it tomorrow. 'When is it?'

'A few weeks.'

She might not be living with him in a few weeks. But she didn't need to know that now. 'Who asked you?'

Her eyes lit up even more and she moved farther into the room. 'Zack Anderson. He's a senior.'

Shit.

'He's in a band! He's got a lip ring and his nose and eyebrows are pierced. He has a tattoo. He's sooooo hot!'

Double shit. Luc had nothing against a tattoo. But piercings? Christ. 'What's the name of his band?'

'The Slow Screws.'

Great.

'I need to get a dress. And shoes.' Marie sat on the edge of his bed and shoved her hands between her knees. 'Mrs. Jackson said she'd take me.' She looked up, her eyes pleading. 'But she's old.'

'Marie, I'm a guy. I don't know anything about buying prom dresses.'

'But you have lots of girlfriends. You know what looks good.'

On women. Not on girls. Not on his sister. Not to go to a prom she probably wouldn't be here to attend anyway. And even if she was, not with Zack of the Loose Screws. The guy with the lip ring and pierced nose.

'I've never been on a date,' she confessed.

His hands fell to his sides and he looked at her closely. At her brows that were too thick and hair that looked a bit on the dry side. Damn, she needed a mother. A woman to help her. Not him.

'What do boys like girls to wear?' she asked.

As little as possible, he thought. 'Long sleeves. We think long sleeves and high necks are hot. And long dresses with big puffy skirts so we can't get very close.'

She laughed. 'That's not true.'

'I swear to God it is, Marie,' he said and pulled the tie from around his neck and tossed it on the bedside table. 'We don't like anything that shows too much skin. We like anything a nun would wear.'

'Now I know you're lying.'

She laughed again and he thought it was a shame he didn't know her better. She was his only sibling and he didn't know her at all. And there was a possibility that he wouldn't know her either. A part of him wished things could be different. Wished that he was home more, and that he knew what she needed.

'After school tomorrow, I'll give you my credit card.' He sat next to her and untied his shoes. 'Get what you need and I'll take a look when you bring it home.'

She stood, her shoulders hunched, a frown pulling at her bottom lip. 'Okay,' she said and walked from the room.

Jesus, he'd made her mad again. But she really didn't expect him to shop for a prom dress with her, did she? Like he was her girlfriend? How could she be mad at him for that? He didn't even like to shop with girls his own age.

Gassed: Cut from the Team

When Jane finally forced herself from bed the next morning, she pulled on her laundry-day underwear and sweatsuit and hauled her dirty clothes to the Laundromat. As the machines washed and spun, she flipped open a *People* magazine and caught up on her reading.

There was no place she had to be today. No deadline breathing down her neck. She didn't have anything work-related until tomorrow night's game. She bought a Coke from the vending machine, sat back in a hard plastic chair, and enjoyed the mundane pleasure of watching her darks tumble dry. She grabbed the real estate section from the local newspaper and checked out properties for sale. With her added income from the hockey columns, she estimated that by summer she'd have enough money saved to put twenty percent down on a home of her own, but the more she looked, the more discouraged she got. Two hundred thousand sure didn't buy much these days.

On the way home, she stopped at the grocery store to

pick up a week's worth of food. She had today off, but tomorrow the Chinooks were playing the Chicago Blackhawks at Key Arena. They had home games Thursday, Saturday, Monday, and Wednesday nights. Three days off after that, then it was back on the road. Back on the jet. Back on the bus and back to sleeping in hotel rooms.

Reporting the Chinooks' six–four loss to the Sharks was one of the hardest things she'd ever done. After she'd trash-talked and played darts with them, she felt a bit like a traitor, but she'd had a job to do.

And Luc . . . watching the horror unfold in the net had almost been as bad as watching him sitting on the bench. Staring straight ahead, his handsome features devoid of expression. She'd felt bad for him. She'd felt bad that she had to be the one to report the details, but again, she'd had a job to do, and she'd done it.

When she returned home, there was a message on her machine from Leonard Callaway asking her to meet him the following morning in his office at the *Times*. She didn't think the message bode well for her further employment as a sports reporter.

And she was right. He fired her. 'We've decided it's best if you no longer cover the Chinooks games. Jeff Noonan is going to fill in for Chris,' Leonard said.

The paper was letting Jane go and giving her job to the Nooner. 'Why? What happened?'

'I think it's best if we don't get into that.'

The Chinooks hadn't played their best games the past week, ending in Luc's spectacular blowout. 'They think I jinxed them. Don't they?'

'We knew it was a possibility.'

Good-bye to her chance to write an important article. Good-bye to twenty-percent down on her own home. And all because some stupid hockey players thought she was bad luck. Well, she couldn't say that she hadn't been warned or that she wasn't half expecting it. Still, knowing it didn't make it any easier to take. 'Which players think I brought them bad luck? Luc Martineau?'

'Let's not get into that,' Leonard said, but he didn't deny it.

His silence hurt more than it should. Luc was nothing to her, and she was certainly nothing to him. Less than nothing. He'd never wanted her to travel with the team in the first place, and she was sure he was behind her getting the boot. Jane pushed up the corners of her mouth when what she really wanted was to scream and yell and threaten to sue for wrongful termination or sexism or . . . or . . . something. She might even have a case too. But *might* wasn't a good enough guarantee, and she'd learned long ago not to let her hot temper burn bridges. She still had the *Single Girl* column to write for the *Times*.

'Well, thank you for the opportunity to write the sports column,' she said and shook Leonard's hand. 'Traveling with the Chinooks was an experience I won't forget.'

She kept her smile on her face until she left the building. She was so angry, she wanted to hit someone. Someone with blue eyes and a horseshoe tattooed above his private parts.

And betrayed. She'd thought she'd made progress, but the players had turned on her. Maybe if she hadn't beat them at darts, talked trash, and they hadn't called her

Sharky, she wouldn't feel so betrayed now. But she did. She'd even felt bad for doing her job and reporting the facts of their last game. And this was how they repaid her? She hoped they got athlete's foot. All at the same time.

For the next two days, she didn't leave her apartment. She was so depressed she cleaned all the cupboards. While she recaulked the bathroom, she cranked the volume on the televison and felt only slightly vindicated when she heard that the Chinooks lost to the Blackhawks four to three.

Who would they blame now?

By the third day, her anger hadn't diminished, and she knew there was only one way to get rid of it. She had to confront the players if she was to reclaim her dignity.

She knew they would be at the Key Arena for the game-day skate, and before she could talk herself out of it, she dressed in her jeans and black sweater and drove into Seattle.

She entered on the mezzanine level, and her gaze immediately fell on the empty net. Only a few players practiced on the ice below, and with her stomach in knots, she walked down the steps and headed for the locker room.

'Hello, Fishy,' she said as she strolled toward him in the tunnel, a blowtorch in his hand as he warmed the blade of his stick.

He looked up and shut off the torch.

'Are the guys in the locker room?' she asked.

'Most of them.'

'Is Luc in there?'

'I don't know, but he doesn't like to talk on game days.'

Too damn bad. The soles of her boots squeaked on the

rubber mats in the hallway and heads swiveled in her direction when she walked into the room. She raised a hand. 'Keep your pants up, gentlemen,' she said as she moved to stand in the middle of the half-naked players. 'I'll just take a moment of your time, and I'd prefer you not do your synchronized jock-dropping thing.'

She turned to face them and stood with her shoulders straight and her head high. She didn't see Luc. The rat bastard was probably hiding. 'I'm sure you've all heard that I will no longer be covering Chinooks games, and I wanted to let you know that I will not forget our time together. Traveling with you guys was . . . interesting.' She walked to Captain Mark Bressler and stuck out her hand. 'Good luck with your game tonight, Hitman.'

He looked at her a moment as if she made the two-hundred-and-fifty-pound center a bit nervous. 'Ah, thanks,' he said and finally shook her hand. 'Are you going to be in the seats tonight?'

She dropped her hand to her side. 'No. I have other plans.'

She turned to face the room one last time. 'Good-bye, gentlemen, good luck, and I hope this is your year to win the Stanley Cup.' She even managed a smile before she turned to go. She'd done it, she thought as she walked down the hall. They hadn't chased her away with her tail between her legs. She'd shown them that she had class and dignity and that she was magnanimous too.

She hoped they all got jock itch. Really, really bad jock itch. She looked down at the rubber mats as she walked into the tunnel, but she stopped short when she came face to naked chest with sculpted muscles, ripped abs, and a horseshoe tattoo rising out of a pair of hockey shorts. Luc Martineau. Her gaze lifted up his damp chest to his chin and mouth, up the deep furrow of his top lip, past his straight nose to the beautiful baby blues staring back at her.

'You!' she said.

One brow rose slowly up his forehead and her temper exploded.

'You did this to me,' she said. 'I know you did. I guess it didn't matter to you that I actually needed that job. You screw up in the net and *I'm* out.' She felt the backs of her eyes sting and that made her all the madder. 'Who did you blame your loss on last night? And if you lose tonight, who will you blame? You . . . you . . .' she stammered. One rational part of her brain told her to shut up, to quit while she was ahead. To just walk around him and leave while she still had her dignity.

Too bad she was too far gone to listen to that part of her brain.

'You called him a big dumb dodo?' Caroline asked later that night as the two of them sat on Jane's couch watching the gas fireplace lick the fake logs. 'Why didn't you go for broke and call him a poo-poo head too?'

Jane groaned. Hours later she was still writhing with embarrassment. 'Don't,' she pleaded and pushed her glasses up the bridge of her nose. 'The only consolation I have is that I will never see Luc Martineau again.' But she didn't ever think she'd forget the look on his face. Kind of stunned surprise, followed by laughter. She'd wanted to die right there, but she couldn't even blame him for laughing at her. He probably hadn't been called a big dumb dodo since grade school.

'Bummer,' Caroline said as she raised a glass of wine to her lips. She'd pulled her shiny blond hair back into a perfect ponytail and, as always, looked gorgeous. 'I thought maybe you could introduce me to Rob Sutter.'

'The Hammer?' Jane shook her head and took a drink of her gin and tonic. 'His nose is always broken and he always has a black eye.'

Caroline smiled and got a little dreamy-eyed. 'I know.'

'He's married and has a baby.'

'Hmm, well, someone single, then.'

'I thought you had a new man.'

'I do, but it's not going to work out.'

'Why?'

'I don't know,' she said through a sigh and put her wine on the cherrywood coffee table. 'Lenny is handsome and rich but soooo boring.'

Which meant he was probably normal and didn't need fixing. Caroline was a born fixer-upper.

'Do you want to turn on the game and watch it?' Caroline asked.

Jane shook her head. 'Nah.' She'd been tempted, real tempted, to grab the remote and surf by the game to see who was winning. But that would only make everything worse.

'Maybe the Chinooks will lose. That might make you feel better.'

It wouldn't. 'No.' Jane leaned her head back on the floral print sofa. 'I don't ever want to see a hockey game again.' But she did. She wanted to be in the press box or a seat near the action. She wanted to feel the energy run through her, watch a flawless play, a fight break out in the corners, or Luc reach for the perfect glove save.

'Just when I thought I was making progress with the team, I get the sack. I beat Rob and Luc at darts, and they all kidded me about having lesbian glasses. And that night I didn't get nuisance calls in my room. I know we weren't friends, but I thought they were beginning to trust and accept me into the pack.' She thought a moment and added, 'Like wild dingos.'

Caroline glanced at her watch. 'I've been here fifteen minutes and you haven't gotten to the good stuff.'

Jane didn't have to ask what her friend was talking about. She knew Caroline too well. 'I thought you came over to cheer me up, but you just want to hear about the locker room.'

'I did come to cheer you up.' She turned toward Jane and laid an arm across the back of the sofa. 'Later.'

It wasn't like she owed any of them any sort of loyalty. Not now. And it wasn't as if she were going to put it in a tell-all book. 'Okay,' she said, 'but it wasn't like you're thinking. It wasn't all really hard bodies and me the only woman. Well, it was, but I had to keep my eyes up and every time I walked past a player he dropped his cup.'

'You're right,' Caroline said as she leaned over and plucked her wine off the table. 'It isn't what I was thinking. It's better.'

'It's harder than you think to talk to a naked man while you're fully clothed. They're all sweaty and flushed and they don't want to talk. You ask them a question, and they just sort of grunt out an answer.'

'Sounds like my last three boyfriends during sex.'

'It wasn't as much fun as sex, believe me.' She shook her head. 'Some of them wouldn't talk to me at all, and that made it really difficult to do my job.'

'Yeah, I know that part.' She waved a dismissive hand. 'So, who has the best body?'

Jane thought a moment. 'Well, they're all incredibly built. Powerful legs and upper bodies. Mark Bressler probably has the biggest muscles, but Luc Martineau has this horseshoe tattoo low on his abdomen that makes you want to fall right to your knees and kiss it for good luck. And his butt . . . perfect.' She held her cool glass to her forehead. 'Too bad he's a jerk.'

'Sounds like you like him.'

Jane lowered the glass and looked over at Caroline. Like him? Like Luc? The guy who got her fired? More than all the other players combined, she felt most hurt and betrayed by Luc. Which, when she thought about it, probably wasn't all that rational, since she didn't really know him and he didn't know her. It was just that she'd thought they'd developed a tentative friendship, and if she was honest, she'd admit that she'd also developed a slight infatuation for Luc. No, *infatuation* was too strong a word. *Interest* better described what she'd felt. 'I don't like him,' she said, 'but he does have one of those Canadian accents that is only detectable with certain words.'

'Uh-oh.'

'What, uh-oh? I said I didn't like him.'

'I know that's what you said, but you've always been a sucker for a man with an accent.'

'Since when?'

'Since Balki on *Perfect Strangers*.'

'The sitcom?'

'Yep, you were mad for Balki all because he had that accent. No matter that he was a loser who lived with his cousin.'

'No, I was mad for Bronson Pinchot. Not Balki.'
She laughed. 'And that same year, you were mad for
Tom Cruise. How many times do you think we saw
Top Gun?'

'At least twenty.' Caroline took a drink of her wine.
'Even back then you were attracted to losers.'

'I call it having realistic expectations.'

'More like selling yourself short because you have
typical abandonment issues.'

'Are you high?'

Caroline shook her head and her ponytail brushed her
shoulders. 'No, I read all about it in a magazine while I
was in my gynecologist's office last week. Because your
mother died, you're afraid everyone you love will leave
you.'

'Which just goes to show, there's a lot of made-up
crap in magazines.' And she should know. 'Just last week
you told me I had issues with leaving a relationship
because I have a fear of getting dumped. Make up your
mind.'

Caroline shrugged. 'Obviously it's all the same issue.'

'Right.'

They watched the fireplace for a few more minutes,
then Caroline suggested, 'Let's go out.'

'It's Thursday night.'

'I know, but neither of us has to work tomorrow.'

Maybe a night of blowing out her ears with a garage
band was just what she needed to take her mind off the
hockey game she should have been covering but wasn't.
Get her out of the apartment so she couldn't turn on the
television and surf past the game. She looked down at her
green T-shirt, black fleece, and jeans. She also needed

new material for her *Single Girl* column. 'Okay, but I'm not changing.'

Caroline, who'd dressed down tonight in a *Tommy* sweater with a flag on the chest and butt-tight jeans, looked at Jane and rolled her eyes. 'At least put your contacts in.'

'Why?'

'Well, I didn't want to say anything because I love you and all, and because I'm always telling you what to wear and I didn't want you to feel self-conscious and have bad self-esteem, but those horrid people at Eye Care lied to you.'

Jane didn't think her glasses were that bad. Lisa Loeb had a pair just like them. 'Are you sure they don't look good on me?'

'Yes, and I'm only telling you this because I don't want people to think I'm the girl and you're the boy.'

Not Caroline too? 'What makes you think people would assume *you're* the girl and *I'm* the boy?' she asked as she got up and moved into the bathroom. 'It's possible that people would think *you're* the boy.' There was silence from the other room and she stuck her head around the door. 'Well?'

Caroline stood at the fireplace applying red lipstick in front of the mirror hanging above the mantel 'Well, what?' She replaced the lipstick in her cute little handbag.

'Well, what makes you think people would assume *you're* the girl and *I'm* the boy?' she asked again.

'Oh, was that a real question? I thought you were trying to be funny.'

*

The next morning at nine o'clock, Jane's telephone rang. It was Leonard phoning to tell her that he and Virgil and the Chinooks management had reconsidered their 'hasty decision.' They wanted her to resume her job ASAP. Which meant they wanted her in the press box for tomorrow night's game against St. Louis. She was so shocked, she could only lie in her bed and listen to Leonard's complete about-face.

It seemed that after her talk with the team, they'd all played brilliant hockey. Bressler had scored a hat trick after she'd shaken his hand, and Luc was back in his zone. He'd kept the score at six–zero, and for the moment surpassed his rival Patrick Roy in shutouts.

Suddenly Jane Alcott was good luck.

'I don't know, Leonard,' she said as she threw aside her yellow flannel duvet and sat on the edge of her bed. Her head and mouth felt as if they were stuffed with cotton, a result of too much late-night fun, and she was having a hard time grasping her thoughts. 'I can't take this job and wonder if I'm going to get fired every time the Chinooks lose a game.'

'You don't have to worry about that anymore.'

She didn't believe him, and if she did decide to take the job again, she wasn't going to jump at the opportunity like last time. And truthfully, she was still severely ticked off. 'I'm going to have to think about it.'

After she hung up the phone, she brewed a pot of coffee and ate a little granola to take away the hollow feeling. She hadn't gotten to bed until around two the night before, and she was sorry she'd even spent the money and wasted her time going out. She'd been unable to think of anything besides getting fired and she'd been bad company.

While she ate, she thought about Leonard's new offer. The Chinooks had pretty much treated her like a leper and blamed their losses on her. Now they suddenly thought she was good luck? Did she really want to subject herself to more of their superstitious craziness? Their synchronized cup-dropping and nuisance calls?

When she finished eating, she jumped into the shower and closed her eyes as the warm water ran over her. Did she really want to travel with a goalie who could look right through her? Even as he made her heart race? Whether she wanted it to race or not? And she most definitely did not. Even if she and Luc liked each other, which they obviously didn't, he only had eyes for tall gorgeous women.

She wrapped her hair in a towel and put on her glasses as she dried her body. She pulled on a sheer bandeau bra, a white University of Washington T-shirt, and a pair of old jeans with holes in the knees.

Her doorbell rang, and when she looked through the peephole, a man wearing a pair of silver Oakley sunglasses stood on her little porch all windblown and gorgeous, and looking exactly like Luc Martineau. She opened the door because she'd just been thinking of him, and she wasn't certain this wasn't a figment of her imagination.

'Hello, Jane,' he greeted. 'May I come in?'

Wow, a polite Luc. Now she *knew* she was imagining things. 'Why?'

'I hoped that we could talk about what happened.' That did it. He said *aboot* instead of about, and she knew she was talking to the real Luc.

'You getting me fired, you mean?'

He reached for his sunglasses and stuck them in the pocket of his leather bomber jacket. His cheeks were flushed, his hair messed, and behind him at the curb he'd parked his motorcycle. 'I didn't get you fired. Not directly anyway.' When she didn't respond, he asked, 'Are you going to invite me inside?'

Her hair was in a towel and the cold air was giving her goose bumps. She decided to let him in. 'Have a seat,' she said as he followed her into the living room of her apartment. She left for a moment to take the towel from her head and to brush the tangles from her hair. Of all the men in the world, Luc was the last man she'd thought would ever be standing in her living room.

She brushed and towel-dried her hair the best she could, and for one brief moment she thought of maybe putting on some mascara and lip gloss. But she dismissed the thought just as quickly. She did, however, exchange her glasses for her contact lenses.

With her hair damp and the ends starting to curl, she returned to the living room. Luc stood with his back to her, studying a few photographs sitting on her mantel. His jacket lay on the sofa, and he wore a white dress shirt, the cuffs folded up his thick forearms. One wide pleat ran down the middle of his back and was tucked into a pair of Lucky Brand jeans. His wallet bulged one back pocket and the denim hugged his butt. He looked over his shoulder at her, his blue gaze moving from her bare feet, up her jeans and T-shirt to her face.

'Who's this?' he asked and pointed to the middle photo of her and Caroline in their caps and gowns standing on the porch of her father's house in Tacoma.

'That's my best friend Caroline and me the night we graduated from Mt. Tahoma High School.'

'So you've lived around here all your life?'

'Yep.'

'You haven't changed that much.'

She stood next to him. 'I'm a lot older these days.'

He looked across his shoulder at her. 'How old are you?'

'Thirty.'

He flashed a white smile that slid past her defenses, warmed her up, and curled her toes into the beige Berber carpet. 'That old?' he asked. 'You look pretty good for your age.'

Oh, God. She didn't want to read more into that statement than he'd intended, which she was certain was absolutely nothing. She didn't want him to dazzle her with a smile. She didn't want to feel tingles or warm flushes or have bad sinful thoughts. 'Why are you here, Luc?'

'I got a call from Darby Hogue.' He shoved one hand in the front pocket of those Lucky jeans and rested his weight on one foot. 'He told me they'd offered you your job back and you turned them down.'

She hadn't turned them down. She'd said she'd think about it. 'What does that have to do with you?'

'Darby thought I could talk you into coming back.'

'You? You think I'm the archangel of gloom and doom.'

'You're a cute archangel of doom.'

Oh, boy. 'You were the wrong choice. I don't—' she stopped because she couldn't lie and say she didn't like him. She did. Even though she didn't *want* to like him. So she settled on a half lie. 'I don't know if I even like you.'

He chuckled as if he knew she lied. 'That's what I told Darby.' The corners of his mouth slid into a smile filled with charm, and he rocked back on his heels. 'But he thought I could change your mind.'

'I doubt it.'

'I figured you might say that.' He walked to the couch and pulled something out of the pocket of his leather jacket. 'So I brought you a peace offering.'

He handed her a thin trade-sized paperback with a pink ribbon tied around it. *Hockey Talk: The Jargon, the Lore, the Stuff You'll Never Learn from TV*.

Shocked, she took it from him. 'You did this?'

'Yeah, and I had the girl at the bookstore put that bow on it.'

He'd given her a gift. A peace offering. Something she could actually use. Not something generic men typically gave women, like flowers or chocolate or cheap underwear. He'd given it some thought. He'd paid attention. To her.

'They didn't have black ribbon, so she had to use pink.'

Jane's heart pinched in her chest and she knew she was in trouble. 'Thank you.'

'You're welcome.'

She looked up past his smile and into his blue eyes. Big bad trouble. The kind all wrapped up in a white shirt and Lucky jeans. The kind that dated Barbie Dolls because he could.

Deke: To Outmaneuver an Opponent

Luc looked down into Jane's green eyes, and he knew his gift had worked. He'd softened her up, maneuvered her right where he wanted. But just before he had her completely and she dropped into his hand like a puck from heaven, her gaze turned wary. She took a step back and skepticism pulled her brows together.

'Did Darby tell you to butter me up with this?' she asked and held up the book.

Damn. 'No.' The little dweeb had suggested he bring her flowers, but the book had been Luc's idea. 'That was my idea, but everyone wants you to come back and cover the games.'

'I find it hard to believe that everyone wants me back. Especially the coaches.'

She was right. Not everyone did want her back, especially management. After the disgraceful loss in San Jose, the team had been looking for something to blame.

Something in the air or the alignment of the stars. Something other than their pathetic performance. That something had been Jane. They'd groused and bitched in the locker room, but none of them had thought she'd get fired. Especially Luc. After she'd told him she'd needed the job, he'd been able to think of little else but Jane living on the streets because of something he'd said. And looking at the size of her apartment, she probably did need the money. It was clean and, surprisingly enough, not everything was black, but the whole thing could easily fit into his living room. He was glad he'd come.

'I told management you're our good-luck charm,' he said, which was true. After she'd called him a big dumb dodo, of all things, he'd played one of the best games of his life. And Bressler pulled his first hat trick of the season after she'd shaken his hand.

A frown pulled at the corners of her lips. 'Do you really believe that?'

Luc never questioned the source of good luck. 'Of course, but mostly I'm here because I know what it's like to need a job and have the opportunity taken from you.'

Jane looked down at her bare feet and Luc studied the part in her damp hair. The ends had begun to curl about her shoulders as if she'd twisted them around her finger. He wondered what they'd feel like curled around his own finger. Standing so close, he was reminded of how short she was. How small her shoulders were, and how young she looked in her University of Washington T-shirt. Not for the first time he noticed her nipples poking at the front of her shirt, and again he wondered if she was cold or turned on. Warmth spread through his veins and settled in his groin. He felt himself get semi-hard and was shocked as hell at his response to Jane Alcott. She was short and flat-chested and too smart. Despite all of that, he heard himself say, 'Maybe we could start over. Forget about the first time we met when I offered to piss in your coffee.'

She looked up again. Her skin was smooth and flawless and her lips full and pink. He wondered if her cheeks were as soft as they looked and he lowered his gaze to her mouth. No, she wasn't his kind of woman, but there was something about her that intrigued him. Perhaps it was her humor and her grit. Perhaps it was nothing more than her puckered nipples and his sudden interest in her soft curls.

'Actually, that wasn't the first time we met,' she said.

He raised his gaze to her eyes. Shit. There were several months of his life that were a blur to him. When he'd done things he'd only heard or read about later. He hadn't lived in Seattle at that time, but he'd certainly traveled with Detroit here. He was almost afraid of the answer, but he had to ask. 'When did we meet?'

'Last summer at a press party.'

Relief poured through him and he almost laughed. He would have remembered if he'd slept with Jane last summer. It was the summer before that his memory got a bit dicey. 'The press party at the Four Seasons?'

'No, at the Key Arena.'

He tilted his head back and looked at her. 'There were a lot of people there that night, but I'm surprised I didn't remember you,' he said, even though he wasn't at all surprised. Jane wasn't the sort of woman he would have remembered on first meeting. And yeah, he knew what that said about him, and he still didn't really care. He lived his life a certain way, looked at things a certain way. He'd lived it so long, he was comfortable with himself. 'But maybe not all that surprising, since you were probably wearing black,' he joked.

'I remember exactly what you were wearing,' she said and moved across the room to the kitchen. 'Dark suit, red tie, gold watch, and a blonde woman.'

He let his gaze slide down her back to her round booty. Everything about Jane was small but her attitude. 'Were you jealous?'

She glanced over her shoulder. 'Of the watch?'

'That too.'

Instead of answering, she moved into the kitchen and asked, 'Do you want a cup of coffee?'

'No, thanks. I don't drink caffeine.' He followed but stopped in the doorway of the narrow kitchen. 'Are you going to take your job back?'

She set the book he'd given her on the counter and poured coffee into a tall Starbucks mug. 'I might.' She opened the refrigerator and pulled out a quart of milk. The door had Post-its stuck all over it with notes reminding her to buy everything from pickles and saltines to Comet. 'How much is it worth?' she asked as she put the milk away and shut the refrigerator.

'To me personally, or the team?'

She raised the mug to her lips and looked across at him. 'You personally.'

She was going to take advantage of the reversal of circumstances. Squeeze it for all it was worth. He couldn't say he wouldn't have done the same thing if the situation was reversed. 'I gave you a peace offering.'

'I know, and I appreciate the gesture.'

She was good. Maybe he'd fire Howie and hire Jane to negotiate his next contract. 'What do you want?'

'An interview.'

He folded his arms across his chest. 'With me?'

'Yes.'

'When?'

'After I've had time to do some research and get my questions together.'

'You know I hate interviews.'

'I know, but I'll make it painless.'

He rocked back on his heels and looked down at the front of her shirt. 'How painless?'

'I won't ask you personal questions.'

She was still cold and should probably put on a sweatshirt or something. 'Define *personal*.'

'Don't worry, I won't ask you about your women.'

He slid his gaze to the delicate hollow of her throat, past her lips to her eyes. 'Some of that stuff you've probably read about me isn't true,' he said and didn't know why he was defending himself to her.

She blew into the mug. 'Some?'

He dropped his hands to his sides and shrugged. 'I'd say at least fifty percent was made up to sell books or papers.'

From behind her coffee, one corner of her mouth lifted. 'Which fifty percent is true?'

She looked so cute looking up at him, smiling, he was almost tempted to tell her. 'Off the record?'

'Of course.'

Almost. 'None of your business. I don't talk about the women in my past or my time in rehab.'

She lowered the mug. 'Fair enough. I won't ask you

anything about rehab or your sex life. There's been enough written about that, and it's boring.'

Boring? His sex life wasn't boring. Lately he hadn't had a lot of action, but what he did get wasn't boring. Well . . . maybe just a little. No, *boring* was the wrong word. Too strong. There was something missing in his sex life lately. Besides the sex itself. He didn't know what that something was, but once he had the Marie situation resolved, he'd have more time to figure it out.

'And besides,' she added, 'I don't want anything you tell me to blow my illusions of you.'

'What illusions?' He leaned one shoulder against the doorway. 'That I have threesomes every night?'

'You don't?'

'No.' He looked at her standing there telling him his sex life was boring and he decided to shock her a little bit. Just a bit with something she'd probably read about anyway. 'I tried it once, but the girls were more interested in each other than me. Which didn't do much for my self-esteem.'

She started to laugh and he couldn't remember the last time he'd been alone with a woman in her apartment, laughing and talking with her, and not trying to maneuver her toward the bedroom. It was kind of nice.

The night after Luc's visit, Jane sat next to Darby in the press box for the Chinooks' Vancouver game. An octagonal scoreboard with four video screens hung from the center of the pyramid-shaped roof. Lights bounced off the big green Chinooks logo below at center ice, and the pregame laser show had yet to begin. It was half an hour until the scheduled puck drop, but Jane was ready with a pad of paper and her recorder in her bag. She was back and more excited than she let on. Except for Darby, management had yet to arrive, and she wondered if they'd give her the cold shoulder.

She looked across at him. 'Thanks for getting my job back for me.' His forearms rested on his knees as he gazed out at the arena. Tonight he'd applied a little less hair gel than usual, but beneath his blue suit jacket, he wore his trusty pocket protector.

'It wasn't just me. The players felt bad after you came to the locker room and wished them luck. They thought anyone that gutsy should have her job back.'

'They wanted me back because they think I'm lucky now.'

'That too,' he said through a smile as he gazed at the ice below. 'What are you doing next Saturday?'

'Aren't we on the road?'

'No, we leave the next day.'

'Then nothing.' She shrugged. 'Why?'

'Hugh Miner is having his jersey retired at a big banquet at the Space Needle.'

The name sounded familiar, but she couldn't place it. 'Who's Hugh Miner?'

'Chinooks goalie from '96 to his retirement last year. I was wondering if you'd want to go.'

'With you? On a date?' she asked as if he were crazy.

His pale cheeks flushed, and she realized that had come out all wrong. 'It doesn't have to be a date,' he said.

'Hey, I don't mean that like it sounded.' She patted his shoulder through his jacket. 'You know I can't date anyone involved in the Chinooks organization. It would only cause more speculation and rumor.'

'Yeah, I know.'

Now she felt really bad. He probably couldn't get a real date to go with him, and she'd added insult to injury. 'I suppose I'd have to dress up.'

'Yes, it's black tie.' He finally looked at her. 'I'd pick you up in a limo, so you wouldn't have to drive.'

How could she possibly say no? 'What time?'

'Seven.' The cell phone hooked to Darby's belt rang and he turned his attention to the call. 'Yes,' he said. 'Right here.' He glanced at her. 'Right now? Okay.' He disconnected and returned the phone to his belt clip. 'Coach Nystrom wants you in the locker room.'

'Me? Why?'

'He didn't say.'

Jane stuffed her notebook in her bag and headed out of the press box. She took the elevator to the ground level and moved through the hall to the locker room, wondering the whole time if she was about to get fired again; if she was, she feared that this time she just might go ballistic.

When she walked into the room, the Chinooks were all suited up and imposing in their battle gear. They sat in front of their stalls listening to the coach, and Jane stopped just inside the door as Larry Nystrom talked of the weakness in Vancouver's second line and how to score against their goalie. She looked across the room at Luc. He wore his big goalie pads and white jersey with the blue and green Chinook on the front. His gloves and helmet were beside him as he stared at a point just beyond his skates. Then he looked up and his eyes locked with hers. He simply looked at her for several heartbeats, then his blue gaze began a leisurely journey down her gray sweater, over her black skirt and tights to her black penny loafers. His interest was more curious than sexual, but it pinned her in place and made her heart feel heavy in her chest.

'Jane,' Larry Nystrom called to her. She pulled her attention from Luc and looked at the coach. He motioned her forward, and she moved to stand beside him. 'Go ahead and say what you said to the guys the other day.'

She swallowed. 'I can't remember what I said, Coach.'

'Something about us keeping our pants up,' Fish provided. 'And traveling with us being an experience.'

They all looked so serious she almost laughed. Until now, she'd never really believed they were this superstitious. 'Okay,' she began to the best of her recollection, 'keep your pants up, gentlemen, I have something to say and it will just take a minute. I won't be traveling with you any longer, and I wanted you to know that traveling with you all has been an experience I won't forget.' They all smiled and nodded except Peter Peluso.

'You said something about synchronized jock-dropping. I remember that part.'

'That's right, Sharky,' Rob Sutter agreed. 'I remember that too.'

'And you said you hoped this was our year to win the Cup,' Jack Lynch added.

'Yeah, that's important.'

Did it really matter? Sheesh! 'Do I have to start from the beginning?'

They all nodded and she rolled her eyes. 'Keep your pants up, gentlemen, I have something to say and it will just take a minute and I don't want any of that

132

synchronized pants-dropping crap.' Or something like
that. 'I won't be traveling with you any longer and I
wanted you to know that traveling with you guys has been
an experience I won't forget. I hope this is your year to
win the Stanley Cup.'

They all looked pleased and she started to leave
before they made her crazy.

'Now you have to come and shake my hand,' the
captain, Mark Bressler, informed her.

'Oh, that's right.' She walked up to him and took his
hand. 'Good luck with the game, Mark.'

'No, you said Hitman.'

This was just weird. 'Good luck with the game,
Hitman.'

He smiled. 'Thanks, Jane.'

'You're welcome.' From outside, she could hear the
pregame entertainment begin, and she once again
headed for the door.

'You're not finished, Jane.'

She turned and looked across the room at Luc. He
stood and crooked a finger at her. 'Come here.'

No way. No way was she going to call him a dodo in
front of the guys.

'Come on.'

She looked around at the faces of the other players. If
Luc played badly, they'd blame her. As if her shoes were
lead, she walked across the dense carpet with the
Chinooks logo in the center. 'What?' she asked as she
came to stand in front of Luc. In his skates, he was taller
than usual, and she had to look way up.

'You have to say what you said to me the other day. For
luck.'

That's what she'd suspected, but she tried to get out of it. 'You're so good, you don't need luck.'

He grasped her arm and gently pulled her closer. 'Come on, now.'

His heated palm warmed her through her sweater. 'Don't make me, Luc,' she said just loud enough for him to hear. She could feel her face catch on fire. 'It's too embarrassing.'

'Whisper it in my ear.'

The creaking of leather pads filled the vanishing space between them as he bent over her. The scent of his shampoo and shaving cream filled her nose combined with the leather of his pads. 'You dumb dodo,' she whispered beside his ear.

'That's not right.' He shook his head and his cheeks touched hers for the briefest of seconds. 'You forgot *big*.'

Oh, Lord. Before this was over, she was either going to die of shame or pass out or combust from pent-up lust. She really didn't want to do any of the three. Especially the last one, but his testosterone level was like a heavy force field pulling her in against her will. She closed her eyes and locked her knees so she wouldn't lean into him. 'You big dumb dodo.'

'Thanks, sweetheart. I appreciate it.'

Sweetheart. She opened her eyes. He turned his face, and with his lips inches from hers, he smiled. 'Am I going to have to do this before every game?' she managed, though her voice sounded more breathy than she would have liked.

He didn't seem to notice her voice. He straightened and tiny creases appeared in the corners of his eyes. ''Fraid so.'

Finally, she felt as if she could breathe again. 'I'm asking for a raise.'

He slid his big warm hand up her arm to her shoulder. He gave her cheek a light pat, then dropped his hand to his side. 'Ask for a bigger expense account too. The next time we're on the road, I'm going to win back that fifty I lost at darts.'

Jane shook her head and turned to go. 'Not going to happen, Luc,' she said over her shoulder.

She made her way back up to the media booth and again sat beside Darby. King-5 was there as well as ESPN, broadcasting the Chinooks' battle with Vancouver. With Luc Martineau securely back in his zone, Seattle came out on top in the three–one scrum. Seemingly without effort, he snagged the puck from the air and reminded everyone who watched exactly why he was considered a premier goalie.

In the locker room after the game, the team answered Jane's questions. Although they didn't keep their pants up, their disrobing seemed less calculated.

That night, once Jane sent her column off to the paper, she phoned Caroline and made her friend's day, week, and year with four simple words. 'I need a makeover,' she said as soon as Caroline picked up.

'Who is this?'

'Very funny. I have a fancy banquet to go to next week and I need to look good.'

'Thank you, Jesus, for this gift I am about to receive,' Caroline whispered. 'I've waited for this for years. The first thing we need to do is make an appointment with Vonda.'

'Who's Vonda?'

'The woman who's going to wax you all over and shape that wild hair.'

Jane looked at the receiver in her hand. 'Wax?'

'And hair.'

'The last time I let you do my hair, I ended up looking like Buckwheat.'

'That was tenth grade, and *I* won't be doing it. After the hair, we'll hook you up with Sara at the MAC counter where I work. The woman is a true artist.'

'I was thinking just a little mascara and some lip gloss. A nice black cocktail dress and some cheap pumps.'

'And we got in some fabulous Ferragamos today,' Caroline rattled on as if Jane hadn't spoken. 'In red. They'll look prefect with a killer little Betsey Johnson I saw upstairs.'

Boomer: A Hard Shot

Luc pulled the cuffs at his wrists, then slipped onyx studs through each. That morning at practice, he'd heard Jane would be at tonight's banquet with Darby. He was curious to see what she'd show up wearing – something black, no doubt. He raised his hands and popped the last stud in the banded collar of his starched white shirt. He hadn't spoken with her since the game against Vancouver.

The second-string goalie had played the last two games, giving Luc a much-needed break, and he hadn't had the chance to talk to her. Not that he had anything that he wanted to say. But he liked to talk to her, and he liked to provoke her a bit to see her reaction. To see if she'd laugh or if her gaze would narrow and her lips get all pinched. Or if he could bring a blush to her pale cheeks.

He buttoned his charcoal suspenders to the waistband of his pleated trousers and wondered if Jane and Darby were dating now. He didn't think they were. At least he didn't *like* to think they were. Jane was fiery and had a smart mouth, and a geeky pencil pusher was all wrong for her. Especially *that* pencil pusher. It was no secret that Darby had been against Luc's trade to the Chinooks and that the two men tolerated each other because they had to. As far as Luc was concerned, Darby Hogue was nutless, while Jane had guts. He guessed that's what he liked about her. She didn't run from adversity. She faced it head-on. All five feet of her.

Luc grabbed his black bow tie and moved to his closet's mirrored doors. He laid it flat against his collar and threaded one end beneath the other. Dissatisfied with the lengths on each side, he pulled it off and started over. It took him three tries before he'd tied it perfectly around his neck. He usually didn't mind throwing on his tux and attending banquets – especially banquets honoring fellow goalies – but there was nothing usual about tonight. Tonight his little sister was going to a high school dance with a guy who had his nose pierced.

Luc grabbed his watch from his bedside table and slipped it on his wrist as he made his way to Marie's room. He wasn't about to leave until her date appeared for her. He knew what went on in the minds of teen boys, and he planned to look this Zack over and let the kid know that he'd be home when Marie returned, waiting up for her. He had to be here to shake Zack's hand a little too hard, give him the don't-mess-with-my-sister stare, and put some fear into him. Luc might not be a great brother – in fact, he wasn't anywhere near great – but he would protect Marie as long as she was with him.

He'd decided to put off any discussion of boarding school until sometime after the dance. She'd had so much fun picking out her dress and shoes, it just hadn't seemed like the right time to talk about it.

Luc knocked on Marie's door, and when she mumbled a reply he entered the room. He expected to see her in the black velvet dress with the square neck, puffy sleeves, and little pink roses sewn on it. She'd shown him the dress the other day, and he'd thought it real sweet for a girl her age. Instead of being dressed, though, she lay on top of her bed wearing her pajamas. Her hair was pulled back in a ponytail, and she'd been crying.

'Why aren't you getting ready? Your date's going to be here in a few minutes.'

'No, he's not. He called and canceled last night.'

'Is he sick?'

'He said he forgot that he has to do something with his family and can't take me. But that's a lie. He has a girlfriend now and he's taking her.'

Something white and hot flashed behind his eyes. Something that clenched his jaw and tightened his hands into fists. No one stood up his sister and made her cry. 'He can't do that.' Luc moved farther into the room and looked down at Marie. 'Where does he live? I'll go talk to him. I'll make him take you.'

'No,' she gasped, mortified, and sat up on the edge of her bed, her eyes wide as she gazed up at Luc. 'That's so embarrassing!'

'Okay, I won't make him take you.' She was right. Being forced would embarrass her. 'I'll just go over there and kick his ass.'

Her dark brow rose almost to her hairline. 'He's a minor.'

'Good point. Well, I'll kick his dad's ass. Anyone who

raises his son to stand a girl up deserves to get his ass kicked just on principle.' Luc was serious, but for some reason, that got a smile out of Marie.

'You'd kick Mr. Anderson's ass for me?'

'I meant butt. Not ass. And of course I would.' He sat next to his sister. 'And if I couldn't get the job done, I know a few hockey players who would feed him his lunch.'

'That's true.'

He took her hand and studied her stubby fingernails. 'Why didn't you tell me he'd called and canceled?'

She looked away. 'I didn't think you'd really care.'

With his free hand, he brought her gaze back to his. 'How can you say that? Of course I care. You're my sister.'

She shrugged. 'I just didn't think you cared about stuff like dances.'

'Well, you might be right. I don't care that much about dances and dancing. I never went to any dances at my school because . . .' He paused and hit her arm with his elbow. 'I can't dance worth a damn. But I care about you.'

One corner of her mouth turned down as if she didn't believe him.

'You're my sister,' he said again, as if there were nothing else to explain. 'I told you I'd always take care of you.'

'I know.' She looked at her lap. 'But *taking care of* and *caring about* aren't the same thing.'

'They are to me, Marie. I don't take care of people I don't care about.'

She pulled her hand from his and stood. She moved across the room to a dresser with a pile of bracelets, stuffed bears, and four dried roses on top. Luc knew the white roses had come from her mother's casket. He didn't know why she'd taken them or why she kept them now, especially when they made her cry.

'I know you want to send me away,' she said with her back to him.

Oh, boy. He didn't know how she'd found out, but he supposed that wasn't important. 'I've been thinking that you might be happier living with girls your own age instead of me.'

'Don't lie, Luc. You want to get rid of me.'

Did he? Was getting rid of her so he could go back to his life his major motivation for looking at boarding schools? Maybe a little more than he'd like to admit to himself. Guilt he could no longer ignore squeezed the back of his neck as he stood and walked toward his sister. 'I won't lie to you.' He put his hand on her shoulder and turned her to face him. 'The truth is, I don't know what to do with you. I don't know anything about teenage girls, but I know you're unhappy. I want to make it better for you, but I don't know how.'

'I'm unhappy because my mom died,' she said in a small voice. 'And nobody and nothing can make that better.'

'I know.'

'And no one wants me.'

'Hey.' He squeezed her shoulder. 'I want you and you know Aunt Jenny wants you.' Actually, Jenny only wanted Marie to 'visit summers,' but Marie didn't need to know that. 'In fact, she threatened to take me to family court to demand custody. I think she had visions of the two of you wearing matching housecoats.'

Marie's nose wrinkled. 'How come I never heard of that?'

'At the time, you had enough worries,' he evaded. 'I have more money than Aunt Jenny if it came to a court battle, so she backed down.'

Marie frowned. 'Jenny lives in a retirement village.'

'Yeah, but look on the bright side. She'd make you her special prune pudding every night.'

'Blech!'

Luc smiled and pulled back the cuff of his shirt to look at his watch. The banquet was just about to start. 'I've got to get going,' he said, but couldn't quite bring himself to actually leave her alone. 'Why don't you put on your new dress and come with me?'

'Where?'

'To a banquet at the Space Needle.'

'With old people?'

'Not that old. It'll be fun.'

'Don't you have to go right now?'

'I'll wait for you.'

She shrugged. 'Oh, I don't know.'

'Come on. The press will be there, and maybe you'll get your picture in the paper looking so good, old Zack will kick his *own* ass.'

She laughed. 'You mean butt.'

'Right. Butt.' He pushed her toward her closet. 'Get your *butt* in gear,' he said as he left the room and shut the door behind him. He grabbed his tuxedo jacket and moved into the living room to wait. He shrugged into the four-button jacket and hoped Marie shook her tailfeathers, but, typical of all females he'd ever known, she took her time getting ready.

He stood in front of the eight-foot windows and looked out at the city. The rain had stopped, but drops still clung to the glass and smeared the glittering image of Seattle at night, of the towering high-rise buildings and Elliott Bay beyond. He'd purchased this apartment for the view alone, and if he walked through either the kitchen or his bedroom doors on the other side of the apartment, he'd be on the balcony, which had a perfect view of the Space Needle and north Seattle.

Looking out the numerous windows was spectacular, but Luc had to admit that the condo had never really come to feel like home to him. Perhaps because of the modern architecture, or maybe because he'd never lived on top of a city before and it felt a bit like living in a hotel. If he opened the windows or stood out on the balcony, the sounds of cars and buses floated up to the nineteenth floor and reminded him of a hotel too. Even though he was beginning to like Seattle and everything it had to offer, sometimes he had a vague antsy feeling to go home.

When Marie finally emerged from her bedroom, she wore a little rhinestone necklace and a matching headband holding the curls back from her face. Her hair was cute, but the dress – the dress looked awful on her. About two sizes too small. The black velvet fit too tight across her breasts and behind and the small sleeves cut into her arms. Even though Marie usually wore big T-shirts and sweatshirts, he knew she wasn't fat. But that dress made her look like a chunkster.

'How do I look?' she asked as she turned in a circle for him.

The seam running up the back of the dress pulled to the left across her behind. 'You look beautiful.' And above the shoulders, she did look good. Her silver eye shadow was a little strange, though, sparkly like the kind of glitter he'd used in grade school.

'What size is that dress?' Luc asked, and by the look she gave him he immediately realized his mistake. He knew better than to ask a woman her dress size. But Marie wasn't a woman. She was a girl and she was his sister.

'Why?'

He helped her on with her wool peacoat. 'You always wear big shirts and pants, and I don't know what size you wear,' he improvised.

'Oh, it's a zero. Can you believe I fit into a size zero?'

'No. A zero isn't even a size. And if you are a zero, you should fatten up, maybe eat some mashed potatoes and gravy. Chase it down with some whipped cream.' She laughed, but he wasn't joking.

They left for the short drive to the Space Needle, and by the time he turned the keys of his Land Cruiser over to the valet, they were more than an hour late. The SkyLine level of the Needle was perched at the one-hundred-foot mark within the structure. The SkyLine had a three-hundred-and-sixty-degree panoramic view of the city, and Luc and Marie arrived just in time for the serious partying. Stepping off the elevator, they hit a wall of noise, the combination of hundreds of voices, the clatter of dishes being cleared, and the three-piece band tuning their instruments. A sea of black tuxedos and bright dresses mixed and mingled within the dimly lit room. Luc had been here before. Not this location, not this occasion, but at a hundred or so other banquets he'd attended since signing to play in the NHL.

As Luc checked Marie's coat, he spotted Sutter, Fish,

and Grizzell and introduced Marie to his teammates. They asked her about school, and the more they spoke to her, the more she slid behind Luc, until only about half of her showed. He didn't know if she was intimidated or shy.

'Have you seen Sharky?' Fish asked.

'Jane? No, I haven't seen her. Why?'

He raised his beer and shrugged.

'Where is she?'

Fish lifted his finger from his glass and pointed to a woman several feet away with her back to Luc. She had short dark curls about her head. A deep red halter dress plunged to the small of her back, and a slim gold chain hung between her shoulder blades, catching the light and scattering gold across her white skin. The dress fit loose about her hips and behind and fell to her calves. On her feet she wore a pair of shiny red shoes with about three-inch heels. She stood talking to two other women. One he recognized as Hugh Miner's wife, Mae. He'd last seen her in September when she'd been about nine months pregnant. The other woman looked vaguely familiar and he wondered if he'd seen her in *Playboy*. None of the women looked like Jane.

'Who's the woman in black?' he asked, referring to the centerfold.

'That's Kowalsky's wife.'

He turned his attention back to his teammates. Now he knew why she looked familiar. A photograph of her and John hung on the wall in Coach Nystrom's office. 'Kowalsky's here?' John Kowalsky was a hockey legend and had been the Chinooks' captain until his retirement. Kowalsky had not only dominated with his size, but his slap shot had been clocked at over a hundred miles an hour. There wasn't a goalie alive who'd wanted to see 'the Wall' coming at him.

Luc glanced about the room until he saw Hugh and John standing within a group of front-office management. They all laughed about something, and Luc's attention returned to the woman in red. He ran his gaze up her smooth spine and neck to the dark curls on her head. Fish was mistaken. Jane wore black or gray and had shoulder-length hair.

Luc reached for the top button closing his jacket as Darby Hogue approached the woman and said something next to her ear. She turned in profile and Luc's hand froze. The archangel of gloom and doom wasn't wearing black tonight, and she'd cut her hair.

'There's someone else I want you to meet,' he said to Marie. They wove their way through the guests but were stopped by Bekah Brummet, a five-ten beauty queen and sometime friend. He'd met her at a fund-raiser last summer, and within hours he'd discovered three things about her. She liked white wine, men with money, and was a natural blonde. He hadn't seen her since Marie had come to live with him.

He quickly introduced the two, and returned his gaze to Jane. She laughed at something Darby said, and Luc couldn't imagine the little weasel saying anything remotely funny.

'I haven't seen you for a while,' Bekah said and pulled his attention to her. She looked as gorgeous as always in a silky little dress that exposed her deep cleavage. There'd been a lot of Bekahs in his life. Beautiful women who wanted to be with him because he was Luc Martineau, notorious goalie. Some of them had become friends, others had not. He'd never minded taking advantage of what they'd been only too happy to give him. But he was standing next to his sister, who was in a dress that didn't fit while she tried to disappear behind him, and he didn't want her exposed to that part of his life.

'I'm out of town a lot.' He placed his hand in the small of Marie's back. 'It was good to see you,' he said and left Bekah looking after him. He propelled his sister away before she could figure out his real relationship with Bekah. He didn't want Marie to think for one second that casual sex was okay. He wanted her to know that she was worth more than that. And yeah, he knew that made him a hypocrite, and he didn't care.

'Jane,' he said as he approached. She looked over her shoulder, and a soft curl fell across one eye. She pushed it back and smiled. Her short hair made her look young and so damn cute. He couldn't help but return her smile. Her new haircut made her green eyes look huge, and she wore makeup that turned them all smoky, sexy. Her lips were painted dark red, his favorite. The heat in the room seemed to rise several degrees and he unbuttoned his jacket.

'Hello, Luc.' Her voice sounded smoky too.

'Martineau,' Darby said.

'Hogue.' With his hand on Marie's back, he forced her to stay by his side. 'This is my date, Marie,' he said, and Jane sent him a look out of the corner of her eye that told him she thought he should be arrested. 'Marie is my sister.'

'Ah, then I take back what I was thinking of you.' Jane stuck out her hand and smiled at Marie. 'I like your dress. Black is my favorite color.'

Luc figured that was pretty much an understatement.

'Have you met Mae Miner and Georgeanne Kowalsky?' Jane asked and moved to widen the circle to include him and Marie.

Luc turned his attention to Hugh's wife, a short blonde with big brown eyes and very little makeup. She was one of those natural girls. Like Jane. Except for tonight. Tonight Jane had painted lips. He shook hands with both women, then said, 'I met Mae last September.'

'When I was about nine months pregnant.' She dug around in her little black purse and pulled out a photo. 'This is Nathan.'

Georgeanne reached for her pictures. 'This is Lexie when she was ten, and that's her little sister Olivia.' Luc didn't mind looking at kid photos – really – but he did wonder why parents always assumed he wanted to see them. 'Cute kids.' He looked them over, then handed the photographs back to both women.

The conversation around him turned to the speeches he'd missed by arriving late, and he took the opportunity to check out Jane's dress. The front scooped low over her small breasts, and he'd bet that if she hunched her shoulders a bit, he could see down the front. The room was hot, yet her nipples poked out like she was in a deep freeze.

'Luc,' Marie said, pulling his attention away from Jane's dress. He looked over his shoulder at his sister. 'Do you know where the rest rooms are?'

'I know,' Jane answered for him. 'Follow me. I'll take you.' With her high shoes, Jane was about the same height as Marie. 'On the way, you can tell me all your brother's deep dark secrets,' she added as they walked away.

He figured he was safe, since Marie didn't know any of his secrets. Deep dark or otherwise. The two were quickly swallowed within the crowd, and when he turned back, Mae and Georgeanne excused themselves and he was left staring at Darby.

Darby spoke first. 'I saw the way you were looking at Jane. She's not your type.'

He brushed aside his jacket and stuck his hand in his pocket. 'What type is that?'

'A rink bunny.'

Luc never went with rink bunnies, and he wasn't so sure he had a type anymore. Not when he could look at Jane Alcott and wonder what she'd do if he pulled her into a linen closet and kissed off her red lipstick. If he ran his fingers down her spine and slid his hand around the front and cupped her small breast. Of course, he could never do that. Not with Jane. 'What's it to you?'

'Jane and I are friends.'

'Aren't you the same guy who called and asked me to talk her into taking her job back?'

'That was business. If you mess with her, she could lose her job. Permanently. I'd be really pissed off if you did something to hurt her.'

'Are you threatening me?' Luc looked down into Darby's pale face and almost developed some respect for the guy.

'Yes.'

Luc smiled. Maybe Darby wasn't the dickless wonder he'd always thought. The band struck its first chords and Luc walked away. The sort of jazz crap that got on his nerves filled the room and he wove his way to the man of the hour, Hugh Miner. John Kowalsky joined them, and they talked hockey, discussing the Chinooks' chances of winning the cup that year.

'If the team stays healthy,' Hugh predicted, 'we have a good shot at the cup.'

'A sniper wouldn't hurt either,' the Wall added.

Their conversation turned to what they'd both been up to since retirement and Hugh pulled a wallet out of the back pocket of his trousers and flipped it open. 'This is Nathan.' Luc didn't bother telling him that he'd already seen the photograph.

Rock Head Move: Dumb Move

Jane dried her hands with a paper towel and tossed it
in the garbage. She looked in the mirror above the
sink and hardly recognized herself. She wasn't sure that
was a good thing.

She opened the little purse she'd borrowed from
Caroline and pulled out a tube of red lip gloss. Marie
joined her at the sink, and Jane studied Luc's sister as she
washed her hands. Brother and sister looked nothing
alike, except that their eyes were the same shade of blue.

Earlier, when she'd turned and seen Luc with such a
young girl, she'd been shocked. Her first thought had
been that he should be arrested, but then he'd shocked
her further a moment later when he'd introduced his
sister.

'I'm not good at this,' Jane confessed as she leaned
forward and smeared the gloss on her mouth. Before the
banquet, Caroline had put some sort of semi-permanent
color on her lips, and all Jane had to do was reapply the
gloss. She thought she'd done a good job, but she had no

experience and wasn't certain. 'Tell me the truth. Do my lips look messy?'

'No.'

'Huge?' She had to admit that getting this made up was kind of fun. Not something she would want to do every day, though. Or even very often.

'No.' Marie dropped the paper towel in the trash. 'I like your dress.'

'I got it at Nordstrom.'

'Me too!'

She handed Marie the gloss. 'My friend helped me pick it out. I'm not very good with color.'

'I picked mine out, but Luc bought it.'

If that was the case, she wondered why Luc let his sister buy a dress that was too small. Jane might not be a slave to fashion, but even she could see it. 'That was very nice of him.' Through the mirror, she watched Marie coat her lips a bit too much. 'Do you live in Seattle?'

'Yep, I live with Luc.'

Shock number three of the evening. 'Really? That must be a flaming hell. Are you being punished for something?'

'No, my mom died a month and a half ago.'

'Oh, no.' Jane's chest squeezed. 'I'm so sorry. I was trying to be funny and I said something insensitive. I feel like such an ass.'

'It's okay.' Marie gave Jane half a smile. 'And living with Luc isn't *always* a flaming hell.'

Jane took back her gloss and turned to face Marie. What was there to say? Nothing. She tried anyway. 'My mother died when I was six. It's been twenty-four years, but I know . . .' she paused, searching for the right word.

There wasn't one. 'I know the hole it leaves in your heart.'

Marie nodded and she looked down at her shoes. 'Sometimes I still can't believe she's gone.'

'I know how you feel.' Jane dropped the tube back in her purse and put her arm around Marie's shoulders. 'If you ever want to talk about it with someone, you can talk to me.'

'That might be okay.'

Tears filled the corners of Marie's eyes and Jane gave her a little squeeze. It had been twenty-four years, but Jane clearly recalled the emotions that were so close to the surface. 'But not tonight. Tonight we're going to have fun. Earlier I met some of Hugh Miner's nephews. They're here from Minnesota and I think they're your age.'

Marie dabbed at her eyes with her fingers. 'Are they hot?'

Jane thought about that. If she were Marie's age, she might think so, but she wasn't, and thinking teenage boys were hot made her uncomfortable. She could almost hear the song 'Mrs. Robinson' in her ears. 'Well, they live on a farm,' she began as they left the bathroom. 'I think they milk cows.'

'Yuck.'

'No, that means they're buff, and as far as I could tell, they don't smell like a barn.'

'That's good.'

'Very good.' Jane looked across her shoulder at Marie. 'I like your eye shadow. It's very sparkly.'

'Thanks. You can borrow it sometime.'

'I think I'm a little old for eye glitter.' Jane dropped her arm as they wove their way through the crowd. She found Hugh Miner's nephews looking out over the city and introduced Marie to the two teenage boys. Jack and Mac Miner were seventeen-year-old twins and were dressed in matching tuxedos with scarlet cummerbunds. They had spiky crew cuts and big brown eyes, and Jane had to admit that they were kind of cute.

'What grade are you in?' Mac, or perhaps Jack, asked Marie.

A blush stained her cheeks, and she hunched her shoulders. Looking at Marie brought it all back, the horrid insecurity of adolescence, and Jane thanked God she never had to go through it again.

'Tenth,' Marie answered.

'We were in tenth last year.'

'Yeah, everyone picks on the tenth-graders.'

Marie nodded. 'They throw tenth-graders in Dumpsters.'

'We don't. At least not the girls.'

'If we were at your school, we'd look out for you,' one of the twins said, impressing Jane with his gallantry. They were really nice young gentlemen, and their parents had raised them right and should be proud. 'Tenth blows,' he added.

Maybe not. Maybe someone should inform him that he shouldn't talk like that in front of girls.

'Yeah, it blows,' Marie agreed. 'I can't wait till next year.'

Okay, maybe Jane was just getting old. And she supposed, that when you got right down to it, saying something blew was the same as saying it sucked.

The more the teens talked, the more Marie seemed to relax. They talked about where they went to school, what sports they played, and what music they liked. All of them agreed that the jazz band playing at the opposite side of the room was lame.

While Marie and the twins talked about what 'blew' and what was 'lame,' Jane glanced about the room, searching for more adult conversation. Her gaze skimmed over Darby, who was in a deep conversation with General Manager Clark Gamache, and landed on Luc where he leaned against the end of the bar, talking to a tall blonde woman in a white slip dress. The woman had her palm on his arm and his head was lowered over hers as she spoke. He brushed aside the edge of his jacket and shoved one hand in his pants pocket. Charcoal suspenders lay flat against the white pleats of his shirt, and Jane knew under those formal clothes the man had the body of a god and a horseshoe tattooed on his flat belly. Luc laughed at something the woman said, and Jane looked away. Something alarming that felt a lot like jealousy landed in the pit of her stomach and her hand tightened on her little purse. She couldn't be jealous. She had no claim to him, and she didn't even like him. Well, not that much. What she felt was anger, she reasoned. While she babysat Luc's sister, he trolled for Vanna White lookalikes.

Rob Sutter asked her to dance and she left Marie in the care of the Miner twins. The Hammer led her to the middle of the floor and surprised her with how well he moved. His hand on her side, he led her around the dance floor. If it hadn't been for his black eye, he would have looked utterly respectable in his black tux.

After Rob, she danced with the Stromster, who'd dyed his Mohawk a light blue to match his tuxedo. At first conversation with the young Swede was difficult, but the longer she listened to him, the better she understood his heavy accent. When the band paused between songs, she thanked Daniel and made her way to Darby, who waited for her on the edge of the dance floor.

'I'm sorry, Jane,' he began as she approached him, 'but I have to take you home now. An acquisition we've been working on is finally taking place tonight. Clark has already left for the office. I have to meet him there.'

The Space Needle was a stone's throw from the Key Arena and, depending on the time of day, about half an hour from her apartment. 'Go ahead. I'll take a taxi.'

He shook his head. 'I want to make sure you get home.'

'I'll make sure she gets home.' Jane turned at the sound of Luc's voice. 'Marie's up on the observation deck with the Miner twins. When she comes back down, we'll take you home.'

'That would help me out a lot,' Darby said.

Jane glanced behind Luc for the blonde, but he was alone. 'Are you sure?'

'Sure.' He looked at the assistant general manager. 'Who's involved in the acquisition?'

'Keep it under your hat until morning.'

'Of course.'

'Dion.'

Luc smiled. 'Oh, yeah?'

'Yeah.' Darby turned to Jane. 'Thanks for coming with me tonight.'

'Thank you for inviting me. The ride in the limo was wild.'

'See you two at the airport in the morning,' Darby said and headed for the elevator.

As Jane watched him go, she asked, 'Who's Dion?'

'Boy, you really don't know much about the game.' Luc took her elbow and, without bothering to ask, pulled her out onto the crowded dance floor. Luc took her small purse and stuffed it in the pocket of his jacket. He folded one of her hands in his and placed his warm palm on her side.

In her new heels, her eyes were level with his mouth, and she set her hand on his shoulder. The light on the dance floor cast a diagonal shadow across his face, and she watched his lips while he spoke. 'Pierre Dion is a veteran sniper,' he said. 'He knows the ice. When he shoots from his sweet spot, the puck stings like a son of a bitch.'

Watching his mouth did funny things to Jane's nerve endings, and she raised her gaze to his. It was probably best not to talk about sweet spots. 'Your sister seems like a very nice girl.'

'Really?'

'You sound surprised.'

'No.' He looked over her head. 'It's just that she's moody and unpredictable, and tonight hasn't been a real good night for her. She was asked to a high school dance, but the boy decided to take someone else at the last minute.'

'That's horrible. What a little bastard.'

His gaze returned to hers. 'I offered to kick the kid's ass, but Marie thought it would embarrass her.'

For some bizarre reason, Jane felt herself fall deeper into infatuation with him. She couldn't help it, and all because he'd offered to kick some ass on his sister's behalf. 'You're a good brother.'

'Actually, I'm not.' His thumb brushed the back of her

hand and he pulled her a little closer. 'She cries a lot, and I don't know what to do about it.'

'She just lost her mother. There's nothing you *can* do.'

His knee bumped hers. 'She told you that?'

'Yes, and I know how she feels. I lost my mother too. I told her if she needed to talk to someone, to give me a call. I hope you don't mind.'

'I don't mind at all. I think she really needs a woman to talk to. I've hired someone to stay with Marie while I'm on the road, but she doesn't seem to like her.' He thought a moment, then said, 'What she really needs is someone to take her clothes shopping. Every time I give her my credit card, she comes back with a bag of candy and something two sizes too small.'

That would explain the tight dress. 'I could hook her up with my friend Caroline. She's really good at making people over.'

'That would be great, Jane. I don't know anything about girls.'

Even if she hadn't read up on him, she would have known within five seconds of meeting him that Luc knew a lot about girls. It was the look in his eye and the confident curve of his smile. 'You mean you don't know anything about sisters.'

'I don't know anything about *my little* sister,' he said through a wicked grin. 'But I did date twins once.'

'Yes.' She frowned. 'You and Hef.'

He laughed, deeply amused with himself. 'You're so gullible,' he said as the music ended and she stepped back. Instead of releasing her, he pulled her against his chest. The band struck up another number. 'What did you and Hogue do in the limo?' he asked next to her hair.

'What?'

'You thanked Darby for a wild limo ride.'

She and Darby had drunk champagne and played with the television, as the driver drove them around the city as if they were Bill and Melinda Gates. But she figured that wasn't really what Luc wanted to know. His mind was in the gutter, and she decided to give him something to think about. 'We got freaky.'

He stopped. 'You got freaky with Hogue?'

She almost laughed, and looked up into his face. The only thing freaky about her was her imagination. 'Beneath that hair gel, he's a wild man.'

He started to move once more. 'Tell me about it.' His breath whispered across her temple and her fingers curled into his shoulder.

'You want the details?'

'Yes, please.'

She did laugh then. He'd probably done things that even Honey Pie hadn't thought up. She doubted she could shock him if she tried. 'Unless I make something up, I'm afraid you're doomed to disappointment.'

'Then make something up.'

Could she? Right here on the dance floor? If she closed her eyes, could she become Honey Pie? The woman who made men want her with a smile. Men like Luc.

'Something good,' he added. 'No whips, though. I'm not into pain.'

It was tempting. Tempting to sink into his chest and pretend she was the kind of woman to satisfy a man like Luc. The kind who whispered naughty suggestions and made men beg. For her next article in *Him*, she'd been thinking of writing Honey into a co-ed fantasy. Men loved co-ed fantasies. 'Do you like to watch?'

'I'm more of a doer,' he said close to her ear. 'It's more interesting that way.'

But she couldn't do it. Alone in her own apartment was one thing, but standing within Luc's arms in the SkyLine was entirely different. She couldn't take it any further and the best she could come up with was, 'Darby is an animal. Neither of us may ever recover. In fact, I better go sit down now. I'm exhausted.'

Luc pulled back and looked into her face. 'Don't tell me that's the best you can do. You're better at trash-talking. And you pretty much suck at that.'

'Let's talk about something else.' Something safe.

He was quiet for a moment, then said, 'You look good tonight.'

'Thank you. You're looking pretty good yourself.' He pulled her close once more, and she brushed her fingers across his shoulder, feeling the texture of his jacket. If she leaned in just a fraction, the smell of his cologne and the starch of his shirt filled her nose. 'Very nice.'

'I like your hair.'

'I got it cut this morning. It looks good now, but the real test will come in the morning when I have to wash it.'

When he spoke again, his voice was a smooth rumble next to her ear. 'I just wash mine and go.'

She closed her eyes. Good, a nice, safe, boring subject. Hair care.

'I like your dress.'

Another safe subject. 'Thanks. It's not black.'

'I noticed.' He slid his hand from her side to the small of her back, his warm palm and fingers against her bare skin. 'Do you think you might ever wear it backward?'

His touch seemed to warm her up from the inside out, and startled laughter escaped her lips. 'No. I don't think so.'

'Too bad. I wouldn't mind seeing it on backward.'

The music flowed around Jane as everything within her stilled. Luc Martineau, with his wicked grin and horseshoe tattoo, wanted to see her naked. Impossible. Just beneath the surface, her skin tingled, hot and alive with sensation. Want and need pooled low in her abdomen and she wondered if he'd notice if she leaned into him. Just enough to smell the side of his neck. Right above the black band of his tie and starched collar.

'Jane?'

'Hmm?'

'Marie is back. We have an early flight and better get going.'

Jane looked up into the shadows caressing his face. While impure thoughts sullied her mind, he appeared unaffected. *I wouldn't mind seeing it on backward*, he'd said. No doubt he was pulling her chain again. 'I'll get my coat.'

He removed his hand from her back, and cool air replaced his warm touch. He took her arm, and as they walked from the dance floor, he handed her Caroline's little bag. 'Give me your ticket. I'll get your coat when I get Marie's.'

Jane fished around in the purse and pulled out the piece of paper. While he retrieved the coats, she talked to Marie, but her mind was on Luc, and there was no denying it. She lusted after him. Bad. She wondered if he'd noticed. She sincerely hoped not. She hoped he would never find out. She could happily live her entire life without anyone knowing that Jane Alcott wanted to jump bad-boy hockey player Luc Martineau. If he suspected, he'd no doubt run long and hard in the opposite direction.

When he returned, he helped her on with her black raincoat. His fingers brushed the back of her neck as he fixed the collar for her, and she wondered what it would be like to feel his arms slide around her as she leaned back into him. But even if she'd had the nerve to act on her impulse, she was too late; he stepped away and held his sister's coat open for her.

While they waited at the bottom of the Space Needle for the valet to bring around Luc's white Land Cruiser, he fastened the four buttons on his jacket and stuck his hands in the pockets, his broad shoulders hunched against the cold. They talked about the weather and about the early flight in the morning. Nothing important. Marie told them about the view from the observation deck, and Jane cast glances at Luc's dark profile. Light from the Needle lit up one side of his face and wide shoulders and cast a long shadow across the concrete.

When the valet returned, Luc opened the front passenger door for Jane and the back for his sister. He climbed into the driver's side and they headed for Bellevue. Within a few blocks, Luc broke the silence.

'Mrs. Jackson knows she's to come over tomorrow before you get home from school,' he told his sister. 'Do you need money for anything?'

Jane looked over at him through the corner of her eye. His profile was just a black outline within the dark interior. Golden light from the dash shone on his wristwatch and sent slivers of gold on to the front of his jacket. Jane turned and gazed out her window.

'I need lunch money and I haven't paid for ceramics class.'

'How much do you need?'

Jane listened to their conversation, feeling like an intruder, sitting within the rich leather interior of Luc's SUV while he talked to his sister about their everyday life. A life that did not include her. This was his life. Not hers. She had her own life. One she'd made for herself, and she did not belong in his.

When the vehicle pulled up to the curb in front of her apartment, Jane reached for the door. 'Thanks so much for bringing me home,' she said.

Luc reached across the distance and grabbed her arm through her thin coat. 'Don't move.' He glanced in the backseat. 'I'll be right back, Marie,' he said as he got out of the vehicle.

The headlamps briefly spotlighted him as he walked in front of the Land Cruiser, then he opened her door. He helped her out and moved beside her up the short walkway. Beneath her illuminated porch, she opened her little bag and pulled out her keys, but just as he had the night he'd walked her to her hotel room in San Jose, he took the key from her and shoved it in the lock.

Inside, she'd left on a floor lamp, and the light spilled across the carpet and lit up the front door. 'Thanks again,' she said as she stepped into the apartment. She held her hand out for her keys and he grasped her wrist and placed the keys in her palm. Instead of letting go, he followed her inside.

'This is not a good idea,' he said and brushed his thumb across her pulse.

'What? Bringing me home?'

'No.' He pulled her against him and lowered his face to hers. 'You've been driving me crazy. With your hair that makes me wonder what it'd feel like tangled around my fingers.' His hand grasped the back of her raincoat, twisting the material in his fist and pulling it tight. 'Your red lips and your little red dress give me all kinds of crazy ideas. Stuff I shouldn't think about you, but I am. Questions that are better left alone.' His blue eyes stared into hers, hot and intense. 'But I can't leave them alone,' he whispered against her mouth. 'So tell me, Jane, are you cold?' His lips brushed hers and he said through a hot breath, 'Or turned on?' Then he kissed her, and the shock stunned her for several seconds. She could do nothing more than just stand there as he placed tender kisses on her lips.

What did he mean, was she cold or turned on? She definitely was *not* cold.

He pressed his warm mouth to hers and brought his free hand to the side of her face, cupping her cheek and running his fingers through the hair at her temples. A little moan stuck in her throat, the keys dropped from her hand, and she no longer cared what he meant about her being cold. She ran her palm up the front of his jacket to the side of his neck. This couldn't be happening. Not to her. Not with him.

His lips teased and pressed harder until she opened her mouth. His tongue slipped inside and touched her, wet and oh so welcome.

For a man who spent his time hitting people and

pucks with a hockey stick, his touch was surprisingly gentle. The little moan worked free, escaped into his mouth, and she let herself go. She let herself slide into the hot passion spreading across her skin, pounding in her chest, and aching between her thighs. She let herself fall face first into the lust she'd been trying to hold at bay. His big hand cupped her breast through the layers of her dress and coat, and she leaned into him. His thumb brushed her nipple and she raised onto her toes. There was no more thought of letting, just doing. Just kissing him as if she wanted to eat him up in one sitting. Her tongue sliding across his as if she wanted to binge on Luc Martineau.

He pulled back and looked into her face, his eyes dazed, his voice a bemused rasp. 'You make me want to suck a bruise on you just to kiss it better.'

Jane licked her moist lips and nodded. She wanted that too.

'Damn,' he said through a harsh breath. Then he turned on his heels and was gone. Leaving Jane stunned and bewildered. Shocked for the fourth time that night.

Blindsided: Hit from Behind

Jane closed her laptop on Honey Pie and her latest victim, a hockey player Honey had met on the observation deck of the Space Needle. A hockey player who looked a lot like Luc Martineau.

She rose from the chair, pushed aside the heavy drapes, and looked out the hotel window at downtown Denver, Colorado. She'd definitely developed an infatuation for Luc. Probably an unhealthy one too. In the past, she'd sometimes based Honey's victims on real people. She'd changed their names, but readers could still figure it out. A few months ago, she'd put Brendan Fraser into a coma for subjecting moviegoers to *Monkeybone*, *Dudley Do-Right*, and *Blast from the Past*. But this was the first time Jane had written someone she knew personally into the column.

People might recognize Luc when the magazine hit the shelves in March. Definitely the readers in Seattle would. He'd probably hear about it too. She wondered if he'd mind. Most men wouldn't, but Luc wasn't most men.

He didn't like to read about himself in books, news-papers, or magazines. No matter how flattering. And the Honey article was extremely flattering to him. Hotter and more passionate than she'd ever written. In fact, it was the best thing she'd ever written. She hadn't decided if she was actually going to send it in. She had a few days before her deadline to decide.

The drapes fell from her hands and she turned back to the room. It had been about sixteen hours since Luc had kissed the breath out of her. Sixteen hours of reliving and analyzing every word and action. Sixteen hours later, she still didn't know what to think. He'd kissed her and changed everything. Well, actually, he'd done more than just kiss her. He'd touched her breast and told her she drove him crazy, and if his sister hadn't been sitting out in the car, Jane might have thrown him down and checked out that lucky tattoo, which was driving *her* crazy every time she saw it in the locker room. And that would have been bad. Very bad. For a lot of reasons.

Jane kicked off her shoes and pulled her sweater over her head. She tossed it on the bed as she moved to the bathroom. Her eyes were scratchy and her brain fuzzy, and instead of locking herself in her room working on her Honey Pie article, she should be at the Pepsi Center, talking to the coaches and players before tomorrow night's game. Darby had mentioned that the best time to talk to the coaches or front-office management was during practice. And Jane wanted to ask them about their new acquisition, Pierre Dion.

She jumped into the shower and let the warm water pour over her head. That morning when Luc boarded the jet, wearing his dark glasses, blue suit, and striped tie, her stomach had fluttered like she was thirteen again with her first junior high school crush. It was horrible, and she was old enough to know that having a crush on the most popular boy in school would only bring her heartache.

After fifteen minutes, she stepped out of the shower and grabbed two towels. If she was honest with herself, something she tried to avoid if possible, she could no longer fool herself into thinking that what she felt for him was nothing more than a crush. It was more. So much more, it scared her. She was thirty. Not a girl. She'd been in love and she'd been in lust and she'd been somewhere in between. But she'd never allowed herself to fall for a guy like Luc. Never. Not when she had so much to lose. Not when there was more at stake than just her contrary heart. Something more important: her job.

A broken heart would mend; she could get over that. But she didn't think she could get over blowing the best opportunity she'd been given in a long time. Because of a man. That was plain stupid, and she wasn't stupid.

A knock interrupted her thoughts, and she moved to the door. She looked out the peephole, and Luc stood on the other side, all windblown and perfect. He glanced down at the ground and she took a moment to study him. He wore his leather coat and a gray wool sweater, and he must have just come from outside because his cheeks were pink. He looked back up and his blue eyes stared at her through the peephole as if he could see her. 'Open up, Jane.'

'Just a sec,' she called out, feeling foolish. She moved to the closet and pulled out a terrycloth bathrobe. She tied the belt around her waist, then opened the door.

His gaze rose to the towel wrapped around her head,

lowered to her mouth, then, in no great hurry, slipped to the tips of her bare toes. 'Looks like I caught you just out of the shower again.'

'Yes. You did.'

He slid his gaze back up her legs and robe and looked at her without expression. He either was uninterested or doing a really good job of appearing uninterested. 'Do you have a minute?'

'Sure.' She stepped aside and let him in. 'What do you need?'

His long strides took him to the center of the room and he turned to face her. 'When I saw you this morning, you seemed uncomfortable. I don't want you to feel uncomfortable around me, Jane.' He took a long deep breath and stuck his hands in the pockets of his jacket. 'So I think maybe I should apologize.'

'Apologize for . . . ?' But she knew and she wished he wouldn't.

'For kissing you last night. I'm still not sure how it happened.' He looked over her head as if the answer were written on the wall. 'If you hadn't cut your hair and been looking so good, I don't think it would have happened.'

'Wait.' She held up one hand like a traffic cop. 'Are you blaming my hair?' she asked, just to make sure she was hearing him right. Hoping she wasn't.

'Probably had more to do with that dress. That dress was designed with ulterior motives.'

He'd kissed her, and she'd fallen so deep into infatuation that she wasn't sure it even was infatuation anymore. Now here he was, blaming her hair and her dress as if she'd purposely tricked him. As if he wouldn't have kissed her if he hadn't been tricked. Knowing how he felt hurt more than it should have. He was a jerk, no doubt about it, but she was a fool. The latter was the hardest to take.

Pain and anger tangled into a knot around her heart, but she was determined not to let it show. 'It just was an ordinary red dress.'

'It didn't have a back and had only two strips of material up the front.' Luc rocked back on his heels and lowered his gaze from the towel wrapped around Jane's head, down the front of her robe to her bare toes again. Since last night, he'd been thinking about that kiss in her apartment, and he wasn't certain what had driven him to kiss her. The dress. The lips. Curiosity. All of those. 'And the little gold chain hanging down your back was there for only one reason.'

'What? To hypnotize you?'

She was being sarcastic, but she wasn't that far off. 'Maybe not hypnotize, but it's there so any man seeing it will think about unhooking it.'

She raised one brow and looked at him as if he were an idiot. He sort of felt like an idiot. 'I'm telling you the truth. All the guys last night were thinking of unhooking your dress.' None of the guys had mentioned it to Luc, but he figured that if he'd been thinking it, they had too.

'Is this your idea of an apology or your way of rationalizing what happened?' She grabbed the towel from her head and tossed it on her bed.

'It's a fact.'

She combed her fingers through her hair. 'It's delusional.'

If she were a guy, she'd see the logic in it.

'And it's stupid.' Her wet curls tangled about her fingers as she pushed them back from her face. 'It puts the blame on me, and I didn't walk into your apartment last night and kiss you. You kissed me.'

'You didn't protest.' He didn't know what had shocked him more. Him kissing her, or her response. He never would have guessed that so much passion could be contained in so little a package.

She let out a long sigh as if she were bored. 'I didn't want to hurt your feelings.'

He laughed even as he wanted to cross the room and press his mouth to hers. To slip his hand inside that robe and cup her breast, even as he knew it was a hell of a bad idea. Luc leaned a hip into the desk as he lowered his gaze from her mouth and thought about how her mouth had tasted last night. He glanced somewhere safe, down at Jane's laptop. 'The way you kissed, I thought you were trying to climb inside me.' An open day planner sat beside the laptop. Several Post-its were stuck on the inside. A couple of the notes had to do with hockey trivia and questions she wanted to ask for her sports columns.

'There you go, being delusional again.'

On one pink note the words, *Feb. 16/Single Girl deadline*, were printed. While another read, *Honey Pie/make decision by Wednesday at the latest*. Honey Pie? Did Jane read Honey Pie? The nympho who humped men into comas? He just couldn't picture her reading porn. 'You were so hot for it,' he said in a slow and deliberate drawl as he looked back up at her, 'I could have had you naked in no time.'

'You're not only conceited beyond belief, and delusional, you're . . . you're deranged!' she sputtered.

'Probably,' he admitted as he walked past her on his way to the door. He felt deranged.

'Wait a minute. When do I get the interview you promised me?'

With his hand on the doorknob, he turned and looked at her. 'Not now,' he said.

'When?' she pushed.

'Sometime.'

'Sometime tomorrow?' She raised her arms and brushed her hair behind her ears.

'I'll let you know.'

'You can't back out on me now.'

He didn't plan to. He just wasn't going to do it now. Here. In a hotel room with a king-sized bed and a woman wearing a bathrobe begging him to prove just how deranged he was. 'Yeah, says who?'

Her brows lowered and she pinned him with her gaze. 'Me.'

He laughed again. He couldn't help it. She looked like she was gearing up to kick his ass.

'You gave me your word.'

For a split second he thought about shutting her up with his mouth. Kissing her until she turned soft and melted into him again. Until she fed him that little moan of hers that had urged him on last night, to take it further. To touch her where his mind had been taking him since that first morning on the team jet when he'd looked back and seen her.

'When, Luc?'

Instead of giving in to the urge, he opened the door and said over his shoulder, 'When you get a bra, Jane.'

Luc unzipped his jacket the rest of the way as he

walked down the hall. A repeat of last night couldn't happen again. The instant he'd kissed her, he'd gone from zero to hard in under a second, and that hadn't happened to him in a very long time. If Marie hadn't been waiting in the car, he didn't know if he would have stopped. He liked to think he would have. He liked to think he was mature and experienced enough to stop before he did anything he'd regret, anything colossally stupid, but he wasn't sure. He'd kissed a lot of women in his thirty-two years. A lot of women had kissed him too, but never like Jane. He didn't know what it was about her, and he really didn't want to take the time to figure it out. She already spent too much time in his head.

The very last thing he needed in his life right now was a woman. Any woman. Especially *that* woman. The reporter traveling with the team. Sharky, their good-luck charm.

There was only one solution to his Jane problem. He'd have to avoid her as much as possible. Not as simple as it sounded, granted. Not when she traveled with the team, covered every game, and had to call him a 'big dumb dodo' for luck.

Over the course of his career, Luc had developed the kind of intensity that held up under the pressures of overtime and point-blank shooters. During the next few days, he planned to use that intensity to keep his focus on winning. He needed to concentrate on his game and do what needed to be done.

That night against Colorado, he shut down twenty-eight of thirty goal attempts and the Chinooks boarded the jet with a three–two victory over their biggest contenders for the Stanley Cup. As soon as the BAC-111 evened out, the glow of Jane's laptop illuminated the space three rows up. Luc hadn't needed the light to tell him where she sat – he knew. But just because he knew didn't mean he had to do anything about it. During the flight from Denver to Philadelphia, he noticed some of the guys talking to her. Daniel said something that made her laugh, and Luc wondered what the young Swede told her that could possibly be so damn funny. Luc grabbed a pillow and sacked out for the rest of the trip.

Avoiding Jane turned out to be easier than anticipated but not thinking about her proved impossible. It seemed the more determined he was to avoid her, the more he thought about her. The more he tried not to think about her, the more he wondered what she was doing and who she was doing it with. Probably that 'wild man' Darby Hogue.

He only saw Jane once in Philadelphia, but the second she entered the locker room at the First Union Center, he noticed her red lips. And he *knew* she'd worn lipstick on purpose just to drive him insane. She gave her good-luck speech, then walked toward him where he sat in front of an open stall.

'Good luck, you big dumb dodo,' she said, then she lowered her voice to just above a whisper. 'And for your information, I have several bras.'

As Luc watched her breeze from the room, he worried that her full red lips had fucked up his concentration. For a few tense moments, his focus was on Jane's mouth and imaginary black lace bras. He closed his eyes and cleared his head, and by sheer force of will, he got it back ten minutes before he hit the ice.

That night, the Chinooks shut out the Flyers, but not

before the boys from Philly laid on the lumber and sent Sutter to the hospital with a concussion. Rob was still on the injured list when the Chinooks landed in New York to take on the Rangers. In the locker room before the game, Luc waited for Jane to wish him luck before he said, 'If you own several bras, you might try wearing one.'

She tilted her head to one side and looked at him. 'Why?'

Why? He could tell her exactly why, but not in a locker room full of hockey players. Then again, it wasn't his job to tell her that her nipples were at full salute. He was avoiding her. He was finished talking to her and thinking about her, he told himself as he skated to the net and turned his attention to winning against the Rangers. But without their best lunch pailer, the Chinooks took a thrashing against the boards and in the corners and ultimately lost the game when the Rangers' captain broke away and shot at Luc on the long side.

Then it was on to Tennessee, the birthplace of Elvis and the Nashville Predators. That night in the locker room there was no mention of bras.

The young Tennessee expansion team easily fell victim to the more experienced Chinooks, and when the team boarded the jet for the long flight to Seattle, Luc was glad to be heading home. His right knee was bothering him and he was exhausted.

Once the BAC-111 evened out, he shrugged out of his jacket and raised the arm between the seats. Grabbing a duffel, he stuffed it against the side of the plane and leaned his back against it. With his fingers woven together and his hands resting on his stomach, he sat in the dark and looked across the aisle at Jane. The light directly above her poured over her head and filtered through her loose curls as she typed out her column. The tips of her fingers lightly touched the keyboard. She paused, stroked backspace several times, then started again. He thought of a few places on his body he'd like to feel those talented hands stroke.

A curl fell across her cheek and she pushed it behind her ear, drawing Luc's gaze to her jaw and the side of her throat. A few rows back, some of the guys played poker, but most of them slept, their snores mixing with the sound of Jane's typing.

For the past seven days, he'd kept himself busy, distracted. Now, with nothing to occupy his thoughts, he took the time to study her. To figure out exactly why he suddenly found Jane Alcott so interesting. What it was about her that wouldn't let go and leave him alone. She was short, small-breasted, and had a smart mouth. In fact, she was just too damn smart. Luc didn't like those qualities in a woman. And yet . . . he liked Jane. Tonight, she wore one of those cardigan sweater sets like old women and Ivy League girls wore. Black. No pearls. A pair of gray wool pants, and she'd kicked off her shoes.

Within the darkness, Luc studied her soft hair and smooth white skin. The first time he'd seen her, he'd thought her too plain. A natural girl. Now he was having a hard time remembering exactly why natural girls had never appealed to him before. He wondered what it would be like to slide his hands all over her soft skin. For the first time since he'd stood in her hotel room in Denver, he let himself wonder what it would feel like to hold her naked body against him. To lose himself in the pleasure of touching her. Of kissing her mouth and breasts and smooth thighs.

The tapping stopped, and Jane brought her fingers to her mouth. She pinched her bottom lip and moaned, followed by a long drawn-out sigh that could be either frustration or pleasure. The sound of her moan brought Luc to full painful attention, and he decided that picturing Jane naked hadn't been such a grand idea after all.

Through the variegated shadows that separated them, he watched her tap backspace a dozen or so times and begin again. Luc closed his eyes and turned his thoughts toward home. While he'd been away, Mrs. Jackson hadn't reported any more problems with Marie, and when he'd talked to his sister, she seemed somewhat stable. She'd made friends with a girl in their building, and Marie hadn't burst into tears or gotten angry during any of the calls. He still hadn't ruled out boarding school, because he did think she would ultimately benefit from a female environment. He just didn't believe she was ready to talk about it yet, and for some reason he couldn't explain, there was a part of him that wasn't ready to talk about it either. Not yet.

Somewhere over Oklahoma he fell asleep, and didn't wake up until the jet was about to set down at SeaTac. Once the jet landed and came to a stop, Luc grabbed his bags and headed for general parking. Jane walked at a distance in front of him, pulling a huge suitcase on wheels and lugging her laptop and briefcase. His longer stride easily overtook her and they stepped into the elevator together. They pushed the same button to the same floor of the garage and the doors slid closed. Luc leaned back against the wall and glanced over at Jane. Her head was tilted to one side as she studied him. She looked worn out, but so damn cute.

'What?' he asked.

'Are you going to give me the interview this week?'

She might be tired, but she was obviously on the job. While he was thinking how cute she looked and had been fantasizing about her soft skin and talented fingers, she was thinking about her work. Damn. 'Are you wearing a bra?'

'Are we back to that?'

'Yes. Why don't you wear a bra like most women?'

'Why do you care?'

His gaze lowered to the front of her wool coat, but of course he couldn't see anything. 'Your nipples stick out, and it's distracting.' When he raised his gaze to her face, her brows were drawn and her mouth was open as if she'd been about to say something but forgot what. The elevator doors slid open. 'You look like you're turned on all the time,' he added and held the door open while she wheeled her big suitcase out. The stunned look on her face was classic and he started to laugh. 'Don't tell me that no one's ever told you that before.'

'No. You're the first.' She shook her head, and together they started across the parking lot. 'You're just yanking my chain again. Like when you offered to pee in my coffee and told me you were going to a strip bar.'

'I was serious about the coffee and I'm serious now.' He stopped at the rear of his Land Cruiser.

'Ah-huh. Right,' she said as she continued to her Honda Prelude parked a few spaces from his SUV.

He tossed his bags in the back of his Toyota, then

looked over at her. The trunk of her car was open and she was making little huffing sounds as she tried to get her big suitcase inside. Luc walked past the two cars separating them, and the heels of his shoes echoed in the near-empty lot. At the sound of his footsteps she looked up. The lights in the garage cast deep shadows in the corner where she'd parked her car. A lock of her hair fell over one eye and she pushed it back. Her lips were slightly parted as she breathed.

'Need help?' he asked.

She pointed to the big suitcase still on the ground. 'You can help me with that. I bought some books last night and they've made it really heavy.'

Luc easily heaved the suitcase into the trunk.

'Thank you.' She put her laptop and briefcase inside, then shut the trunk.

'You're welcome.'

'Did Marie tell you I'm going to pick her up Saturday?' she asked as she moved to the driver's side door.

'Yep.' He followed and took the key from her fingers. He unlocked the door and added, 'She sounded real excited.'

She held out her hand and he dropped her keys in her palm. 'I'm glad to hear it. We haven't talked in a while, and I didn't know if you were okay with the plan.'

He lowered his gaze from her hair, past her green eyes and straight nose, the bow of her top lip. 'We've talked.'

'You may not know this, but me calling you a big dumb dodo and you razzing me about my bra isn't considered talking.' The corners of her mouth turned down. 'At least it isn't outside of the locker room.'

He returned his gaze to hers and he wondered if she was trying to piss him off on purpose. He suspected she was. 'What's put your panties in a twist, sweetheart?'

She folded her arms across her chest and took a step back – Luc figured so she didn't have to bend back her head so far to look up at him. 'I think we both know.'

'I'm just a stupid hockey player, so why don't you go ahead and spell it out real slow for me?'

'I never said you were stupid.'

He took a step closer so she'd have to look up at him again. 'You implied it, Jane, and I'm not so stupid that I didn't get the implication.'

She stepped back. 'I didn't mean that you're stupid.'

'Yes, you did.'

'Okay, but I don't think you're stupid. You're . . .'

He followed her. 'I'm . . . ?'

'Rude.'

He shrugged. 'That's true.'

'And you say inappropriate things to me.'

'Like?'

'That I look like I walk around turned on.'

She did.

'You wouldn't say that to a male reporter.'

That's true, but if a male reporter walked around with full wood, chances were Luc wouldn't even notice. Now, Jane, he noticed. 'I'll work on that.'

She took one more step and her back hit the wall behind her. 'And you're spoiled. You get everything you want and everything is your way.'

She was talking about the interview again. 'Not everything.' He moved forward and placed both of his hands on the cold concrete beside her head. 'Some of the things I want aren't good for me. So I have to leave them alone.'

'What?'

'Caffeine. Sugar.' He lowered his gaze to her lips. 'You.'

'Me?'

'Most definitely you.' He slid his hand to the back of her neck and he lowered his mouth to hers. 'I've never had *you* my way,' he said, and he kissed her because he couldn't seem to stop himself. Her lips were warm and sweet and instant desire settled heavy in his groin. With nothing more than his hand on the back of her head and his mouth pressed to hers, lust rolled over him like a Zamboni.

He pulled back with every intention of walking away, of leaving before he did something he would regret, but she looked up at him and licked her moist lips. Instead of turning on his heels, he wrapped one arm around the small of her back and brought her body against his. He was used to tall women and he had to pull her up on her tiptoes. His mouth opened wide over hers and he fed her a hot wet kiss. He held her to him as her hands ran across his shoulder and up the sides of his neck. His tongue touched and mated with hers as she combed her fingers through his hair. His scalp tingled from her touch. She moaned deep in her throat, that sound of lust and frustration and yearning that had urged him on the other night and had him thinking about having sex with her right there against the wall now.

In the weak light of the parking garage, he unbuttoned her coat, then shoved his hand under her sweater. Her flat stomach was warm and he slid his hand to her breast. She wasn't wearing a bra, and her breast hardly filled his hand. Her puckered nipple poked the middle of his palm like a hard little raspberry, and his testicles squeezed and his scrotum tightened and his knees almost buckled. He slid his mouth to the side of her cheek and took a deep breath. This was the most sexual excitement he'd felt in a long, long time, and he had to stop.

'Luc,' she gasped, then she grabbed the sides of his head and brought his mouth right back to hers. She ran her hands over his shoulders and chest and kissed him like a woman who wanted to end up in bed. A hot openmouthed feeding kiss that had him thinking of security cameras and of the likelihood of arrest. He rolled her hard nipple beneath his palm and she wrapped her leg around his waist. He shoved his erection against her crotch. The heat of their bodies nearly did him in. He ground against her and forgot about stopping.

'Not here,' he said as he ended the kiss. 'We'll get arrested. Believe me, I know.' He tilted his head back and took a deep breath. 'There's a Best Western or a Ramada within a few miles.' He blinked. He was fairly sure there was anyway. 'I'll grab a room while you wait in the car.'

'What?'

God, he wanted her. He wanted to fall on top of her and stay there for a good long while. 'We'll have sex all night. Half the morning too. And just when you think you can't take anymore, we'll go at it again.' It had been a long time since he'd wanted it so bad that he could hardly think beyond the throbbing in his pants. 'I'm going to fuck you real good.' She didn't say anything and he looked down into her face.

She unwrapped her leg from his waist and lowered her foot to the ground. 'In a motel room?'

'Yes. We can take my car.'

'No.'

'Where?'

She pushed his hand from her breast. 'Nowhere.'

'Why the hell not? I'm hard, and I don't have to stick my hand down your pants to know you're wet.'

Her eyes were wide and a little glassy. 'You're talking to me like I'm one of your groupies.'

He'd never even thought of her in those terms. Had he? No, he hadn't. 'You don't like *wet*? What do you call it?'

'I don't call it anything, and I don't fuck. I make love. Groupies fuck.'

'Jesus,' he swore, 'who cares? When you get down to it, it's all the same thing.'

'No, it's not, and I care.' She shoved at his chest and he took a step back. 'I'm not one of your women. I'm a professional reporter!'

He didn't know who she was trying to convince. Him or herself. 'You're a tease and a damn prude,' he said and turned on his heels. He shoved one hand in the pocket of his jacket and his hand curled around his keys until they cut into his palm. He was sorry he'd ever met Jane. He was sorry he'd ever laid eyes on her, and sorrier that she made him so insane that he'd kissed her and now he was going home hard. Again.

As he walked to his vehicle, he heard her car start and by the time he unlocked the driver's side door of his Land Cruiser, she was gone, the glow of her red taillights the last remnants of her.

That and the ache in Luc's groin and the pounding in his brain and the knowledge that he'd have to see her again in three days.

I make love, she'd said. The first time he'd met her, he'd figured her for one of those uptight, probably-hadn't-had-sex-in-five-years women. And he'd been right.

'"Make love,"' he scoffed as he climbed into his vehicle and started it up. Jane didn't want to make love. He hadn't misinterpreted her signals. A woman who wanted him to 'make love' to her didn't kiss like a porn queen. A woman who wanted to 'make love' wanted to take her time. She didn't wrap her leg around his waist while he had her shoved up against a wall in a parking garage.

He backed out of the parking space and headed home. Someone should teach the little prude a thing or two about being a tease. But it wasn't going to be him. He was through with Jane Alcott.

This time he meant it.

Juke: To Fake an Opponent

Three days after the parking garage incident, Jane sat in the press box at the Key Arena, staring down at the ice.

'Do we get free food and booze up here?' Caroline asked her.

'There's free food and booze in the media lounge.' She'd brought Caroline along so that she'd have someone to talk to. Someone to help take her mind off her current man problems. 'I don't usually go there until later.'

Caroline was dressed in an extremely tight Chinooks T-shirt and equally tight jeans. She was dressed for a fishing expedition, and she'd already caught the attention of the guy operating the video for the game. He'd flashed Caroline up on the screen three times already.

Darby joined them a few minutes before the pregame entertainment was to start. His hair was stiff with gel, and his pocket protector was stuck in his black silk shirt. Jane introduced him to Caroline, and his eyes widened and his mouth fell open a little as he gazed at Jane's beautiful friend. She wasn't surprised by Darby's reaction, but she was a bit surprised when Caroline turned her charm on Darby and reeled him in.

The pregame show started, and Jane knew that in about fifteen minutes she was going to have to go to the locker room and wish the team luck. She was going to have to see Luc for the first time since he'd kissed her and she'd lost her mind and wrapped her leg around his waist. Thank God she'd come to her senses at the last minute and hadn't gone with him to a motel. That would have been bad for a lot of reasons.

There was no denying it, though, she'd fallen madly in lust with Luc. She was drawn to him, pulled like she was a magnet and he was a big hunk of metal, and there didn't seem to be anything she could do about it.

She'd spent the past week on the road avoiding him as much as possible. Avoiding the man who irritated her, and angered her, and made her insides melt. For the most part, she'd kept herself busy. She'd interviewed Darby for her *Single Girl* column, and she'd written a piece about nice guys who finished last. She'd told her readers that they should avoid those guys who set women's hearts on fire and instead give nice guys a second look. She'd quoted Darby and made him sound good, and in return he was supposed to talk her up to the coaches who still didn't want her around.

She'd taken her own advice and done fairly well at avoiding the one guy who set *her* heart on fire. Then he'd backed her against that wall and kissed her. She should have been shocked and appalled, but seeing him come at her, his lids lowered to half mast and lust heavy in his blue eyes, she'd gone all weak and excited at the same time. The moment his lips had touched her, she'd given in to her heart and fed it what it so desperately wanted. Luc.

Even though her feelings for him were a tangled mess, she could no longer avoid the truth. She wanted Luc. She wanted to be with him, but she wanted to be more than just another woman to take to just another hotel.

More than a groupie.

He'd called her a prude. She was anything but a prude. She didn't care if men used rough language during sex. She wrote *Honey Pie*, for goodness' sake. No, she was no prude. She was a woman hanging on to her dignity, fighting him and herself. Fighting not to fall completely in love with an unattainable man.

If he ever found out that she was Honey Pie, she supposed she wouldn't have to fight it anymore. He might never speak to her again. He might even hate her.

After he'd stood in her hotel room in Denver last week and told her it was her dress's fault that he'd kissed her, she'd sent in the March serial she'd written featuring a handsome Seattle goalie. She'd been so angry and hurt and she'd pressed send and had zipped it across cyberspace.

If Luc found out and read the March column, he'd know he was Honey's latest victim. She told herself that he should be flattered. That maybe he would be flattered. Not every man in America had the honor of being put into a coma by Honey Pie. But she really didn't believe Luc would feel honored, and that made her feel a little guilty. Of course, there was no way he'd ever connect her with Honey. He'd never know what she'd done. That didn't assuage her guilt, however.

Darby laughed at something Caroline told him and pulled Jane's thoughts from Luc. For a brief second, Jane wondered if she should warn Darby that he wasn't her friend's type, that she'd probably throw him back, but Darby looked more than happy to be caught up in Caroline's smile. Instead of warning him, Jane left him to figure it out for himself. She put her briefcase beneath her seat and forced herself to take the elevator to the ground level.

She glanced down at the navy blazer she wore over her white turtleneck. She buttoned the jacket to make sure it covered her breasts. Before Luc had mentioned that her nipples stuck out, she hadn't really given them a lot of thought. She really didn't notice her breasts much. They were small and weren't her best feature, and she just figured no one else noticed them either.

No one but Luc.

Her feet dragged a little as she approached the locker room, and she stopped by the door and listened to Coach Nystrom's inspirational speech. When he wound down, she straightened her shoulders and walked into the room. She refused to look at Luc, but she didn't need to see him to know he was in the room. She could feel him watching her. And it wasn't a good vibe.

'Hey, Sharky,' Bruce called out to her.

'Hey, there, Fishy,' she said and turned her attention to the rest of the team. She took her place in the middle of the room and recited the good luck ritual. 'Keep your pants up, gentlemen. I have something to say. It will just take a minute, and I don't want you to do that synchronized jock-dropping crap. Traveling with you guys has been an experience I won't forget. I hope this is your year to win the Stanley Cup.' She walked over to the team captain, who was in the process of pulling his jersey over his head. 'Good luck with the game, Hitman.'

He shook her hand. Although the cut on his lip must have caused him pain, he smiled. 'Thanks, Jane.'

'You're welcome.'

Rob had been cleared to play tonight and she moved to his stall. 'How are you feeling, Hammer?'

'One hundred percent.' He stood and towered over her in his skates. 'It's good to be back.'

'It's nice to see you back.' Finally she turned to Luc and walked toward him. Several locks of his dark blond hair touched his forehead, and he sat with his helmet resting on one knee. His clear blue eyes watched her approach, his gaze carefully blank. With each step she took, her stomach twisted tighter into a knot. She almost preferred his anger. Something. She stopped in front of him and took a deep breath. 'You big dumb dodo.'

'Thank you,' he said, completely devoid of any emotion.

'You're welcome.' She told herself to leave, but she couldn't make herself go. 'I interviewed Dion last week.'

'So? Haven't you been told not to irritate me before a game?'

Okay, so maybe he wasn't completely without feeling. He was obviously mad. Good. Mad was better than indifferent. 'Yes. And you've told me not to irritate you after a game too.'

'So why are you still standing here?'

'I have everything ready for your interview.'

'Too bad.'

Time to get rough with him. 'We had a deal,

Martineau. If you don't keep it, I won't ever call you a dodo again.'

He stood and looked down at her. 'Fine. Tomorrow after you finish shopping with Marie. When you bring her home, bring your questions.'

She smiled. 'Fabulous.' Then she left before he changed his mind. When she returned to the press box, Darby and Caroline were deep in conversation about his Hermès suit.

Jane reached beneath her seat and retrieved her briefcase. She dug around inside and pulled out her day planner and a pad of Post-its. *Interview with Luc*, she wrote and stuck it on tomorrow's page of her planner. As if she'd really forget.

During the second period, Caroline leaned over and whispered in her ear, 'Look at all that testosterone on ice.'

Jane laughed. 'Kind of like Campbell's Soup Stars on Ice?'

'No, kind of like a sperm bank.'

The Chinooks lost to the Florida Panthers in the last four seconds of the game, when a Panther ripped a one-timer from the blue line. Luc went down on his knees, but the puck somehow shot beneath his pads. Luc looked behind him in the net and hit his stick on the bar as the final buzzer blew.

When Jane re-entered the locker room, she kept her gaze up and came face-to-face with Vlad Fetisov and his broken nose. She didn't know which was worse, looking at him above the shoulders or below the waist.

As she asked Vlad about his injury, she cast a surreptitious glance a few stalls away. Luc stood with his back to her, stripping off his armor until he was naked from the waist up. Her gaze slid down the indent of his spine to the small of his back. He turned and her throat got tight. Rising out of his shorts like an invitation to sin was his horseshoe tattoo. No wonder she was infatuated with him. Coming or going, the guy was eye candy. No wonder her brain shut down when he touched her. She hadn't had sex since Vinny, and she'd kicked him to the curb almost a year ago.

'. . . Iz just game,' Vlad finished, and she was glad she'd recorded his response because she hadn't heard a word he'd said.

'Thanks, Vlad.' Maybe it was time to get a new boyfriend. Someone to help take her mind off Luc and his lucky tattoo.

A gray mist hung over Seattle the next morning when Jane picked up Caroline and drove to Bell Town. Because of her interview with Luc later that day, Jane had dressed in her usual business clothes, gray wool pants and white blouse. Caroline wore pink suede pants and a red-and-pink-striped body shirt. She looked like she was about thirty-five years too late for her *Laugh-In* audition. On anyone else, the outfit would have been a fashion don't, but on Caroline it somehow worked.

They collected Marie outside Luc's condo and made it just in time for Marie's hair appointment. First Vonda cut the dead ends from Marie's hair, then she feather-cut it just below her chin. The cut was young and cute and aged Marie about four years.

Afterward, they walked to Gap, Bebe, and Hot Topic, where Marie bought a leather belt with big silver studs and a Care Bear shirt. Caroline bought a new belly button ring and a Strawberry Short Cake nail file. Jane got a Batgirl T-shirt. They talked about boys and music and which Hollywood actress was starting to look skanky. Each place they went, Marie gave Luc's Visa a thorough workout.

At the MAC counter in Nordstrom, the makeup artist applied just enough cosmetics to accentuate Marie's big blue eyes and bring out her smooth complexion. Marie chose a deep red lipstick that looked good on her, but added another year. Jane couldn't help but wonder what Luc would think of his sister looking older. She would find out shortly.

When it came to picking out clothing, Marie took Caroline's suggestions without arguing. Caroline had a way of steering people away from faux pas without them knowing they were being steered, and it didn't hurt that Caroline was tall and beautiful and dressed like a supermodel.

'Those run small,' she told Marie when she wanted to try on a size three pair of Calvin Klein stretch jeans. 'Designers design for anorexic girls or little boys,' she said. 'And thank God you don't look anything like a boy.' She handed Marie a size five.

Darby Hogue showed up in the shoe department as Marie tried on a pair of Steve Madden clogs with a five-inch wedge.

'I told Darby I'd help him pick out some shirts,' Caroline said, and if Jane didn't know better, she would have sworn her friend blushed a little. Impossible, because Mensa nerds with flaming red hair were not Caroline's type. She liked them tall, dark, and free of pocket protectors.

Caroline pointed Marie to black boots with big silver buckles on the sides. 'These will look fabulous with that camo skirt and belt you bought.'

Personally, Jane thought the boots were hideous, but Marie's eyes lit up and she said, 'Boo-ya!' which Jane assumed was good. Once again, listening to a teenager made Jane feel old. To counterbalance the feeling, she tried on a pair of rope sandals with two-inch heels.

She sat next to Darby as she strapped them on. 'What do you think?' she asked him as she pulled up the legs of her jeans and looked at the sandals from different angles.

'I think they look like scarecrow shoes.'

She glanced over at him in his favorite silk skull shirt and leather pants and considered the source.

He leaned over and said next to her ear, 'I need you to put in a good word for me with Caroline.'

'No way. You insulted my sandals.'

'If you get me a date with her, I'll buy you the shoes.'

'You want me to pimp for you?'

'Do you have a problem with that?'

Jane glanced at her friend, who was at the Ralph Lauren table eyeing a pair of slides. 'Ah – yeah.'

'Two pairs.'

'Forget it.' She took off the sandals and shoved them back into the box. 'But I'll give you a few pointers. Lose the skull shirt and don't talk about Mensa.'

'Are you sure?'

'Absolutely.'

When they finished in the shoe department, she and Marie rode the escalator up to lingerie, while Caroline and Darby headed to the men's department.

Jane and Marie were loaded down with bags as they found racks of bras.

'What do you think?' Marie asked as she held up a lavender lace bra.

'It's pretty.'

'I bet it's uncomfortable, though.' She tilted her head to one side. 'Don't you think?'

'Sorry, but I'm not going to be able to help you here. I don't wear bras. I never really have.'

'Why not?'

'Well, as you can see, there isn't much need. I've always just worn camisoles or a bandeau or nothing at all.'

'My mom would have killed me if I wore just a camisole.'

Jane shrugged. 'Yeah, well, growing up, my dad didn't like to talk about girl stuff. So I think he just pretended I was a boy for a lot of years.'

Marie flipped over a price tag. 'Do you still miss your mom?'

'All the time, but it isn't so bad now. Just try and recall all the good memories of your mother before she got sick. Don't think about the bad.'

'How'd your mom die?'

'Breast cancer.'

'Oh.' They looked at each other over the rack of bright lacy bras, Marie's big blue eyes staring into Jane's, and neither of them had to say anything about watching a loved one die that way. They knew.

'You were younger than me. Right?' Marie asked.

'I was six, and my mother was sick a long time before she died.' Her mother had been thirty-one. One year older than Jane was right now.

'I still have a few flowers from my mom's casket. They're dried up now, but it makes me feel somehow still connected to her.' Marie looked down. 'Luc doesn't understand. He thinks I should throw them away.'

'Have you told him why you've kept the flowers?'

'No.'

'You should.'

She shrugged and picked up a red bra.

'I have my mother's engagement ring,' Jane confessed. 'My father left her wedding band with her, but he kept her engagement ring, and I used to wear it on a chain around my neck.' She hadn't talked about the ring in years and what it meant to her. Caroline didn't understand, because her mother had run off with a trucker. But Marie did.

'Where is the ring now?'

'In my underwear drawer. I put it away a few years after my mother died. I imagine you'll put your flowers away when the time is right for you.'

Marie nodded and chose a white water bra. 'Look at this one.'

'It looks heavy.' Jane picked one from the rack and squeezed the bottom. It was heavy and squishy and she wondered what Luc would think of his little sister wearing a push-up bra. She wondered what he'd think if *she* wore one. 'Luc might not want you to buy a big ol' padded bra.'

'Oh, he won't care. He probably won't even notice,' Marie said and took four bras and disappeared into the dressing room. While Jane waited for her, she picked up the numerous shopping bags and moved a few feet away to the panties department.

Jane might not know a lot about bras, but she was a panties connoisseur. Two years ago, she'd become a thong convert. At first she'd hated them, but now she loved them. They didn't ride up like conventional panties because, well, they were already up. While she waited, she bought six cotton and lycra thongs with matching camisoles.

Once Marie emerged from the dressing room, she placed a handful of panties and three bras on the checkout counter. The cell phone in her purse chirped and she flipped it open.

'Hello,' she answered. 'Hmm . . . Yeah, I think so.' She glanced at Jane. 'I'll ask her. Luc wants to know if you're hungry.'

Luc? 'Why?'

Marie shrugged. 'Why?' she asked him. She handed the clerk Luc's credit card, then told Jane, 'It's his night to cook. He says since you're coming over to interview him, he'll throw something on for you too.'

Two things occurred to Jane at the same time. That Luc cooked, and that he must not be mad at her anymore. 'Tell him I'm starved.'

Put in the Third Row: Hit Hard

'It's weird not having a yard,' Marie said, talking about the differences in her life now that she lived in Luc's Bell Town condo. 'And I don't do laundry anymore,' she added as they stepped out of the elevator on the nineteenth floor. 'That's nice.'

'Luc does your laundry?'

Marie laughed. 'No.' They moved down the hall to the last door on the left. 'We send it out and it comes back all clean and folded.'

'Even your underwear?'

'Yep.'

'I don't think I'd want anyone touching my panties,' Jane said while Marie opened the door. At least not strangers, she thought as she stepped inside and came to an abrupt halt. The impact of the windows stopped Jane in her tracks and replaced thoughts of strange people folding her thongs. The windows ran from floor to ceiling and took up an entire wall. Beyond the tops of buildings, she could see the ships in Elliott Bay. The room was filled with a deep blue couch and chairs and wrought-iron-and-glass coffee and end tables. The angles of the rooms seemed to flow in on themselves and big potted plants thrived in brushed stainless steel pots. To her left, the Devils battled Long Island on the big-screen televison, while Dave Matthews pumped through the stereo fit into a huge entertainment center.

Luc stood in the open kitchen separated from the living room by a granite bar. The cabinets behind him had glass fronts with chrome handles. The appliances were stainless steel and a bit futuristic-looking. Luc picked up a remote and cut the sound to the stereo. A smile curved his mouth and crinkled the corners of his eyes. 'You look great, Marie.'

Marie dumped her bags on the floor and tossed her coat on the couch. She spun around for her brother. 'I think I look twenty-one,' she said.

'Not quite.' He turned his smile on Jane, and she once again felt like a magnet, pulled by a force stronger than herself. 'Wanna beer, Jane?'

'No, thanks. I don't drink beer.' She set her briefcase and jacket on the couch.

'What do you drink?'

'Water's fine.'

'I'll take Jane's beer,' Marie volunteered, bless her heart.

'As soon as you *are* twenty-one,' he said as he pulled a bottle of water out of a stainless steel refrigerator.

'I bet you drank before you turned twenty-one.'

'Yeah, and look how I turned out.' He shut the door with his foot and pointed the bottle at Jane. 'Don't say it.'

'I wasn't going to say a thing.' She moved across the

room and stepped between two chrome and gray leather barstools.

'Better not.' He tossed a few ice cubes in a glass and twisted the top off the bottle. He'd pushed up the sleeves of a plaster-colored ribbed sweater, and the edge of a white T-shirt showed beneath the crew neck. He wore his gold Rolex and a pair of olive cargo pants. ''Cause I know stuff to blackmail you.'

He knew she melted when he kissed her and that she didn't like to wear a bra. 'You don't know any of the really good stuff.'

A smile tugged at one corner of his mouth. 'How good?'

Stuff that would blow his mind, and she just thanked God he would never figure it out. He would never know that she was Honey Pie.

'What stuff?' Marie wanted to know as she took a seat beside Jane.

'That I'm a Girl Scout,' Jane answered.

Luc lifted one dubious brow and set the glass on the bar.

'Well, I was,' she assured him.

'Me too,' Marie added. 'I still have all my patches.'

'I was never a Boy Scout.'

Marie rolled her eyes. 'Well, duh.'

Luc looked at his sister as if he meant to comment, but at the last second decided against it. Instead, he returned the water to the refrigerator and set a bowl of marinated chicken breasts on the counter.

'What can I do to help?' Jane asked.

Opening a drawer, he took out a fork and turned the chicken. 'Just sit tight and relax.'

'I'll help you,' his sister volunteered and slid off the barstool.

Luc glanced up and smiled, his blue eyes warm as he looked at Marie, and Jane's heart squeezed in a way that had nothing to do with her lust for him. Nothing to do with infatuation, and everything to do with seeing the kinder, gentler side of Luc Martineau. 'That'd be great. Thanks. Grab the pasta and get it boiling.'

Marie walked around the bar and joined Luc in the kitchen. She pulled down a red box from one glass-faced cabinet, then reached for a measuring cup. 'Two cups of water,' she read out loud. 'And a tablespoon of butter.'

'When Marie was little,' Luc said as she turned on the faucet, 'she said "gotter" instead of water.'

'How do you know?' Marie asked as she measured water into a cup.

'I heard you when I came to visit when Dad was still alive. You were probably two.'

'I was cute when I was a baby.'

'You were bald.'

She turned off the water and poured it into a pan. 'So?'

He reached over and messed up her hair. 'You looked like a monkey.'

'Luc!' Marie set the pan on the stove and brushed her hair with her fingers.

He laughed, a deep pleased-with-himself ha-ha-ha. 'You were a *cute* monkey.'

'Okay. That's better.' She turned on the burner and added the butter. 'You're just jealous because you looked like a Teletubby.'

'What's a Teletubby?'

'Oh, my gosh! You don't know what a Teletubby is?' She shook her head at her clueless brother.

'No.' A bewildered crease furrowed his brow as he turned his blue gaze on Jane. 'Do you?'

'Unfortunately, yes. It's a show geared toward very young children. And, as far as I could tell from the one time I watched it, all the Teletubbies do is run around in Teletubbyland babbling and baby-talking.'

'And they show pictures on their tummies,' Marie added.

His mouth fell open a bit, his eyes glazed, and he looked as if he were getting a sudden headache just thinking about it. 'You're kidding.'

'No.' Jane shook her head. 'And in my own defense, I only know this because a few years ago, Jerry Falwell made headlines when he warned parents that there are gay undertones in Teletubbyland. Apparently because Tinky Winky is purple and carries a red purse.'

'Tinky Winky?' Slowly he turned and looked at his sister. 'Holy hell, and you make fun of me for watching hockey.'

'It's not the same thing. You watching hockey is like me watching school.'

She had a point.

He must have thought so too because he conceded with a shrug of his shoulders. 'I can't believe you watch those Telebelly things,' he said, but he did pick up the remote and shut off the hockey game.

'Teletubby,' Marie corrected him. 'When I go to Hanna's, she puts in the tapes for her two-year-old brother. It mesmerizes him so we can paint our fingernails.'

'Hanna?'

'The girl who lives on the third floor. I told you about her.'

'Oh, that's right. I forgot her name.' Once Luc set the vegetables steaming, he turned on the stovetop grill and put the chicken on.

'I'm going to the movies with her after dinner.'

'Do you need a ride?'

'No.'

Luc had an innate grace about him, whether it was reaching for a puck or turning chicken breasts on a grill, an economy of motion and fluid style that was fascinating to watch. Almost as fascinating as the way his butt filled out those cargo pants. The bottom edge of his sweater hit just below his hips and right above the Nautica label sewn on his back pocket.

Jane listened to Luc and his sister talk about her day. Everything Marie had bought, and her plans for later. Jane knew from her conversations with Luc that he didn't think he was doing a good job with Marie. Seeing them together, Jane wasn't so sure he was right. They seemed to get along pretty well. They were a family. Perhaps not an average family, maybe not always easy, but family just the same. They stood at the stove, cooking, talking, trying to include Jane, but she still felt a little left out. Marie in the too-tight jeans she'd worn when Jane had picked her up that morning, and Luc in his pants that were just right.

Luc flipped chicken and Marie filled him in on the different designers Caroline had told her about. 'I hope you finally bought some jeans that aren't too tight,' he said as he checked on the steaming vegetables.

Marie looked across her shoulder at her brother and her blue eyes got a bit squinty.

Perhaps if Luc had glanced his sister's way he would have noticed she'd just taken serious issue with him and he wouldn't have added, 'Your pants are so tight it's a wonder you don't blow out the seams.'

Uh-oh.

'That's soooo mean! I don't tell you your jeans are too tight.'

'That's because they're not. I don't like anything up my butt.' Finally, he glanced at Marie. 'What are you so mad about?'

Marie opened her mouth, but Jane headed her off. 'Marie picked out some nice things and she looks really cute in them.' Well, except that studded belt. 'Caroline helped her out. I'm not any good at fashion stuff or that whole color chart thing. That's why I wear a lot of black.'

Luc moved to lean his behind into the counter. 'I thought it was because you were the Queen of the Damned.'

She glanced into his smiling eyes and frowned. 'No, rude guy,' she said and turned her attention back to Marie. 'The next time I go get waxed, you should come along. I used to shave, but I'm a wax job convert now. It hurts like hell ... ah, I mean the dickens ... but it's worth it.'

'Okay.' Marie smiled at her brother. 'Can I keep one of your Visas, Luc?'

'Hell, no.' He crossed his bare feet and folded his arms over his wide chest. 'You'll buy twenty pounds of candy and bad Britney Spears CDs.'

Marie was back to glaring. 'That only happened once, and it wasn't twenty pounds. And I don't buy bad CDs.'

'Twice. All that sugar is bad for you and Britney Spears

is a mind-suck.' Tension strained the air, yet Luc didn't
seem to notice. Either that or he was just good at ignoring
it. He straightened and checked on their meal. 'Someday,
when you still have all your teeth and your brain hasn't
turned to Jell-O because of Britney, you're going to thank
me.'

By the look on Marie's face, that someday was a
looooong way off.

By the time they all sat down at the dining room table,
Marie had pretty much gone mute. Even though Jane
had been a teenage girl once, she didn't recall ever being
so moody. Then again, she didn't have a brother who told
her her pants were too tight and her music sucked. Just a
father who used to aggravate and creep her out by
blaming everything on her 'woman's time.'

Luc sat at the head of the table with Jane and Marie
on opposite sides. Three glasses of milk sat beside their
plates, even though Jane recalled telling him she didn't
drink milk when he'd asked. No one had served her milk
since grade school, she thought as she placed her napkin
on her lap and dug into her meal. She'd had men try to
force alcohol on her before, but never milk.

Not only had Luc managed to make cooking look
good, he made it taste good also. A guy who looked good
enough to eat *and* could cook? If it wasn't for his Barbie
collection, and forcing milk on her, he'd be too good to be
true.

'The chicken is wonderful,' Jane complimented him.

'Thanks. The secret is in the orange juice.'

'You make the marinade yourself?'

'Sure, the stuff—'

'Did you know,' Marie interrupted, 'that dolphins are

the only mammals other than man that have sex for pleasure?'

Luc's fork stopped in midair and he looked at his sister. Marie was purposely baiting him and Jane was interested to hear his response, to see if he'd freak out and give her the reaction she wanted.

'Where did you hear that?' he asked.

'My biology teacher told me. And a kid in the class went to Disney World and swam with the dolphins, and he says they're really horny.'

The fork continued to his mouth and he chewed thoughtfully. 'I don't remember learning about horny dolphins in school. We just dissected frogs.' He turned his attention to Jane. 'I feel cheated.' Then he took all the wind out of Marie's sails. 'What about you, Jane? Did you get to learn about horny dolphins?'

She shook her head and tried not to smile. 'No, but I saw on the Discovery Channel that they found some homosexual monkeys in Africa. So they're fairly sure some species of monkeys also mate for pleasure.'

Luc's brows rose up his forehead. 'Homosexual monkeys? How did they determine that?'

She laughed and shook her head.

A smile pushed up the corners of his mouth and little lines appeared at the corners of his blue eyes. 'Black-rimmed glasses and cow pajamas?'

'Don't start that again.'

'What?' Marie wanted to know.

Jane returned his smile as she dug into her pasta. 'He thinks I have ugly glasses.'

'And pajamas.'

'How do you know what Jane's pajamas are like?'

Luc looked at his sister. 'I caught her at the candy machine at the hotel in Phoenix wearing the ugliest cow pajamas you can imagine.'

'I was on a chocolate run,' Jane explained. 'I thought the players were all in their rooms.'

'Luc doesn't understand chocolate runs.' Marie rolled her eyes. 'He only eats *healthy* stuff.'

'My body is a temple,' he said around a big bite of cauliflower.

'And anyone with long legs and big boobs is welcome to worship,' Jane added and immediately wished she could take that one back.

Marie laughed.

Luc smiled like a sinner.

Jane changed the subject before he could comment. 'Who's Mrs. Jackson?'

'The old lady who stays with me when Luc is gone,' Marie answered.

'Gloria Jackson is a retired schoolteacher and a very nice woman.'

'She's old.' Marie took a bite of pasta. 'She eats slow too.'

'Now, there's a reason to hate her.'

'I don't hate Gloria. I just don't think I need a babysitter.'

Luc let out an exasperated breath as if they'd had this conversation before. A lot. He reached for his glass of milk and took a long drink. When he lowered it again, a slim white mustache rested on his top lip and he sucked it off. 'Why aren't you drinking your milk?' he asked Jane.

'I told you I don't like milk.'

'I know, but you need the calcium. It's good for your bones.'

'Don't tell me you're worried about my bones.'

'Not worried.' A sexy grin curved his mouth. 'Curious, though.'

His words and the look in his eyes slipped inside and warmed her up in places that were better left cooled.

'Better just drink it, Jane,' Marie warned, missing the sexual innuendo between the two adults. 'Luc always gets what he wants.'

'Always?' Jane asked.

'No.' He shook his head. 'Not always.'

'Most of the time,' Marie insisted.

'I hate to lose.' His gaze drifted to Jane's mouth. 'I'm a do-or-die-trying kind of guy.'

Jane glanced at Marie, who was busy pushing her broccoli to the edge of her plate. 'Whatever it takes?' she asked and returned her attention to Luc.

'Absolutely.'

'What about finesse?'

'Depends on my odds.' He looked back up into her eyes and said, 'Sometimes I'm forced to play dirty.'

'Forced?'

A wicked grin curved his mouth. 'Sometimes I just like to play dirty.'

Yes, Jane knew that about him. She'd seen him shove and hook skates and run roughshod in front of his net. But she didn't think he was talking about hockey.

'When can I get my driver's license?' Marie broke in and thankfully changed the subject.

Both adults looked at her, then Luc leaned back in his chair and Jane breathed easier. 'You're not old enough.'

'Yes, I am. I'm sixteen.'

'When you're eighteen.'

'No way, Luc.' She gulped down her milk and placed it on her empty plate. 'I want a new Volkswagen Beetle. I can buy it with my own money.'

'You can't have your money until you're twenty-one.'

'I'll get a job.'

He watched her take her plate and utensils and move into the kitchen. 'She's in one of her moods tonight,' he said out of the corner of his mouth.

'She's mad because you told her her jeans are too tight.'

'They are.'

Jane gathered her napkin in her hand and laid it on the table. 'I don't think she'll have that problem now. Caroline talked her into buying clothes that fit.'

'It was very nice of you and your friend to give up your Saturday and take my sister shopping,' he said as both of them watched Marie leave the kitchen and move down the hall to her bedroom. 'I can't imagine anything worse.' Luc slid his palm beneath Jane's and he studied her fingers.

'Caroline did everything.' Her hand appeared small and very white within the warmth of his, and her chest suddenly felt too tight. 'I can barely dress myself. I wear a lot of black because I don't know what colors look good on me.'

'Red.' He turned her hand over and looked at her palm. Slowly, his gaze slid up her wrist and arm, past her shoulder to her mouth once more. He leaned closer, and his voice got a little deeper, hotter. 'You look good in red, but I believe we've already talked about that little red dress of yours,' he said. His voice chased warm flutters across her flesh to the pit of her stomach.

'The one that hypnotized you into kissing me?'

'I've decided it wasn't the dress. It was the woman in the dress.' His thumb brushed the side of hers. 'You have soft girl skin.'

She placed her free hand on her stomach as if she could still the butterflies. 'I am a girl.'

'I noticed. Even when I don't want to notice you. Sitting in the back of the plane or bus or walking into the locker room after a game, ready to take on a bunch of guys twice your size, I've always noticed you, Jane.'

Nervous laughter got stuck in her throat. 'Probably because I'm the only female traveling with thirty men. I'm kind of hard to miss.'

'Maybe at first.' His gaze took in her hair and face. 'I'd look around and see you, and I'd be surprised because you weren't supposed to be there.' He lowered his gaze to hers. 'Now I look for you.'

Even as his words made her heart beat a bit harder, what he said was hard for her to believe. 'I thought you didn't want me traveling with the team.'

He placed her hand back on her napkin. 'I didn't.' He stood and gathered the plates and utensils. 'I still don't.'

Jane grabbed the glasses and followed him into the kitchen. 'Why? I told you I'm not interested in a tell-all book.' And she wasn't. *Honey Pie* was a fictional column. Erotic fantasy. Her erotic fantasy.

He set everything in the sink, and instead of answering, he took her full glass of milk and drained it. When he lowered the glass again, she repeated her question. 'Why don't you want me traveling with the team?'

His blue eyes stared into hers as he sucked his milk

mustache from his top lip, and she had a feeling his answer was very important. To her. Because, though she wished it weren't happening, and no matter how hard she tried to prevent it, she was falling in love with Luc. The harder she resisted, the more the force of it pulled her under.

'I'm leaving,' Marie said as she re-entered the kitchen.

For a few brief moments, Luc continued to look at Jane before dragging his gaze to his sister. 'Do you need money?' he asked and set the glass in the sink.

'I have a twenty. That ought to cover it.' Marie shrugged into a snowboarding jacket and pulled her hair from the back collar. 'I might spend the night with Hanna. She has to ask her mom, though.'

'Let me know either way.'

'I will.' She zipped up her coat and bade Jane goodbye. As Jane watched Luc walk his sister to the door, her gaze fell on her briefcase and she was reminded why she was in his apartment in the first place. They might be attracted to each other, but they were both professionals and she was here to do a job. She wasn't his kind of woman, and she didn't want to fall in love with a man who would break her heart like a Dorito.

She moved from the kitchen to the sofa in the living room. She unzipped her briefcase and pulled out a pad of paper and her tape recorder. Jane didn't want her heart broken. She didn't want to love Luc Martineau, but each beat of her heart told her it was too late.

When Luc shut the door behind Marie, Jane looked up at him. 'Ready to get busy?' she asked.

'Are we officially on the clock?'

'Yep.' She took a pen from the pocket of her briefcase.

He moved toward her, his long stride closing the distance between them. What was it about him walking toward her, looking at her through his beautiful blue eyes, that melted her beneath his molten mojo?

'Where do you want to do it?' she asked.

'Now, there's a question,' he said through a warm sexy smile.

Hat Trick: Player Scores Three Goals in One night

'Are you going to sexually harass me?'

Luc folded his arms across his chest and stared down at Jane. 'Do you have a problem with that?'

'Yes. I'm here to interview you for the *Times*.'

Damn. Her shoulders straight, her gaze direct, she was all business. Too bad. He liked harassing her. 'Have a seat.' It had been a long time since Luc had seen a woman other than Gloria Jackson in his home. Since before Marie had come to live with him.

Earlier, when he'd first looked up and Jane had been standing in the living room, it had been a shock to see her, surrounded by his things. Like it had been in the beginning when he'd looked around and had seen her sitting on the team jet or bus. An out-of-place female in an unexpected place. Now, as then, it didn't take long before she seemed to fit. As if she'd always belonged.

He took a seat at one end of the couch and Jane sat in

the middle. Several dark curls fell across her temple and cheek as she looked at the notepad and tape recorder in her lap. She wore her usual black pants and white blouse, and he knew her skin was as soft as it looked.

'How much of your past do you want to talk about?' she began, keeping her head bent over her notebook as she asked her first question.

'None.'

'There's been a lot written about it. You could clear the air.'

'The less said about it, the better.'

'Which bothers you the most, the stuff written about you that is true?' She looked at him out of the corner of her eye. 'Or the total fabrications?'

No one had ever asked him that question, and he thought about that for a moment. 'Probably the stuff that isn't true.'

'Even if it's flattering?'

'Like what?'

'Oh, I don't know.' She sucked in a breath and blew it out. 'The women. The all-night sex stuff.'

He was a little disappointed that she would bring it up. Since she hadn't turned on her tape recorder yet, he said, 'There was never any all-night sex. If I stayed up all night, it was because I was high.'

She looked down at her lap again and chewed on the inside of her lip. 'Most men would probably be flattered if they were portrayed as some sort of sexual marathoner.'

He figured he must trust her or he wouldn't have told her as much as he had. So much so that he added, 'If I was high and up all night, I wasn't up sexually, if you get my meaning.'

'So none of that stuff about you and the different women is flattering?'

He wondered if she asked because she was a bit of a prude and was intrigued by that sort of thing. 'Not really. I'm trying to rebuild my career and that shit gets in the way of what's important.'

'Oh.' She clicked her pen and flipped on her tape recorder. 'In the *Hockey News*'s ranking of the top fifty players so far this season, you are number six, second among goaltenders,' she said, moving the interview away from his private life. 'Last year you didn't make the list at all. What do you think contributed to your startling improvement over last season?'

She had to be kidding. 'I didn't improve. I didn't play much last season.'

'A lot has been made this year about your comeback from your injury.' She sounded stiff, as if she were nervous, which was a bit of a surprise. He didn't think there was much on the planet that made her nervous. 'What has been the single biggest obstacle for you?' she asked.

'Getting a chance to play again.'

She pushed her hair behind her ear and glanced up at him. 'How are the knees?'

'One hundred percent,' he lied. His knees would never be what they had been before the injury. He'd have to live with the pain and worry as long as he played.

'I've read that when you started out in the junior league in Edmonton, you played center. What made you decide to become a goalie?'

Apparently she'd researched more than his sex life. For some reason, that didn't irritate him like it used to. 'I played center from about the age of five to twelve. Our team goalie quit midseason and the coach looked around and said, "Luc, get between the pipes. You're goalie."'

She laughed and seemed to relax a bit. 'Really? You weren't born with a burning desire to stop pucks with your head?'

He liked her laugh. It was sincere and shone from her green eyes. 'No, but I got real good real fast so I wouldn't get a concussion.'

She scribbled something on the notepad. 'Did you ever think of going back to your former position?'

He shook his head. 'Nah. Once I was in the net, I never wanted to leave. I never even thought about it.'

She looked back up at him. 'Did you know that you say *aboot* instead of *about*?'

'Still? I've been working on that.'

'Don't. I like it.'

And he liked her. A lot more than he knew was wise, but looking at her, with her shiny hair and pink lips, he suddenly didn't care about being wise. 'Then I guess I won't work on it – eh?' he said like a true son of Edmonton.

A smile tugged at both corners of her mouth, and she turned her attention back to the notebook on her lap. 'Some people have said that goalies are different from other players. That you are a whole different breed. Would you agree?'

'That's probably true to a certain degree.' He leaned farther back into the sofa and rested his arm along the top. 'We play a different game than the other players. Hockey is a team sport, except for the guy between the pipes. A goaltender plays much more one-on-one. And if we mess up, there's no one to cover for us.'

'Lights don't flash and the crowd doesn't cheer when one gets by the wingers?' she asked.

'Exactly.'

'How long does it take you to shake off a loss?'

'That depends on the loss. I review the game tape, figure out how to do it better next time, and am usually over it the next day.'

'What are your pregame rituals?'

He remained silent until she finally turned her head toward him, then he asked, 'Besides you calling me a dodo?'

'I'm not printing that.'

'Hypocrite.'

She shrugged. 'Sue me.'

There were several things he could see himself doing to her, but suing her wasn't one of them. 'I eat a lot of protein and iron the night before and the day of the game.'

'Retired goalie Glenn Hall was quoted as saying he hated every minute that he played. How do you feel about the position?'

Interesting question, he thought as he tilted his head and studied Jane. How did he feel about it? Sometimes he hated it as much as Hall had. Sometimes it was better than sex. 'On the ice I am very focused and competitive. There is no greater feeling than when I'm in my zone, blocking shots and snagging pucks from midair. Yeah, I love what I do.'

She wrote something in the notebook, then flipped the page. She raised the pen and pressed it to her bottom lip, drawing Luc's attention to her mouth.

There was something about Jane that intrigued him

more than any woman he'd ever known. Something more than the contradictions between Jane the prude, and the Jane who kissed like a porn queen. Something that made him want to run his fingers through her shiny curls and hold her face in his palms. Luc had been with many beautiful women in his life, physically perfect women, but he'd always been in control of his desire. Except with Jane. Skinny little Jane, with her small breasts and wild curls and deep green eyes that could look through him and see that he was up to absolutely no good. Ever since the night of the banquet when he'd kissed her, he'd envisioned taking off her clothes and exploring her body with his hands and mouth. He'd tried to avoid her, and instead he'd come close to having sex with her against a parking garage wall. And his desire for her had only gotten stronger over the past few days.

Watching her now, with her soft skin and shiny hair, he wondered why he should avoid her at all. She was in his life. She wasn't going anywhere, and neither was he. They were both adults. If he ended up with his mouth on her breasts while buried deep in her warm wet body, well, there was absolutely nothing wrong with two adults giving each other pleasure. In fact, it was probably just what they both needed. He lowered his gaze to the front of her blouse and the thrust of her small breasts. He knew it was just what *he* needed.

The telephone next to Luc rang, interrupting his study of Jane's breasts. He picked up the receiver, and it was Marie, telling him that she would be spending the night at Hanna's. 'Call me in the morning,' he said and hung up.

'Marie?'

'Yes. She's staying at Hanna's.'

Jane turned toward him, pulling one knee on the couch and leaning a shoulder into the cushion next to his hand. 'Do you want to talk about Marie?'

'No. I wouldn't want to say anything that would make her life any harder.'

'I think that's wise.' She glanced at the notepad, then looked up at him again. 'When you look into the future, where do you see yourself?'

Luc hated that question. He was just trying to survive the season without injury, and he didn't like to think too far ahead. One play, one game, one season, that's as far as he liked to look. 'I figure I'll have time to decide what to do with my life once I retire.'

'When do you think that will be?'

'I'm hoping I have at least five more years. Maybe more.'

'You are notorious for not giving interviews. Why are you so hesitant to talk with reporters?'

Luc brushed his fingers across her arm. 'Because they usually ask the wrong questions.'

She watched his fingertips slide to her shoulder, and her lips parted on a soft breath. 'What are the right questions?'

He placed his fingers beneath her chin and brought her gaze to his. 'Ask me again why I don't want you traveling with the team.'

'Why?'

He slid his thumb across her bottom lip. 'Because you drive me insane.'

'Oh,' she whispered.

He reached for her tape recorder and shut it off. 'I thought if I quit looking around for you, I would forget you. I thought if I avoided you, I could get you out of my head. But it didn't work.' He took the pad of paper and pen from her hand and tossed them on the floor. Then he indulged himself and brushed his fingers through the soft curls at her temples. 'I want you, Jane.' He leaned forward and held her face in his palms. He rested his forehead against hers, and to make sure she understood him completely, he added, 'I want to strip you naked and kiss you all over.'

Her eyes widened. 'Just last night you were really angry with me.'

'Mostly I was angry with myself because I'd made you feel like a groupie.' He brushed his mouth across hers. 'I want you to know that I *don't* think for one second that you're a groupie. I know who you are, and despite my best attempts to ignore you, I can't.'

He softly kissed her lips, then pulled back to look deep into her eyes. 'I want to make love to you, and if you don't stop me now, that's exactly what's going to happen.'

'I don't think that's a good idea,' she said, but she didn't pull away.

'Why?'

'Because I'm a reporter traveling with you. With the Chinooks.'

He kissed the corner of her mouth and felt her melt a little. 'You better come up with a better reason than that within the next three seconds or you're going to find yourself very naked very soon.'

'I'm not one of your Barbie Dolls. I don't have long legs or big breasts. I can't compete with that.'

Again he pulled back to look into her eyes, and he might have laughed if he hadn't seen that she was serious.

'It's not a competition.' He pushed her hair behind one ear.

She grabbed his wrists. 'I'm not the sort of woman who inspires lust in a man like you.'

This time he did laugh. He couldn't help it. He had a hard-on that proved her wrong. 'Ever since that first morning on the team jet when I looked back and saw you, I've been wondering what you look like naked.' He slid one hand down her throat to the buttons closing her blouse. 'You've driven me crazy ever since.' The tips of his fingers brushed her bare skin and some sort of silky material as he popped the buttons. 'Inspiring all sorts of things, but especially lust.' His head dipped and he kissed the shell of her ear. 'A whole lot of lustful thoughts and dirty fantasies that would shock you.'

He tugged the ends of her blouse from her pants and he looked down at a silky camisole. 'The other night when I walked by and saw you in the media lounge, I fantasized about throwing you up on the table and doing you right there on top of the dessert trays.'

'Sounds . . . messy.'

'And fun. I thought about all the interesting places I'd get to lick you clean.'

She sounded as if she were holding her breath when she said, 'I thought you don't eat sugar.'

He laughed. 'I want to eat yours,' he said as he kissed the crook of her neck. 'Does that shock you, little Jane?'

Jane held back a moan threatening deep within her chest. He was shocking her, but not like he thought. That he fantasized about her at all, let alone in the press room, was a huge shock. His warm breath on the side of her throat sent shivers up her spine and his hand slipping across her silk camisole spread heat across her flesh. Warmth pooled in and between her legs. Her nipples puckered painfully tight and she squeezed her thighs together. She wanted him. She wanted him so much, her vision was getting blurry and she could hardly breathe. Oh, yes, she wanted him as much as he wanted her, but she was afraid where all the wanting would lead. If it were just a matter of sex, she would have been naked by now. He'd be naked too, but it was more. At least for her it was. No matter how she wished it otherwise, her heart *was* involved.

She took a shallow breath and parted her lips to tell him that she couldn't do this, that she had to go home now, but his big hand closed over her breast, heating her skin through the silk material, and he whispered in her ear, 'Jane, I want you.' Then his mouth sought hers and the warm male scent of him filled her nose and she breathed him deep into her lungs. He smelled like clean skin and he tasted like sex.

From nineteen floors below, a fire engine sped past and the real world slipped away, taking the last of her reserve with it. Her sanity gone, she grabbed his sweater in her fists and held tight. She wanted Luc as much as he wanted her. Maybe more, and she would worry about the repercussions later. Now all she cared about was his hand brushing her nipple through the silk of her camisole and his hot wet kisses that left her mind numb and her body aching. A defeated moan came from her own throat as she kissed him back, devouring him with a passion bigger than her ability to hold it back any longer. Her inhibitions and reason burned to ash within the hot overwhelming need to have wild and wicked sex with Luc Martineau.

Her mouth fed him kisses, and she pushed herself onto her knees and straddled his lap. She was lost, completely lost to sensations bigger than her. She pulled his sweater and T-shirt up his chest and their hungry mouths parted just long enough for her to pull it over his head. Then her hands were on him. Touching everywhere she could reach. His hard shoulders and chest. Her fingers brushed his skin and slid down his sternum. Then she sat, and the hard length of him pressed into her. Through the material of her pants and his, Luc warmed her flesh with his hot erection. Her heart pounded in her chest and ears and she pressed harder against him as he shoved his pelvis into her. She slipped her hands to his flat belly and he grasped her wrists.

'Damn,' he said, his voice strained, his breathing rapid. 'Slow down or I'll never make it until I'm inside of you. As it is, I'll probably only last five seconds.'

She'd take it. Five seconds of Luc sounded better than anything else she'd had in a very long time. Better than anything she would ever have again.

Luc pushed her blouse from her shoulders and down her arms. He tossed it on the floor, then he stared at her thin silk camisole. His heavy-lidded eyes were slightly glazed. 'Is this what you wear instead of a bra?'

She shook her head and ran her hands across his warm shoulders and chest. 'Sometimes I don't even wear this.' Through her lust haze, she thought back on which thong she'd pulled on earlier, and she thanked God she'd done the laundry and had on something decent.

'I remember,' he groaned. 'Knowing you walk around without half your underwear has been getting me in trouble.' His big hands circled her waist and he lifted her to her knees, then he leaned forward to bury his face in her stomach. He pushed up the silk material and his warm breath heated her flesh as he spoke. 'Take this off,' he said, then placed wet kisses on her abdomen.

Jane pulled the camisole over her head and dropped it on the couch beside her. Luc spread his fingers wide along her ribs and leaned his head back to look at her. His hot gaze touched her breasts and he took in a heavy breath, but he didn't say a word.

Jane sat in his lap once more and felt compelled to speak for him. 'I'm not quite what you're used to,' she said and covered herself with her palms.

'Big breasts can be a big disappointment. You're beautiful, Jane. Better than my fantasies.' He grasped her wrists and shoved them behind her, arching her back and bringing her breasts close to his face. 'I've waited a long time to see you like this. To do this,' he said as his breath whispered against her aching nipple. Then he softly sucked her inside his hot wet mouth. He let go of her wrists, and her hands found the sides of his head and she held him there.

His cheeks drew inward as the suction he created intensified. The backs of his knuckles brushed her belly, and he unbuttoned the waistband of her pants, then he pushed his hand inside. He cupped her crotch though her red lace thong and she moaned with pleasure.

'You're wet, Jane,' he said low in his throat as he pushed aside her tiny panties and touched her hot slick flesh. It would have been so easy just to succumb right there. To let him stroke her to orgasm. It wouldn't have taken much more and she would have been gone, but she didn't want to orgasm by herself, she wanted him to come with her.

'No more,' she said and grabbed his wrist. He slid his hand up her stomach to her breast, and his fingers played with her, spreading moisture across her nipple. He followed with his mouth. A sound of intense male pleasure, primal and possessive, rumbled deep in his throat, pushing her so close to the edge she feared she would orgasm with nothing more than his mouth on her breast.

'Stop.'

He leaned his head back and looked at her, his gaze totally gone with passion. 'Tell me what you want.'

There was a lot she wanted, but since she might never get this chance again, she said, 'I want to lick your tattoo.'

He blinked several times as if hadn't quite heard her, then he spread his arms.

Jane slid from his lap and pulled him to his feet. She kicked off her shoes and socks and her pants followed. Standing in just her thong, she kissed his shoulder and chest. She ran her hands over his hard muscles and kissed a trail downward. Then she knelt before him, hooked her hands in the waistband of his pants, and brought his flat belly to her face. She licked the heels of the tattoo and tasted his flesh on her tongue. 'I've been wondering how big your horseshoe is,' she whispered as she kissed his navel. 'I've wanted to do this for so long.'

'You should have asked before now. I would have let you.' He ran his fingers through her hair and pushed it from her face. 'Next time, you don't even have to ask.'

She smiled against his belly and she would have bitten him if his skin hadn't been tight as a drum. She unbuttoned his pants and shoved them down his hips and thighs. He stood before her, his black horseshoe disappearing beneath his white briefs. An impressive erection filled out the clean white cotton, and she kissed him through his underwear. Then she pushed the underwear down his legs. Freed, he jutted toward her, and she noticed that the toe of the horseshoe disappeared beneath his pubic hair and went clear to the base of his penis. A ribbon was tattooed just above his dark blond pubic hair and was tied from one side of the horseshoe to the other. LUCKY was written across it in bold black ink.

She laughed and kissed the hot velvet tip. 'You don't want me to ask to do this?'

His response was a strangled, 'No!'

For the first time since he'd kissed her, she felt the power shift to her, and she was in control. She took as much of him as she could into her mouth and tested the weight of his testicles in her palm. She'd never done this for a man during their first time together, fearing it would set a bad precedent, but with Luc, she didn't care. She wanted to do it. Not for him but for her. And no matter how it hurt and would kill her later, she knew there was no future with Luc. No precedent to set. She would take all that she could of him. She was Honey Pie. She'd try her hardest to put him into a coma.

Luc grasped her shoulders and pulled her to her feet. He brought his face to hers and his tongue ravished her mouth. His hands slid to her behind and he lifted her and she wrapped her legs around his waist. His hard naked flesh pressed into her through her thong panties and he kicked free of his pants and briefs. He fed her hungry kisses as they moved from the living room down the hall to his dark bedroom. Light from the massive windows spilled across the big bed, and he gently laid her across the deep blue quilt. She raised herself on her elbows and watched him move through the shadows. A drawer to a night-stand slid open and then he was before her.

'I'm thinking I might have to apologize before we get busy,' he said as he rolled a latex condom over the plump head and down the thick shaft.

She pushed her panties from her legs and tossed them aside. Light from outside poured over one side of his face. 'Why?'

He covered her with his warm body and rested his weight on his elbows. 'Because I don't think I can last very long.'

Then she felt the head of his penis, smooth and hard and hot, and she didn't think he had to worry, because she wasn't likely to last long herself. He slid partway into her, and her body resisted the intrusion. She placed her hands on his shoulders to stop him and he took her face in his hands and kissed her gently. Then he withdrew and pushed a little farther inside.

'You're so tight around me,' he gasped. She sucked in a breath, his breath, as he pulled out almost completely, only to bury himself so deep she felt him against her cervix. A deep groan tore through his chest and echoed around her heart.

She wrapped one leg around his back. 'Luc,' she whispered as he began to move, setting a perfect rhythm of pleasure. 'Mmm, that feels good.'

With his face just above hers, he asked, 'How do you want it?'

'Just like you're giving it to me.' His athlete's body –

toned and trained to go the distance – strained, and his harsh breath brushed her face. Every cell in her body was focused on the shaft pounding into her body.

'More?'

'Yes. Give me more,' she gasped, and he gave it to her. Faster, harder, and more intense. Over and over, his harsh breath brushing her cheek as he drove her farther up the bed. And just when she didn't think she could take any more, she cried out and her hands curled into fists. Her climax was so exquisite she saw and heard nothing over the pounding of her heart and the rushing of sensation across her flesh. The fire he ignited deep inside flushed her body, and her inner muscles clenched and drew him deeper until he too climaxed. An explosion of curses were torn from his throat.

Neither of them said anything for a long time. Not until their breathing slowed and their heart rates returned to normal. Luc withdrew from her and moved from the bed to the bathroom. Cool air rushed over Jane's heated skin as she watched him go, walking through the variegated shadows. Her mind was still too numb to think about what she'd just done, but her heart knew. She loved Luc Martineau with a frightening intensity.

When she heard the toilet flush, she looked toward the bathroom door. Luc walked toward her, naked and beautiful within the panels of light falling across the bedroom. Looking at him, her chest got tight as if she were having a heart attack.

'What time did you need to leave?' he asked as he joined her on the bed.

Reality intruded like a bucket of cold water. He hadn't even waited for her afterglow to fade. She'd just had mind-blowing sex, and he was ready for her to go. She sat up and looked around for her underwear, hoping like hell she didn't do something mortifying like burst into tears before she got out the door. 'I don't have a curfew.' As modestly as possible given that she was naked, she scooted on her stomach to the far edge of the bed and looked over the side. No panties. 'If I can just find my underwear, I'll get out of here. I'm sure you need your rest for tomorrow night's game.'

He grabbed her ankle and pulled her across the bed toward him again. 'Second string's between the pipes tomorrow night, and I asked because I want you to stay.'

He turned her onto her back, and she looked up into his face. 'You do?'

'Uh-huh. I figure I'm going to want to do that a couple more times before I let you out the front door.'

'A couple more?'

'Yeah.' He pulled her tight against his body, and she felt him rock-hard again. 'Is that a problem?'

'No.'

'Good, because I'm planning on scoring a hat trick.'

14

Sin Bin: Penalty Box

Jane wished she'd brought Caroline with her to the hockey game the next night. She needed something to keep her from thinking too much – from overanalyzing what she'd done the night before. But really, she'd analyzed her actions to death already. She'd had sex with Luc Martineau three times. Three mind-blowing, earth-shattering, set-your-hair-on-fire times. And each time, with each touch, each word uttered from his mouth, she'd fallen more in love with him, until she didn't think her heart would ever recover.

Around two a.m., he'd fallen asleep in a tangle of sheets and moonlight spilling in through the windows. One second he'd been talking about growing up in Edmonton, then he'd gone out as if someone had flipped a switch. She'd never seen anyone fall asleep that fast, and she watched him for a few moments to make sure he was okay. She pushed a lock of hair from his forehead, and she touched his cheek and the rough stubble on his jaw. Then she gathered her clothes and left without waking him.

She'd never fallen so fast and so hard for a man, and she'd left without waking him mostly because she hadn't known what to say. *Thanks? Let's get together again sometime? See ya at the game tomorrow night?* She'd left because that was the rule with a one-nighter. Someone always left before dawn.

She'd also left without her panties. She hadn't been able to find them in his dark bedroom, and she hadn't wanted to wake him by turning on the light. She'd left them there and now her biggest fear was that his cleaning lady, or worse, Marie, would find them.

No, that was wrong. Her biggest fear wasn't the discovery of her missing panties. It was seeing Luc tonight and feeling the horrible push and pull of her heart. In the past, she'd had boyfriends and one-night stands. She'd been hurt, and she'd hurt others too. But nothing compared to how Luc would hurt her. She knew it. She knew it was coming, and yet she couldn't seem to stop it.

It was all so horrible and wonderful, and in the middle of all the confusion was guilt. He'd confirmed for her last night what she'd pretty much known. She could no longer tell herself that he'd find the Honey Pie article flattering. That he wouldn't mind. He would, and there was nothing she could do about it now. There was no way to make it up to him, and knowing that he would never find out she was behind it did nothing to help with the guilt churning in the pit of her stomach.

She loved him and she didn't even bother lying and telling herself that she hadn't dressed for him. She wore red lipstick and a red silk blouse beneath her black blazer and wool pants. She felt silly, running out and buying a blouse because he said he liked her in red. Like that would make him love her.

A half-hour before the game, she headed to the locker room. 'Keep your pants up, gentlemen,' she began as she entered. While she recited her good-luck ritual, she could feel Luc's gaze on her, hot and vibrant, and she absolutely refused to look at him. Not after last night. Not after the things they'd done together in his bedroom. When she was through, she tucked her chin and headed for the door.

'You forgot something,' Luc called out to her.

No. She hadn't forgotten. She kept her gaze on the toes of her boots as she turned and walked back across the room. When she stood before him, she finally raised her gaze from his skates, up his bulky pads, past the fish on his jersey to the mouth that had kissed her passionately the night before. All over her body. 'I thought you weren't playing tonight.'

'I'm not, but if the goalie gets pulled, I'll have to go in for him.'

'Oh, all right,' she sighed. By sheer force of will, she kept her cheeks from turning red and finally looked up into his amused blue eyes. 'You big dumb dodo.'

'Thanks,' he said through a wicked grin, 'but that wasn't what I was talking about when I said you forgot something.'

She'd given her pants-dropping speech, shaken the captain's hand, and called Luc a dodo. She hadn't forgotten anything. 'What are you talking about?'

He leaned forward and said just above a whisper, 'You forgot your panties in my bed last night.'

Everything within her stopped and she couldn't

remember how to breathe. She looked around to see if anyone had heard him, but they all seemed busy elsewhere.

'I found them under my pillow this morning and I wondered if you put them there on purpose. Maybe a good-morning present.'

Her face and neck were on fire and her throat closed. All she could manage was a squeaky, 'No.'

'Why didn't you wake me up before you left?'

She clenched her hand and cleared her throat. 'You were asleep.'

'I was resting up for round two. God, you were hot last night.' He looked closer at her and his brows lowered. 'Are you embarrassed?' he asked, genuinely perplexed.

'Yes!'

'Why? No one can hear me.'

'Oh, my God,' she whispered and walked away before her hair caught fire. When she returned to the press box, Darby was there. And he'd brought Caroline.

'Hey, you two,' she greeted as she sat down. 'If I'd known you wanted to come to another game, Caroline, I would have invited you to come with me.'

'It's okay. I'm really not much of a fan, but Darby called and I wasn't doing anything else.' She shrugged. 'I tried to call you last night. Where were you?'

'Nowhere. I unplugged my phone.'

'I hate when you do that.' Caroline studied her a moment, then leaned closer. 'You're lying.'

'No, I'm not.'

'Yes, you are. I've known you all your life. I know when you're lying.' Her gaze narrowed. 'Where were you?'

Jane leaned forward enough to get a glimpse of Darby. He was on his cell phone. 'I was out.'

'With a man?' When Jane didn't answer, Caroline gasped. 'One of the hockey players!'

'Shhh!'

'Who?' she whispered and looked around as if the CIA were eavesdropping. Caroline considered herself bilingual and resorted to the language she and Jane had spoken since grade school. Pig Latin. 'Ell-tay e-may, ane-jay.'

Jane rolled her eyes. 'Later.' She opened her laptop as the light show started on the ice below. During the game, she took notes and tried to keep her eyes off the goalie sitting on the bench, his arms folded across his chest, watching the game. Several times he turned and looked up into the press box. Three sections up, their gazes met and her heart got stuck in her throat.

And she looked away. She'd never felt so unsure in her life. And for a woman who took charge of things and proceeded accordingly, she hated feeling so uncertain. It put knots in her stomach and made her head ache.

'Jane?' Caroline shook her shoulder as if she'd been trying to get her attention.

'What?'

'I called your name three times.'

'Sorry, I'm thinking about my article,' she lied.

'Darby wants us to meet him for a drink after the game.'

Jane leaned forward and looked at the assistant general manager. She doubted Darby wanted her to tag along. 'I can't,' she said, which was the truth, and which she also figured Darby knew. 'I have to talk to the players and write the article before deadline.' She also had to put together the interview she'd done with Luc. 'You two go without me.'

Darby made an effort to look sorry. 'Are you sure?' he asked.

'Positive.' She almost felt sorry for Darby. She loved Caroline, but her friend was going to stomp Darby's nerdy heart beneath her Ferragamos. Once again she thought perhaps she should warn Darby, but she had her own heart to worry about.

The Chinooks lost to the Bruins two–three. After the game, Jane took a deep breath and entered the locker room again. Luc's pads hung in his stall, but he was gone. She let out her pent-up breath, feeling an odd mix of relief and anger. The horrid push and pull of falling in love. Luc had known she would be in the locker room after the game, and he'd left without harassing her. The jerk.

Jane interviewed Coach Nystrom and the second-string netminder, who'd made twenty saves out of twenty-three shots on goal. She talked to Hammer and Fish, then, with her briefcase and jacket in one hand, she made her way toward the tunnel.

Luc stood near the exit watching her walk toward him. He wore his navy Hugo Boss and a maroon silk tie and he was so handsome he made her mouth water.

'I have something for you,' he said and pushed himself away from the wall.

'What?'

He looked behind her as a sports-beat reporter from Jane's rival paper passed.

'Jim.' Luc nodded his head.

'Martineau.'

The reporter eyed Jane as he walked by, and Jane didn't have to read his mind to know that he was wondering about her relationship with the notoriously tight-lipped goalie.

Luc glanced behind her again, then he pulled her red lace thong panties from the pocket of his jacket. 'These. Although I'm thinking I should probably keep these for luck,' he said and dangled them from his finger. 'Maybe have them bronzed and put on a plaque to hang above my bed.'

Jane snatched them away and shoved them in her briefcase. She looked behind her at the empty hallway. 'They didn't bring you luck. You didn't play tonight.'

'I'm thinking about a different kind of luck.' He reached for her and slid his fingers through her hair. 'Come with me.'

Oh, Lord. She stood perfectly still when what she really wanted was to fall into his chest. 'Where?'

'Somewhere.'

She forced herself to step back, and his hand fell to his side. Push and pull, her heart felt like taffy. 'You know I can't be seen with you.'

'Why the hell not?'

'You know why not.'

'Because you want people to think you're a professional.'

He did get it. 'Exactly.'

'You've been seen with Darby.'

'That's different.'

'How?'

She didn't love Darby. Looking at Darby didn't pull her in different directions. And besides, if she denied a relationship with Darby Hogue, people might actually believe her. If she had to deny a relationship with Luc, *no one* would believe her.

'He doesn't have the bad reputation you do.' And once the March issue of *Him* hit the stands, Luc's reputation was going to get worse.

He simply stared at her as if he couldn't believe what she was saying. 'So, if I was a nancy-boy, you'd be seen with me?'

'For goodness' sake. Darby isn't a nancy-boy.'

'You're wrong about that, sweetheart.'

Sweetheart. She wondered how many different women in how many different states he'd called sweetheart. She wondered how many of those women let it fool them into thinking they were different from the others. She wondered how many were foolish enough to let themselves fall in love with Luc.

Let. As she gazed up at the deep bow of his top lip and his blue eyes and long lashes, *let* sounded as if she'd been in control. As if she'd had a choice. She hadn't and she didn't, or she wouldn't have *let* it happen. With her heart aching, urging her to wrap her arms around his neck and never let go, she forced herself to say, 'Last night was a mistake. We can't let it happen again.'

'Okay.'

Okay! Her heart was breaking and he said *okay*. She didn't know whether to punch him in his Lucky tattoo or run away before she burst into tears. While she decided, he opened a door behind him, grabbed her hand and pulled her into a cleaning closet. He shut the door, then turned on the light.

'What are you doing, Luc?'

'Earning that bad reputation you were talking about.'

She held up her briefcase in front of her. 'Stop.' He smiled, and she didn't know whether it was the smell of cleaning solutions or Luc's mojo, but she felt light-headed.

'Okay.' He reached beside her and locked the door.

She looked at the doorknob and then at him. 'Luc!' He couldn't just drag her off anytime he felt like it. Could he? No! 'I think I gave you the wrong impression last night. I don't usually . . . I mean, I've never slept with someone I've just interviewed.'

He placed a finger on her lips. 'Your sex life is none of my business. I don't care who or how or what different positions you've been in.'

That he didn't care hurt more than it should have. 'But I want—'

'Shh,' he interrupted her. 'Someone might hear you, and you don't want to be seen with me. Remember?' He placed his hands on the door beside her head and leaned into her, forcing her backward. Her briefcase was all that kept their bodies apart. 'I've been thinking about you since I woke up this morning.'

She was too afraid to ask what he'd been thinking about. 'I have to go,' she said, fully aware that if she reached down and unlocked the door, he would let her leave. Yet she couldn't make herself do it. 'I have a column to write.'

'What's a few minutes?'

The scent of his cologne mingled with the cleaning solution, and she couldn't think of one reason why she shouldn't stay for a few minutes. He wrapped one arm around her waist and lowered his face to hers. His voice was a harsh rasp against her mouth when he said,

'Whatever you do, you keep that briefcase in front of your breasts.' Then he kissed her. His lips were warm, his mouth hot and, like everything about him, sexy and provocative. His kiss was aggressive one moment, then he backed off to leave her to chase his tongue. In an instant, awareness rushed across her skin and pooled deep in the pit of her stomach. *Just a few more minutes.* He slid his mouth across her cheek to the side of her throat. He pushed aside the collar of her blouse and gently sucked her skin. 'You're so soft,' he whispered as he worked his way to her ear. 'Inside and out.'

On the other side of the door, male laughter and the Stromster's heavy accent brought Luc's gaze back to hers. His voice was as rough as his breathing when he said, 'You still have a tight grip on that briefcase, sweetheart?'

She nodded and her grasp tightened.

'Good. Don't let go, and don't let me talk you out of handing it over,' he warned. 'Or you're likely to end up on the floor with me on top of you.'

She knew she should be appalled by their behavior. Kissing Luc Martineau in a janitor's closet in the Key was extremely stupid, but a happy little bubble lifted her heart and made her want to laugh. Luc wanted her. It was there in the way he looked at her, the deep hungry timbre of his voice. He might not love her, but he wanted to be with her.

He took a few steps back. 'This wasn't one of my better ideas.'

More noise from the tunnel, and he said, 'I think we might be stuck in here for a while yet.' He grabbed an empty five-gallon bucket and turned it over for her to sit on. 'Sorry.'

She knew she should be sorry too. She had a deadline. She was stuck in a closet with Luc, and if discovered, it could be bad for both of them. She wasn't that sorry, though.

She sat on the bucket and looked up at Luc towering over her. He stared back from beneath heavy lids, and she slid her gaze down his maroon tie, past his black belt, to the zipper of his pants. He was fully erect. She could recall with perfect clarity what he looked like naked. Hard body, harder penis, and hard-to-resist Lucky tattoo. Suddenly she wasn't certain that a repeat of last night was such a bad plan. Not, however, she thought as she placed the briefcase by her side, in a janitor's closet. 'How's your sister?' she asked, changing the subject along with the train of her unruly thoughts. 'I know she liked her hair yesterday, but it's always a shock the next day.'

'What?' Luc looked down into Jane's green eyes and couldn't believe the abrupt shift of her thoughts. Just a second ago, she'd been staring at his dick, and he hadn't mistaken her interest. Now she wanted to talk about his sister. 'She was fine when I saw her at lunch.'

'We talked a bit about her mother the other day.'

Luc took a few steps back and leaned his shoulder into the door. 'What did she say?'

'Not all that much, but she didn't have to. I know how she feels. My mother died when I was six.'

He hadn't realized Jane had been that young when she'd lost her mother, but he wasn't surprised that he hadn't known. All he really knew about her was that she worked for the *Seattle Times*, lived in Bellevue, and had a quick wit and nerves of steel. He liked her laugh and he liked talking to her. Her skin was as soft as it looked. All over. She tasted good to him. Everywhere. He knew she was good between the sheets, better than good. She'd worn him out, and all he'd been able to think about since he'd woken that morning was how to get her to do it again. Now that he thought about it, he guessed he knew more about Jane than he knew about a lot of women. 'I'm sorry about your mother.'

A sad smile tugged at the corners of her mouth. 'Thank you.'

Luc slid down the door until he sat on the floor at Jane's feet. His knees almost touched her. 'Marie's having a hard time, and I don't know what to do about it,' he said, purposely turning his thoughts to his sister and her problems. 'She won't talk to a counselor.'

'You've tried?'

'Of course, but she quit going after two sessions. She's moody and unpredictable. She needs a mother, but obviously I can't give her that. I thought she might be better off at boarding school with other girls her age, but she thinks I'm trying to get rid of her.'

'Are you?'

He unbuttoned his blazer, then hung his wrists over his knees. He never talked about his personal life, not with anyone outside of his family, and he wondered what it was about Jane that made him talk to her – a reporter. Maybe because, for some reason he didn't begin to understand, he trusted her. 'I don't think I'm trying to get rid of her. Maybe I am, though. Either way, I'm a bastard.'

'I'm not judging you, Luc.'

He looked into her clear eyes and he believed her. 'I want her to be happy, but she isn't.'

'No, she isn't, and she won't be for some time. I'm sure

she's scared.' She tilted her head to one side and her curls fell away from her face. 'Where's Marie's father?'

'Our father died about ten years ago. I was living in Edmonton with my mother at the time. Her mother and my father were living in LA.'

'So you know about losing a parent.'

'Not really.' His hand slid from his knee, and he brushed his fingers along the crease of her pants leg. 'I saw my father once a year.'

'Yes, but you still must wonder how your life would have turned out if he'd lived.'

'No. My hockey coaches were more like fathers to me than my father. Marie's mother was his fourth wife.'

'Other siblings?'

'I'm it.' He glanced up. 'I'm all she has and I'm afraid I'm not enough.'

The light overhead caught in her curls, and a sad smile pulled at the corners of her lips. Luc hated to see it there and gave serious thought to grabbing the lapels of her suit and pulling her mouth to his, kissing it all better. But kissing would lead to other things, and those other things weren't going to happen in a janitor's closet with his teammates on the other side of the door.

'At least I still had my dad,' she said. 'He dressed me like a boy until I was about thirteen, and he doesn't have a sense of humor. But he loves me and he was always there.'

Dressed her like a boy? That explained a bit about the clothes and boots.

She chewed on her bottom lip. 'Well, nothing will ever replace her mother. That's for sure. I still miss my mother every day, and I wonder how my life would have been different if she'd lived. But it does get better with time, in that you don't think about it every minute of every day. And you're wrong that you're not enough. If you want to be enough, you will be, Luc.'

The way she looked at him. As if it were that simple. As if she had more faith in him to make the right choices than he had in himself. As if he weren't the selfish bastard that he knew he was. He slid his hand beneath her pants leg and encountered a sock. He slid it to her calf and touched her soft skin. The night before, he'd kissed the backs of her knees as he'd worked his way to her thighs. Her legs had been wet from his Jacuzzi, and even now the memory stirred his groin.

'I'm gone a lot,' he said and brushed her shin with his thumb. 'And if you ask Marie, she'll probably tell you that I'm not a very good brother.'

She pushed her short hair behind one ear and gazed at him a moment before she said, 'When I see you and Marie together, you make me wish I had a brother.'

His thumb stilled. Through the space that separated them, he looked into her green eyes, all thoughts of kissing her came to an abrupt halt, and he felt as if she'd just puck-shot his chest. A hard smack to the sternum that left him stunned. From the tunnel came male voices, but inside the janitor's closet, silence hung between them. Suspended and drawn out until he forced a strained laugh past the knot in his chest. 'Don't tell me you want a brother just like me.'

'No, not just like you.' The corners of her mouth tilted and his world tilted with it. 'If I had a brother just like you, I would be arrested for indecent thoughts.'

He felt as if he were sliding toward her smile, and his

grasp on her leg tightened as if she were the anchor instead of the cause. She didn't seem to notice and he forced himself to let go. He pushed with his feet and slid back up the door. 'You better go. You have that column to write.'

A frown appeared between her brows and she blinked. 'Are you all right?'

'Yeah, I just remembered I have to talk to Marie before she goes to bed.'

'Do you think the tunnel is clear?' she asked as she picked up her briefcase and jacket and rose.

'I don't know.' He unlocked the door and opened it a crack. Hammer walked past talking to the equipment manager. Luc held up one finger until the two men walked out the exit doors, then he stuck out his head and discovered the tunnel was blessedly empty. He and Jane stepped from the closet, and she shoved her arms into her jacket. Normally he would have helped her.

'I have to talk to Nystrom,' he lied and began to walk backward. With each step, he seemed to breathe a little easier.

'I thought you had to talk to Marie.'

Had he said that? 'Later. I have to talk to the coach first.'

'Oh.' She looked at him a moment longer. 'Good-bye.' She held up her hand and turned to go. Luc stared at the back of Jane's retreating head and brushed the edges of his jacket aside. He stuck his hands in the pockets of his trousers and stopped to watch her disappear.

What in the hell just happened? he asked himself as the exit door shut. He wondered if he was coming down with something or maybe inhaled too much ammonia in that closet. One minute he'd been thinking about kissing the backs of her knees, and in the next he couldn't breathe. She thought he was a good brother. So? He didn't think he was, but even if he was the best brother ever, why should Jane's opinion of him matter diddly squat? For some unfathomable reason it obviously did, but he didn't want to think about what that meant. He had too much going on in his life to fall for a short woman reporter with a cute butt and tight pink nipples.

Last night, Jane had blown — among other things — every assumption he'd had of her. She wasn't uptight, and she certainly wasn't a prude. The longer he'd been with her, the longer he'd wanted to be with her. Even when he'd been deep inside her tight body, feeling every ripple of pleasure, he'd wanted her again. When he'd awoken that morning, he'd been seriously bummed that she wasn't there.

But Jane was one complication he didn't need. When she'd told him that last night was a mistake and it couldn't happen again, he should have listened to her instead of pulling her into the closet just to prove her wrong.

'Lucky.' Jack Lynch slapped him on the back as he came to stand beside him. 'Some of us are grabbing a bite and a beer. Come along.'

Luc looked across his shoulder at the defender. 'Where?'

'Hooters.'

Maybe that was what he needed. To go someplace where women wore tiny shorts and tight little tank tops. Where they had big breasts and leaned into him when they served him dinner. Where they flirted and slipped him their phone number. Where the women didn't expect anything from him. Where if he chose to be with them, it didn't mean anything. When it was over, he didn't dwell on it, replay it over and over in his head, like he did with Jane.

He looked at his watch. He had a little time yet. 'Save me a chair.'

'I will,' Jack said, then continued on his way.

Yeah, he should go to Hooters. Be a guy. Do guys things. He didn't have a girlfriend who'd get all bent out of shape if he went.

When I see you and Marie together, you make me wish I had a brother.

Damn. Jane was a dangerous woman. Not only did he think about her too much, but if he wasn't careful, she'd become his conscience. He didn't want a conscience, and he didn't care what that said about him. He was fine just the way he was.

Luc removed his hands from his pockets and pulled out his car keys. He'd have to revert to his original plan and ignore Jane. Of course, that had never worked for him before.

This time he'd just have to try harder.

Mucking It Up: Fighting

Tuesday morning, Jane walked into sports editor Kirk Thornton's office at the *Seattle Times*. Since she'd taken over for Chris Evans, she'd only met with Kirk once. Today he sat behind a desk piled with newspapers and layouts and sports photos. He held the telephone receiver to his ear in one hand and a cup of coffee in the other. He glanced up, and, upon seeing her, a heavy scowl lined his forehead and bracketed his mouth. He raised one finger from the mug and pointed to an empty chair.

She wondered if he was always in a bad mood, or if it was just her effect on him. Suddenly she wondered if coming in was such a good idea. She was crampy and had PMS, and she didn't want to get ugly with him.

'Noonan covers the Sonics,' he said into the receiver. 'I've got Jensen at the Huskies game tonight.'

Jane turned and looked out the door at the bullpen, at some of the other sports reporters sitting at their desks. She would never be one of them. They'd let her know that. But it was okay. She didn't want to be one of the guys. She wanted to be better. Her gaze fell on Chris Evans's empty desk. This job wouldn't last forever; Chris would return to work. But when it ended, she'd have a fabulous addition to her résumé and find something better. Maybe at the *Seattle Post-Intelligencer*.

'How can I help you?' Kirk asked.

Jane turned and looked at the balding editor. 'You didn't run my Pierre Dion interview?'

He took a drink of his coffee, then shook his head. '*Post-Intelligencer* printed an interview with him the day after he signed.'

'Mine was better.'

'Yours was old news by then.' He looked at the papers on his desk.

She didn't believe him. If one of the guys had done the interview, they would have run it as a feature instead of burying it in her regular column.

'Anything else?'

'I got an interview with Luc Martineau.'

That got his attention and he looked up. 'No one gets an interview with Martineau.'

'I did.'

'How?'

'I asked him.'

'Everyone asks him.'

'He owed me a favor.'

He lowered his gaze to her feet, then raised it back up again. He was too smart to say what he was thinking, but she knew. 'What favor would that be?'

She was half tempted to tell Kirk she'd blown Luc, but not until *after* the interview. So technically she hadn't exchanged sexual favors for her story. 'When I was fired,

I only agreed to come back to work if Luc gave me an exclusive interview.'

'And he gave it to you?'

'Yes.' She handed him a hard copy of the interview along with a disk. She could have sent it in an attached e-mail like she did all her columns, but she'd wanted to see his face when he read it. She was proud of the piece and knew every word by heart.

Martineau in His Zone

Controversy is no stranger to Chinook goaltender Luc Martineau. His private and professional lives have been dissected and discussed and written about until no one is quite sure of the truth. Martineau himself claims that most of what has been written about his personal life is fiction and has little to do with the actual facts. Fact or fiction, he will tell you that his past is his own business. These days he is totally focused on what takes place between the pipes.

When I sat down to interview this enigmatic goalie, I discovered that he is by turns forthright and aloof. Relaxed and intense. Contrasts that make this Conn Smythe winner one of the best all-time tenders in the NHL.

What is not in dispute is that two years ago, he was reported to be finished, his days in the NHL all but over. Oh, how wrong those reports were. Currently ranked second, Martineau leads the league in goals against average at 2.00. Fast hands and cool control are the trademarks of this premier goaltender. He has

*as much aptitude as attitude, and when he is in his
zone, his nuclear stare intimidates . . .*

As Kirk read on, a begrudging smile lifted one corner of his
thin lips. A modicum of respect, albeit reluctant, softened
the lines on his face and her mood changed in an instant.
Jane didn't want to feel anything or take any pleasure in
Kirk Thornton's change in attitude toward her. But she did.
She hadn't known how much until now. It burned like a
little light in her chest and filled her with pride.

He looked at the schedule. 'I'll make room for it in the
Sunday edition after next.'

She'd be on the road next Sunday. 'A feature article,
right?' she asked just to make sure.

'Right.'

When Jane left the building, the sun was shining, the
mountain was out, and life was pretty darn good. As she
walked down John Street toward her Honda, she allowed
herself to feel a few moments of triumph. Whether the
guys working the sports beat wanted to or not, they had
to take her seriously now. Or at least they couldn't easily
dismiss her as the bimbo who wrote the silly *Single Girl*
columns. An interview with Luc would get picked up by
the Associated Press, and they would all know it. She
didn't delude herself that this would make things easier
for her in the news-room. The opposite might happen,
but she didn't really care. She'd gotten the interview that
all of them would have killed to get.

Yep, life was pretty good today. Yesterday had been a
different story. Yesterday she'd sat at home staring at the
telephone like she was fifteen again, waiting for it to ring.
After she'd left the Key Arena Sunday night, she'd been

positive Luc would call her. After he'd pulled her into the janitor's closet and made her rethink her decision not to have sex with him anymore, she'd half expected him to call or show up on her doorstep. She'd thought they'd made a personal connection, that they'd talked about something important, something other than her underwear, and she'd been sure he'd contact her.

He hadn't, and as she'd sat on her couch watching birds mate on the Discovery Channel, she'd discovered that falling in love with Luc was the dumbest thing she'd ever done. Of course, she'd known the stupidity of it weeks before it had actually happened, but she'd been powerless against it.

Jane drove to the Laundromat and shoved her dirty clothes into four washing machines. Beneath her suit, she wore a pair of days-of-the-week panties. It was Tuesday, and she had on Saturday's. Not that it really mattered, she supposed. But it did illustrate her life at the moment.

While she watched her clothes tumble dry, Darby called her cell phone and asked her advice. It seemed that he too had fallen for someone unattainable.

'Do you think Caroline would go out with me?' he wanted to know.

'I don't know. How did the drink with her go?' she asked, even though Caroline had called her the next morning with the gory details. The evening had started out okay but had taken a nosedive.

'I don't think I impressed her much.'

'You told her about being a member of Mensa.'

'So?'

'I told you not to do that. Those of us with average intelligence don't want to hear about your big brain.'

'Why?'

She rolled her eyes. 'Do you want to hear Brad Pitt brag about how good-looking he is?'

'It's not the same.'

'Yes, it is.'

'No. Brad doesn't have to brag about his looks. Everyone can see that he's good-looking.'

Hmm. He was right about Brad. 'Okay. How about a porn star? Do you want to hear a porn star brag about his huge package?'

'No.'

She switched the phone to her other ear. 'Look, if you want to impress women, especially Caroline, don't tell her how smart you are. Let it come out subtly.'

'I'm not very good at being subtle.'

He wasn't kidding. 'Caroline will be impressed with a guy who knows what wine to order.'

'Isn't that kind of gay?'

And the flaming skull shirt wasn't? 'No. Take her somewhere nice.'

'And she'll go?'

'Make it someplace really nice. Caroline loves to dress up. Always has.' She thought a moment and asked, 'Are you a member of the Columbia Tower Club?'

'Yes.'

She'd thought so. 'Take her there. It will give her a reason to wear her latest Jimmy Choos. And if she starts talking about shoes and fashion, pretend you're interested.'

'I'm into designer fashions,' he said.

Jane smiled. 'Good luck.' After she hung up, she called Caroline at Nordy's and warned her that Darby would be calling. She was surprised that her friend didn't have stronger objections to a date with him.

'I thought he annoyed you with his talk of Mensa,' Jane reminded her friend.

'He did, but he's sort of cute in a *Revenge of the Nerds* kind of way,' Caroline explained, and Jane decided it was best if she stayed out of it. As she kept reminding herself, she had her own problems.

That night at the Chinooks/Lightning game, Luc hardly paid her any attention when she called him a dodo. He didn't tease her or remind her of the night they'd spent together. In goal, he was his near-perfect self, stopping pucks with his fast hands and big body. The game ended in a tie, and afterward he wasn't waiting to pull her into a closet and kiss her senseless.

Nor was he two nights later, when he recorded his sixth shutout of the season against the Oilers. On the flight to Detroit the next morning, he hardly glanced at her as he passed her seat, and it was excruciatingly obvious to her that he was avoiding her as much as possible. She didn't know what she'd done, and she relived their conversation in the janitor's closet over and over in her mind. The only thing she could think of that might make him avoid her so blatantly was that somehow he'd discerned her feelings for him, and he was running fast in the opposite direction. She'd worn red lipstick and bought a red blouse just for him. She was so pathetic. He'd told her he fantasized about making love to her on a dessert tray, and she'd believed him. She was the worst kind of fool.

Now he was avoiding her almost completely, and she was startled by how much it hurt. They'd made love and she'd thought they'd had a really good time. She hadn't made demands, and if anything, by pulling her into that closet he'd led her to think he wanted more than a one-night stand.

He'd told her he didn't think of her as a groupie, and now he treated her as if she were the worst kind. A groupie that he must avoid at all costs. Not only did that hurt, it made her angry. Beyond angry to the point of doing him bodily harm. She'd even given a few moments' thought to quitting her job just so she wouldn't have to face his disinterest. But the few moments passed quickly when she reminded herself that she would not shoot herself in the foot over a man. Not even a man she loved with her whole aching heart. Not even when seeing that man made her miserable.

Once in her room later that day, she tried to write a rough draft for her *Single Girl* article, but she stared out the window looking over Lake Michigan more than she wrote. Her relationship with Luc would have ended eventually anyway, she told herself. Better sooner than later. At least this way she didn't have to feel as guilty about the *Honey Pie* article. Too bad she couldn't make her conscience listen.

A few hours later, when the telephone didn't ring, she tried to tell herself that Luc was too busy with the team to call. That he wasn't meeting one of his Barbie Dolls. She didn't want to think about him with another woman, but she couldn't help it. And the thought of him kissing and touching one of his women drove her crazy.

At six that evening, she met Darby at one of the hotel restaurants. Over the course of the meal, she drank two martinis while she listened to him rattle on about Caroline.

After dinner, they went to the sports bar inside the

hotel. Five of the Chinooks sat at a table drinking beer, eating bar food, and watching Denver give the Kings a royal trouncing. Luc was with them too. At the sight of him, apprehension and relief lifted her stomach. He wasn't with a Barbie Doll.

'Hey, Sharky,' everyone called out to her. Everyone but Luc.

The pull of his brow and the cool appraisal of his blue eyes told her that Luc wasn't at all happy to see her. Her battered heart took another bruising.

She took a seat between Daniel and Fish and was careful not to make significant eye contact with Luc. She was afraid that every hockey player at the table would see that she was in love with their goalie. That he would see it too, and become even more distant, which probably wasn't possible.

She couldn't quite force herself to ignore him completely, though, and her gaze was drawn to his across the table. He sat back in his chair, his hand at his side, relaxed, at ease. Except for his intense gaze, which appeared for all the world as if he were trying to see to the back of her brain. He reached for his glass and took a drink of water. He sucked an ice cube into his mouth and a drop of water rested on his top lip. He chewed the ice and she looked away.

'I read your last *Single Girl* column,' Fish told her. 'I think you're right that nice guys really do finish last. I'm a nice guy, and I have to give up my house on Mercer to my ex-wife.'

'That's because she caught you with another woman,' Sutter reminded him. 'That really tends to piss off the old lady.'

'Yeah, tell me about it,' Fish grumbled and looked over at Jane. 'What are you writing now?'

She hadn't really come up with much yet. Nothing she wanted to discuss anyway, but she opened her mouth and, 'Is a one-night stand ever a good idea?' popped out. She immediately wished she could take that one back.

'I think it is,' Peluso said from down the table.

'Yeah.'

'I say go for it.'

'Unless you're married,' Fish added. 'You're not planning a one-nighter, are you?'

She shrugged and forced herself to sound cool and emotionless. Detached. Like a man. 'I'm thinking about it. There's a guy with the Detroit press who's very hot. I talked to him the last time I was here.'

Across the table Luc stood, and she watched him move toward the bar. Her gaze slid down the back of his blue-and-white-striped dress shirt to the behind of his Levi's.

'If you ever need help with your columns, we could tell you how guys really think,' Peluso added. 'The real stuff.'

Jane really didn't want to know 'the real stuff.' It was just too scary. 'Maybe I'll get back to you when I have a firmer grasp on the direction I want the column to take.'

'Cool.'

She looked up as Luc returned with two sets of darts. 'You owe me a chance to get my fifty bucks back,' he said. 'Same rules apply as last time.'

'I don't think so.'

'I do.' He grasped her arm and pulled her to her feet. 'Pick the sharpest darts,' he said, then he grabbed her hand and slapped them in her palm. Next to her ear he added, just above a whisper, 'Don't make me carry you to the tape line.'

His brows were lowered and his gaze fierce, as if *he* had something to be mad about. Fine. It would feel good to kick his butt. Since she couldn't do it physically, she'd wipe the floor with him in darts.

'Remember the rules,' he said as she tested the points. 'There's no crying like a girl when you lose.'

'You can't beat me on your best day.' She flipped her hair like a girl and handed over the sharpest three darts. 'This isn't a sport for sissies like you're used to, Martineau. Your teammates can't save you, and there's no hiding behind pads and a helmet in darts.'

'That's low, Sharky,' Sutter told her.

Her mouth dropped open. 'That's trash talk.'

'That was a real cheap shot,' Fish added.

'Last time, you guys said I was a lesbian,' she reminded them. They all shrugged. 'Hockey players,' she said and marched across the bar to the dartboard, with Luc walking beside her. Her shoulder brushed his arm, and she felt the contact all over. She widened the space between them.

'What are you doing here with him?' Luc asked as they stopped at the tape line.

'Who?'

'Darby.'

'We had dinner.'

'Are you sleeping with him?'

If she weren't so mad, she would have laughed. 'That's none of your business.'

'What about the Detroit reporter?'

There was no reporter, but she wasn't about to tell him that. 'What about him?'

'Are you sleeping with him?'

'I thought you didn't care whom or how or what position I preferred.'

He stared at her, then said through clenched teeth, 'Shoot the damn darts.'

She looked up at him. His clenched jaw, his eyes shooting blue flames like when someone dared to shoot a puck in his net. He was clearly angry. At her. He was insane. 'Stand back,' she said as she lined up her first shot. 'I'm gonna kick your butt.' She doubled on with her first throw and scored eighty by the time she was through.

Luc scored forty and slapped the darts in her palm. 'The light sucks in here.'

'No.' She smiled and took great pleasure in announcing, 'You suck.'

His gaze narrowed.

Weeks of anger and hurt poured out of her and she said, louder than she'd intended, 'And worse – you're a whiner.'

A collective intake of breath caught their attention and she and Luc turned and looked at the guys watching a few feet away.

'Lucky's gonna kill Sharky,' Sutter predicted from the sidelines.

By tacit agreement they both went to their respective corners. Jane shot and scored sixty-five. Luc scored thirty-four.

'Now, remind me. Why do they call you Lucky?' she asked as she reached for the darts.

He pulled them back out of her reach as a slow, purely licentious smile curved his mouth. A smile that told her he was remembering her on her knees kissing his tattoo. 'I'm sure if you think long and hard, you'll remember the answer to that.'

'No.' She shook her head. 'Some things just aren't that memorable.' She held out her hand and he placed the darts in her palm.

Instead of moving to stand by the guys, he remained right next to her and said, 'I could remind you.'

'No, thanks.' She shot a triple eight and aimed for a triple twenty. 'Once was enough for me.'

'If that's true,' he said, 'why'd we do it three times?'

'What's the matter?' She looked across her shoulder at him. 'Is your ego in need of stroking tonight?'

'Yes. Among other things.'

He'd decided to talk to her and she was supposed to fall at his feet. He probably thought she'd fall there and kiss his tattoo again. Fat chance. 'Not interested. Find someone else.'

'I don't want anyone else.' His words felt like a warm caress when he added, 'I want you, Jane.'

Her anger fled and all that was left was her deep hurt. It churned in her stomach and twisted her heart. Before she risked bursting into tears like a girl, she shoved the darts at him. 'Too bad,' she said, turned on her heels, and left the bar. She made it to her room on the twenty-first floor before her vision blurred. She would not cry over Luc Martineau, she told herself as she blotted her eyes with a tissue.

She was in her hotel room ten minutes before he

pounded on her door. Afraid that the commotion would alert the security staff, she let him in.

'What do you want, Luc?' She folded her arms across her chest and held her ground.

He moved into the room and forced her back a few steps. 'You,' he answered as the door shut behind him.

'Not interested.' He moved so close that her forearms touched his chest. He was purposely invading her space, and she walked across the room from him, away from the scent of his cologne. 'You told me you didn't think of me as a groupie, but that is exactly how you've made me feel.'

'I'm sorry about that.' His brows lowered and he looked down at the floor between his feet. 'I didn't mean to make you feel like a groupie.'

'Too late. You can't take me to bed, then never give me another thought, as if I'm nothing.'

'I've never thought you were nothing.' He glanced back up at her, his blue gaze direct when he said, 'I've thought about you, Jane.'

'When? When you were with other women?'

'I haven't been with anyone but you.'

She was relieved but still mad as hell. 'Were you thinking of me when you were busy ignoring me?'

'Yes.'

'And avoiding me?'

'Yes. All those times and all the times in between.'

'Right.'

'I think about you, Jane.' He walked toward her until mere inches separated them. 'A lot.'

She'd believed him when he'd told her the same thing a few weeks ago. Not this time. 'I've heard it from you before, and it's not true,' she said, but there was a traitorous piece of her heart that wanted to believe him – *bad*. She took a step back and her calves hit the edge of the bed.

'Oh, it's true. Awake or asleep, I can't get you out of my head.' He grasped her shoulders and pushed her down on the bed. 'You're a complication I don't need.' He followed, placed his hands on each side of her head, and planted his knee between her thighs. 'But you're a complication I want. One I'm going to have.'

She put her hands on his chest to stop him. Through the cotton of his shirt, he threw off heat like a furnace and warmed her palms. 'I don't think you know what you want.'

'Yes. I do. I want you, and being with you feels a hell of a lot better than being without you. I'm not going to fight it anymore.' He kissed her between her brows. 'I'm not going to fight what I feel for you. It's a losing battle, and I just end up pissed off.'

His words defused her anger somewhat, but fear still weighed heavy in her heart. 'What do you feel?' she asked, even though she wasn't completely certain she wanted to know.

He brushed his lips across her forehead. 'I feel like you've hit me between the eyes with the butt end of a stick.'

He hadn't said he was falling in love with her, but getting hit in the head with a stick was pretty good. Instead of pushing him away, she ran her hands over his chest. 'Is that a good thing?'

'It doesn't feel like a good thing. You've put my life in chaos.'

Good, because she was feeling very chaotic herself.

She struggled to hold on to her hurt, but instead she pulled his shirt from the waistband of his jeans. She gazed up into his eyes, then her scrutiny slid to his mouth.

'How did you get the scar on your chin?' she asked.

'Fell off my bike when I was about ten.'

'The scar on your cheek?' She slid her hands beneath his shirt and touched his corrugated muscle and tight flesh.

'Bar fight when I was twenty-three.' He sucked in a breath. 'Any more questions before I undress you?'

'Did it hurt when you got your tattoo?'

'I don't remember.' He lowered his mouth to hers. 'I was pretty wasted at the time.' He silenced any further questions with a kiss that deepened by slow excruciating degrees. The kiss was sweet, gentle, but Jane wasn't in the mood for sweet and gentle. She pushed him onto his back and climbed on top of him, like a mountain she'd conquered before but was looking forward to exploring again. The kiss turned hotter as she unbuttoned his shirt. With his wrists crossed above his head, he watched her from beneath lowered lids as she ran her hands and mouth over him. When she bit his shoulder, he brushed her hair from her face and brought her mouth back to his. He turned her onto her back and stripped her naked while feeding her kisses. Everywhere his hands touched, his mouth followed: her shoulder, her throat, her breast. They lay naked in each other's arms, and when she could stand it no more, she slid a condom on his hot erection and straddled him once again. As she lowered herself, he thrust upward and buried himself deep within her.

'Jane,' he gasped, 'hold still a minute.'

She squeezed her muscles around him and a groan rumbled in his chest. His eyes slid shut, and when he opened them again, raw lust shone up at her, hot and intoxicating. He slid one hand behind her neck and the other to her hip. He pulled her face down to his, and he held her still as he gently kissed her lips. His tongue lightly touched hers, and he created a soft suction as if he were sucking the juice from a peach. As if she tasted sweet and very good to him. He slipped his hand up her back and spine, then down to her hip, stroking her, creating fire inside and out. She tore her mouth from his as she quickened the pace. His blue eyes gazed up at her, shining with his passion. He whispered her name like a gentle caress. The heated tension inside her tightened and coiled until she came apart in hot uncontrollable waves of pleasure.

Her orgasm gripped him hard and his fingers sank into her hips as he drove into her again and again, thrusting harder until he too felt the same ecstasy he'd just given to her.

Jane collapsed on top of Luc, and he held her tight, his breathing labored. Crushed her to his moist chest as if he didn't plan to let her go anytime soon.

'My God,' he said, his harsh breath next to her ear. 'It's better than the last time. And that time was pretty freaking-A fantastic!'

She agreed but was too winded to speak. Something had just happened. Something different. Something better, somehow. Something beyond physical pleasure. Some*thing* she couldn't quite put her finger on.

'Jane.'

'Hmm?'

'Nothing.' She felt him kiss her hair. 'I just wanted to make sure you hadn't passed out.'

She smiled and buried her nose in his neck. The *thing* was in the way he held her, touched her. She didn't fool herself that it was love. But it was something. She'd take that something and run with it, because whatever it was, was a whole heck of a lot better than nothing at all.

Lights Out: Pulling an Opponent's Jersey over His Head

The next evening, when Jane walked into the locker room of the Joe Louis Arena, her emotions were still in chaos. Luc had spent the night in her room, and they'd had breakfast in bed before he'd left for the game-day practice. He'd kissed her at her door and touched her hair and told her he would see her later. But would he be happy to see her later?

'Hi, guys,' she said as she moved to the center of the room.

'Hey, Sharky.'

While the players strapped on their gear, she hurried through her pants-dropping speech. She glanced at Luc, who was in deep conversation with the goalie coach and didn't seem to know she was even in the room.

She shook Bressler's hand. 'Good luck with the game, Hitman.'

'Thanks.' He dropped his chin and studied her face. 'You look different tonight,' he said.

She'd brushed her lashes with a little mascara, covered the dark circles beneath her eyes, and put on some pink lip gloss. She hoped that's what he noticed, and not her serious case of afterglow. 'Is that a good different?'

'Yeah.'

Fish and Sutter joined the captain and complimented her too. As she moved toward Luc, all the horrid fears and the wonderful high of falling in love mixed and tumbled in her stomach. Luc stood in front of his stall still talking to the goalie coach, and as she approached, he cast a sideways glance at her. His gaze held hers for several heartbeats before returning to the coach.

'The Czech always shoots top shelf,' the coach said. 'If he scores on you, that's where he'll aim.' He flipped over a page on his clipboard. 'And Federov will cut across the ice and shoot at you from his sweet spot near the left face-off circle.'

'Thanks, Don,' Luc said and turned to Jane when the goalie coach walked away.

'What were Fish and Sutter saying to you?' he wanted to know.

He towered over her in his gear. 'They thought I looked different tonight.' She would have told him her after-the-afterglow theory, but she didn't want to get him started down that path.

'Were they hitting on you?'

'No. You big dumb dodo.'

He looked around and waited for Daniel to move past before he said, 'I've been thinking.'

'Uh-oh.'

He lowered his voice. 'I think you should kiss my tattoo before every game for good luck.'

She scowled to keep from laughing. 'I think I'm being sexually harassed.'

He grinned. 'Absolutely. What do you say? Wanna kiss my tattoo?'

'Not a chance,' she said and turned away before anyone overheard the conversation. She headed up to the press box and took a seat by Darby. He told her that he was making some headway with management on her behalf, and he told her of a defender they hoped to acquire before the March 19 deadline four weeks away.

'Caroline said she'd go out with me when we get back into town,' he told her after they'd talked business.

'Where are you taking her?'

'Columbia Tower Club, like you suggested.'

She looked at his chili pepper tie hanging halfway down his chest and smiled. If Caroline decided to make Darby Hogue her next fixerupper, she had her work cut out for her. Jane took out her sticky notes, wrote some reminders, and stuck them in her planner. And as soon as the puck was dropped, she pulled out her laptop.

Luc was definitely in his zone, stacking his pads or dropping to his knees and catching shots fired high. He played his angles brilliantly, and Jane had a hard time keeping her attention on the game, and not just on the Chinooks' goalie.

That night on the team jet as they headed to Toronto, she sat within the light shining overhead and wrote her column for the *Seattle Times*. Throughout the flight, she felt Luc's gaze on her and glanced across the aisle at him.

He leaned against the side of the plane, his hands behind his head, watching her work. She wondered what he was thinking and decided it was probably best not to know.

She still hadn't figured out the something that had been different with their sex the night before. She wondered if she'd imagined it, but when he came to her hotel room that night, took her by the hand, and led her to his room, she thought for sure she felt it again. She spent several hours in his bed trying to figure it out. Unsuccessful that night, she tried again in Boston, New York, and St. Louis. By the time they set down again in Seattle, she was tired of trying to figure anything out and decided not to overanalyze every word and touch. She was just going to go with it for as long as it lasted.

She'd fought falling in love with Luc, and she'd lost. Against her better judgment, she was having sex with him. Great sex. Fabulous sex that put her job at risk, but she knew she wouldn't stop no matter the consequences to her career or her heart. She was in love with him and didn't have a choice but to be with him. And over the next few weeks, her love grew and expanded until it filled every part of her. Body and soul. She was in too deep to get out.

One morning shortly after their return from St. Louis, she came home with baskets of her clean laundry to find Luc standing on her porch waiting for her. The mountain was out, and the sky was the same warm blue as his eyes. His dark blond hair was finger-combed and he looked like he should come with a warning label: *Hazardous to your health*. He kissed her hello and helped her carry her laundry inside. Then he led her to his motorcycle parked by the curb.

'No one will see your face,' he said as he handed her a helmet. 'So you don't have to worry about my bad reputation.'

If she didn't know better, she'd think his feelings were hurt. 'It's not your reputation that worries me as much as people assuming I slept with you to get an interview.'

'I've been meaning to talk to you about that article.'

'What about it?'

He fixed her chin strap and his fingers brushed her throat. 'You said I was aloof.'

'So?'

'I'm not aloof. I just don't give interviews.'

She rolled her eyes at him. 'What did you think of the rest of the article?'

He ducked his head and kissed her. 'Next time you mention my fast hands, you could say something about how big they are. And my feet too.'

She laughed. 'Big feet. Big hands. Big . . . heart.'

'Exactly.'

Jane hopped on the bike behind him, and they headed for Snoqualmie Falls. It was fifty-eight degrees, and Jane wore jeans, a sweatshirt, and a pea coat for the thirty-minute ride. The falls were nothing new to Jane. She'd seen them many times, mostly on field trips in grade school, but she never got used to the awesome power and beauty of the 270-foot falls.

They were alone on the observation platform, and Luc stood behind Jane and wrapped his arms around her. The noon sun shot rainbows into the spray rising from the mist below. Beneath their feet, the platform shuddered with the force of nature. Within Luc's embrace, Jane's heart shuddered too, helpless against the natural force that drew her to him. She melted back into his chest as if she belonged there, wrapped in his arms.

He rested his chin on top of her head, and they talked about the falls and about the hockey season. The Chinooks had won forty out of sixty-one games and unless they totally unraveled before April 15, they were pretty much assured a playoff position. Luc's goals against average had risen to an impressive 1.96, the best of his career.

They talked about Marie, who seemed to be making friends and adjusting a bit to life in Seattle with a brother she hadn't known until a few months ago. They talked about boarding school, and how he still hadn't made a decision concerning that. And they talked about growing up, and to her surprise, Luc hadn't been rich and famous all his life.

'I drove a rusted-out truck,' he said. 'I saved for a whole year to buy a stereo and brand-new *Playboy* mud flaps. I thought I was something. Too bad I was the only one.'

'Don't tell me you didn't get a lot of action in high school.'

'I played too much hockey to get any action. Well, not any *good* action. You probably had more dates than I did.'

She laughed. 'I had bad hair, bad clothes, and a Mercury Bobcat with a wire hanger for an antenna.'

He squeezed her against his solid chest. 'I would have dated you.'

She doubted it. 'No way. Even I didn't go out with losers with *Playboy* mud flaps.'

They ate lunch at the Salish Lodge, made famous by the television series *Twin Peaks*. Beneath the table he held her hand while he whispered inappropriate things just to see her blush. And on the drive home, Jane stuck her hands underneath his leather jacket and spread her fingers across his flat belly. Through his shirt, she felt his muscles, and through his Levi's, she felt his full erection.

When they reached her apartment, he helped her off the bike and practically pulled her through her front door. He tossed their helmets and his jacket on the couch. 'You're going to be sorry you decided to tease me for the last half-hour.'

She made her eyes go wide as she shucked her coat and tossed it by his. 'What are you going to do? Feed me my lunch?'

'I already fed you lunch. What I'm going to feed you now is better than lunch.'

She laughed. 'What could be better than Salish burgers?'

'Dessert.'

'Sorry, I don't eat dessert. It makes me fat.'

'Well, I'm going to have some.' He took her face in his hands. 'I'm going to have your sweet spot.'

And he did. Several times. Two nights later, he invited her to his condo for dinner with him and Marie. While he cooked salmon, Jane helped his sister with her English homework. Throughout the evening, there was only one tense moment when Luc made Marie drink her milk.

'I'm sixteen,' she argued. 'I don't need to drink milk.'

'Do you want to be short and stumpy?' he asked her.

Marie's eyes narrowed. 'I'm not short and stumpy.'

'Not now, but look at your aunt Louise.'

Evidently, Aunt Louise must have been an osteoporosis nightmare, because without further argument

Marie picked up her glass and drank her milk. Luc then turned his attention to Jane. He looked at her full glass and then at her.

'I'm already short and stumpy,' she said.

'You're not stumpy – yet. But if you get any shorter, you'll only be waist-high.' Then a beautiful smile curved his lips, and without a word, he reached for her glass and downed her milk.

He was such a bad man.

The night before they were to leave for a ten-day grind, he came to her apartment. When he knocked on her door, she was in the middle of her latest *Honey Pie* story, and not having a lot of success. Mostly because she was thinking of Luc and trying very hard not to write him into the story again. She shut her laptop and let him in.

A heavy rain had wet his hair and the shoulders of his jacket. He dug into the pocket and pulled out a white box about the size of her hand. 'I saw this and thought of you,' he said.

She had no idea what to expect when she lifted the lid off the little box. She really wasn't used to men giving her gifts, except perhaps cheap lingerie. Which she'd always figured was more for them than for her.

Inside the box, nestled on white tissue paper, was a crystal shark. Neither edible nor crotchless, it was the most thoughtful present any man had ever given her. And it touched her more than he would ever know.

'I love it,' she said and held it up to the light. Multicolored prisms shot across the front of Luc's jacket and the hollow of his throat.

'It's not much.'

He was wrong. So wrong. She closed her hand around

the shards of light, but she could not contain the love she felt clear down to the very center of her soul. As she watched him unzip his jacket and toss it on her sofa, she knew she should tell him about the *Honey Pie* column. She should warn him and put a good spin on it. But if she told him, she could lose him. Here. Tonight.

She couldn't tell him. If she did, he'd probably end their relationship, and she couldn't afford for anyone to have that kind of information about her. So she kept quiet. Kept it inside, where it ate at her conscience, while she tried to convince herself that perhaps he'd be okay with the article.

She hadn't taken a look at the column since she'd sent it off. Maybe it wasn't as obvious as she remembered. She wrapped her arms around his neck. She wanted to tell him she was sorry and that she loved him. 'Thank you,' she said, 'I really love it.' Then she took him to her bedroom and apologized the only way she could.

When the first week of March came and went and Luc hadn't seen the *Honey Pie* column, she began to relax. In Los Angeles, she told him she couldn't have sex because she was crampy and had PMS. He'd arrived at her room after practice, carrying a bucket of ice in one hand, a heating pad and Peanut M&M's in the other.

'I got the trainer to give me this,' he said as he handed her the heating pad. 'And I brought the kind of candy you like.'

The night he'd seen her in her cow PJs, she'd been eating Peanut M&M's. He'd remembered. She started to cry.

'What the hell's the matter?' he asked as he wrapped the ice in a towel.

'I just get weepy,' she answered, but it was more. A lot more. Together they sat back against the headboard of her bed, and he placed a pillow beneath his left knee.

'Your knee is bothering you,' she said unnecessarily and helped him place the ice around it.

He downed several Advils. 'Just the left one this time, and just a little.'

Probably more than a little, since he brought ice with him. During her interview with him in his apartment, he'd told her that his old injury didn't bother him. Now he trusted her enough to let her see what she'd wondered about since she'd met him. His knees did in fact bother him sometimes. She sat beside him and took his hand.

'What?' he asked.

She looked across her shoulder at him. 'Nothing.'

'I know that look, Jane. It's not nothing.'

She tried to stop her cheesy smile and utterly failed. 'Does anyone else know that this knee is bothering you?'

'No.' His gaze took in her mouth and then moved up to her eyes. 'And you aren't going to tell anyone, are you?'

She laid her cheek on his shoulder. 'Your secret is safe with me, Luc. I would never tell anyone.'

'I know, or I wouldn't be here.' He put his hand on the side of her face and brought the top of her head to his lips. He kissed her hair, and she settled against him. Maybe everything between her and Luc would work out. He trusted her, and while that pricked her guilt, it also gave her hope for the first time since she'd entered into this relationship with him.

Maybe it didn't have to end. Maybe Ken didn't always choose Barbie. Maybe in the end he'd choose her.

*

Luc popped the last of his pretzel into his mouth and leaned back into the Naugahyde chair. Across the table the Hitman dug into a plate of chicken wings, and Luc lifted his gaze from the captain to the empty entrance of the hotel bar.

Outside the hotel, the Phoenix sun was high in the sky and it was seventy-eight degrees. Some of the guys had hit the links, others milled about, and Jane was up in her room writing her *Single Girl* column. She'd told him she'd meet him in the bar when she was through. That had been over an hour ago, and he was tempted to storm her room. But he didn't because he didn't think she'd appreciate it, and despite his impatience, he respected that she had to work.

'Did you hear about the Kovalchuck suspension?' Hitman asked as he wiped his fingers on a napkin.

'What'd he get?'

'Five games.'

'It was a fairly cheap shot,' Fish added from his chair beside the team captain. 'But I've seen worse.'

Daniel Holstrom and Grizzell joined them, and the conversation turned to some of the worst hits in the NHL, with the Chinooks enforcer, Rob Sutter, leading the pack. Manchester and Lynch pushed their chairs to the table and the talk turned from hockey to who would kick whose ass in a fight, Bruce Lee or Jackie Chan. Luc would put his money on Bruce Lee, but he had other things on his mind and didn't enter into the debate. His gaze drifted to the empty doorway once again.

The only time Jane wasn't on his mind was when he was in the net. Somehow, when he'd taken her to bed, she'd crawled inside his head. Sometimes it felt as if she'd crawled into the rest of him too, and he was surprised that he liked her there.

He couldn't say if he was in love with her. The until-death-do-you-part kind of love. The kind that lasted and settled into the comfortable sort of love he wanted. The kind his mother had never found and that his father never waited around for. He only knew that he wanted to be with her, and when he wasn't, he thought about her. He trusted her enough to let her into his life and the life of his sister. He had faith in her that his trust wasn't misplaced.

He liked watching her and talking to her and just being with her. He liked the twists and turns of her mind, and he liked that he could be himself around her. He liked her sense of humor, and he liked having sex with her. No, he loved having sex with her. He loved kissing her, touching her, and being inside of her, looking down into her flushed face. When he was inside of her, he was already scheming ways to get there again. She was the only woman he'd ever been with for whom that was true.

He loved to listen to her little moans, and he loved the way she touched him. He loved when she took control and he was at her mercy. Jane knew what to do with her hands and mouth, and he loved that about her.

But did he love her? The forever kind? Maybe, and he was surprised that it didn't freak him out.

'Luc?'

He removed his gaze from the entrance and looked at the guys. Most of them stood behind the Stromster, looking at a magazine he had open on the table.

'What?'

Daniel held up a copy of *Him* magazine. He was learning to read English again.

'Have you seen this?' Grizzell asked.

'No.'

Daniel handed it to him, opened to the Swede's favorite choice of educational material. 'Read,' he said.

The guys were looking at him as if they expected something. So he turned his attention to the magazine and read:

The Life of Honey Pie

One of my favorite places in the world is the observation deck of the Seattle Space Needle at night. It's like sitting on top of the world. And anyone who knows me, knows I like it on top. I'd just had dinner in the restaurant below, leaving my date, a real dud, sitting at the table awaiting my return from the ladies' room. I was wearing my little red halter dress, with the gold clasp at the back of my neck and the little gold chain that hung halfway down my spine. I'd worn my five-inch heels, and I was in the mood for more than Pacific swordfish. The date was gorgeous, like all my men. But he'd refused to play beneath the table, and I was turned on and bored. A dangerous thing for the men of Seattle.

Luc paused in his reading to glance at the doorway as two women walked in. He didn't need more than a quick glance to know they were rink bunnies. Uninterested, he returned to his reading.

The elevator to my left opened, and a man wearing a black tuxedo stepped out. My gaze ran up the four buttons of his jacket to his blue eyes. His gaze slid to my perfect breasts barely covered in the red halter. The corners of his mouth rose in an appreciative smile, and suddenly my night got a lot more interesting.

I recognized him right away. He played hockey. A goalie with fast hands, and reportedly a very dirty mind. I liked that in a man. He starred in a million or so female fantasies across the country. A time or two, he'd starred in mine.

'Hello,' he said. 'Nice night for watching the stars.'

'Watching is a favorite of mine.' His name was Lucky, which I thought appropriate since, if his smile was any indication, I was about to get lucky.

Luc stopped and looked up at the guys. 'Jesus,' he said. 'This can't be me.' But he had a bad feeling that it was.

I placed my hands on one of the trivia boxes that talked about how many times a year the Needle got struck by lightning, and I leaned forward. The back of my dress slid up my long tan legs, dangerously close to paradise. I looked up at him out of the corner of my eye and smiled. His gaze was stuck in my cleavage, and I tried to work up some guilt over what I was going to do to him. But guilt and I had parted company about twenty years ago, and all I felt was a flutter in my chest and an ache between my legs. 'What about you? Do you like to watch?'

'I'm more of a doer.' He reached toward me and pushed a lock of my hair out of my face. 'It makes it more interesting that way.'

'I like doers, being that I like to be done in a lot of different positions.' I licked my red lips. 'Does that interest you?'

His blue eyes got all sleepy as he slid his hand up my back and his fingers brushed my spine, spreading fire across my flesh. 'What's your name?'

'Honey Pie.'

'I like that,' he said as he stepped behind me. Then he slipped his hands around my stomach and spoke next to my ear. 'How freaky do you get, Miss Honey Pie?'

I leaned back and pressed my round behind into what felt like at least nine inches of good wood. He moved his talented hands to my breasts and cupped me through the thin material of my halter.

I closed my eyes and arched my back. He didn't know it, but he was so dead. 'The last man I was with hasn't recovered.' That had been two days ago, and Lou was still in a coma after I'd left him inside the service elevator at the Four Seasons.

'What did you do to him?'

'I blew his mind . . . among other things.'

My nipples were hard against his hot palms and I was so turned on, a busload of Japanese tourists wouldn't have stopped me from doing this hockey player with the big hard jock. 'You're making me crazy with your red lips and little red dress.' He bit the side of my neck, and asked in a husky whisper, 'Are you cold, or turned on?'

Luc's gaze stopped on the last line, and he backed up and read it one more time.

'Are you cold, or turned on?'

'What the hell?' he whispered as he continued.

I was hot and definitely turned on.
'You make me want to suck a bruise on you just so I can kiss it better.'
'Where?' I asked as I took his hand and slid it between my legs. 'Here?' He cupped me through my dress and red lace thong.

Stunned, Luc dropped the magazine and sat back. He felt as if he'd been hit in the head with a smoking puck. This absolutely could not be happening. He was imagining things that did not exist.

'Do you know Honey Pie?' Bressler asked, letting Luc know he wasn't imagining things.

'No.' But there was something familiar about it. Something real personal.

'You're famous now,' the captain joked. 'Read on. You've been put into a coma by Honey Pie.'

The rest of the guys laughed, but Luc didn't find it at all amusing. No, he found it disturbing.

'Why'd she pick you this time?' Fish wanted to know. 'She must have seen you play and wanted to get a look at your paraphernalia.'

'Maybe she's someone who's seen the paraphernalia,' Lynch added.

Anger welled up in his chest, but he battled it back and said, 'I can guarantee she hasn't seen the paraphernalia.' Anger would only get in the way. He knew that much from experience. He needed a clear head to think. He felt like he was looking at one of those finger puzzles with a big picture on it – a picture of his life – but all the pieces were mixed up. And if he could just get it all in the right order, everything would become clear.

'I'd think it was cool if Honey Pie screwed me into a coma,' someone said.

'She isn't real,' Lynch told everyone.

'She has to be real,' Scott Manchester argued. 'Someone is writing the columns.'

The conversation quickly turned to speculation over where Honey Pie might have seen Luc. They all agreed she lived in Seattle, but they differed on gender. They wondered if Honey Pie had actually met Luc, and if she was actually a man. The general consensus was that if she wasn't a man, she thought like one.

Luc didn't give a flying fuck if Honey Pie was a man or a woman. He'd spent the last two years trying to live down that kind of shit. And here it was again. Fueling the fire he'd been trying to extinguish. Only this time it was worse than ever before.

'It's all made up,' someone said. But it didn't feel at all made up to Luc. It was all so eerily familiar it raised the hair on the back of his neck. The red dress. The part about hard nipples. About being cold or turned on. The red thong panties. Sucking a bruise.

A piece of the puzzle slid into place. It was Jane. Someone had been eavesdropping on him and Jane, but that was impossible. *You make me want to suck a bruise on you just so I can kiss it better* – Luc remembered saying that as he'd touched her soft skin. The night she'd worn the red dress, he'd wanted to leave a mark on her. His mark. Had they been followed? In his mind, he moved a few more pieces of the puzzle, but he still didn't get a clear picture.

'Hey, boys. What are you all doing?'

Luc glanced up from the glossy pages of the magazine to Jane's green eyes. He would have to tell her. She'd freak out.

'Sharky,' the guys greeted her.

The corners of her lips tilted up slightly as she looked at him. Then her gaze fell on the open magazine and her little smile froze.

'Have you ever heard of *The Life of Honey Pie*?' Sutter asked her.

Jane's gaze locked with Luc's. 'Yes. I have.'

'Honey Pie wrote about Luc.'

Color drained from her already pale complexion. 'Are you sure it's you?'

'Positive.'

'I'm sorry, Luc.'

Luc rose from his chair. She understood what it meant. To him. She understood even what the rest of the guys didn't. Now, when anything was written about him, the Honey Pie article would be mentioned, just one more excuse to dissect his private life. To dig into the stuff that just didn't matter. He moved to her and looked into her eyes. 'Are you okay?'

She nodded, then shook her head.

Without thinking about it, Luc took her arm and they walked from the bar. They crossed the lobby and entered the elevator. 'I'm so sorry, Luc,' she said just above a whisper.

'It's not your fault, Jane.' He punched the number to her floor, then glanced over at her. She stood in the corner of the elevator. Her eyes were huge and filling with water and she suddenly looked very small. By the time they got to her hotel room, tears were falling down her cheeks. He hadn't even told her of his bizarre suspicions and she was already crying.

'Jane,' he began as soon the door shut behind him. 'I know this will sound crazy . . .' He paused to sort it all out in his head. 'There are some things in that Honey Pie piece-of-shit article that are just too close to be a coincidence. Things that were written about you and me that actually happened. I don't know how she knew so much. It's like someone was watching us and taking notes.'

She sat down on the edge of the bed and stuck her hands between her knees. She didn't say anything, and he continued to try and explain what he didn't understand. 'Your red dress, for one. She described your red dress with the chain down the back.'

'Oh, God.'

He sat down beside her and put his arm around her shoulders. The things the writer of the article knew about him were disturbing. Jane was already so upset, he didn't go into any more detail because he didn't want to scare her more than necessary. 'I can't believe this is starting up again. I've been careful to get away from this sort of crap.' He gave her a squeeze. Thoughts tumbled in his head but made no sense 'I feel crazy. Paranoid. A little insane. Maybe I should hire a PI to get to the bottom of this.'

She jumped up as if her pants had caught fire and walked to the chair by the window. She chewed on her bottom lip and gazed somewhere over the top of his head. 'You're not flattered?'

'Hell, no! I feel like some total stranger has been watching me. Us. Sneaking around, hiding in the shadows.'

'We would have noticed someone following us.'

'You're probably right, but I don't know how else to explain the things in that magazine. I know how crazy it sounds.' And it did sound crazy Even to him, and he'd read it. 'Maybe one of the guys . . .' He shook his head as he thought out loud. 'I don't like to think that one of the guys had something to do with this, but who else?' He shrugged. 'Maybe I've lost my mind.'

She looked at him for several long moments, then said in a rush, 'I wrote it.'

'What?'

'I write the *Honey Pie* serial.'

'What?'

She took a deep breath and said, 'I'm Honey Pie.'

'Right.'

'I am,' she said through her tears.

'Why are you saying this?'

'Damn it! I can't believe I'm going to have to prove it to you. I never even wanted you to find out about it.' She wiped her cheeks and folded her arms across her chest. 'Who else would know that you asked me if I was cold or turned on? We were alone in my apartment.'

And then, one by one, the pieces of the puzzle slid into place. The things that only he and Jane knew. The note he'd seen stuck in her day planner reminding her of some 'Honey Pie' decision she had to make. Jane was Honey Pie. She couldn't be. 'No.'

'Yes.'

He stood and looked across the room at Jane. At the

dark curls he loved to touch. Her smooth white skin and pink mouth he loved to kiss. This woman looked like Jane, but if she was really Honey Pie, she was not the woman he thought he knew.

'Now you don't have to hire someone,' she said as if that were some damn consolation. 'And you don't have to suspect one of the guys.'

He stared into her eyes as if he could see the unbelievable truth written there. What he saw was guilt. His chest felt suddenly hollow. He'd trusted her enough to let her into his home and his life. His sister's life too. He felt like such an ass.

'I wrote it the night after you kissed me the first time. You could say I was inspired by you.' She dropped her hands to her sides. 'I wrote it a long time before we became involved.'

'Not that long.' Even to himself, his voice sounded strange. Like his chest, hollow, waiting for his anger to rise up and fill it. It would, but not yet. 'You've always known how I feel about that made-up bullshit being written about me. I told you.'

'I know, but please don't be angry. Or rather, be angry, because you have every right. It's just that . . .' Her tears filled her eyes again and she wiped at them with her fingers. 'It's just that I was so attracted to you, and you kissed me and I wrote it.'

'And sent it in to be published in a porno magazine.'

'I was hoping you'd be flattered.'

'You knew I wouldn't be.' The anger he'd been holding swelled in his chest. He had to get out of there. He had to get away from Jane. The woman he'd thought he was falling in love with. 'You must have had a real good laugh when I thought you were a prude. When I thought my fantasies would shock you.'

She shook her head. 'No.'

Not only had she betrayed his trust in her, she'd made a raging fool of him. 'What else am I going to read about myself?'

'Nothing.'

'Right.' He walked to the door and reached for the handle.

'Luc, wait! Don't go.' He paused. Her voice came to him, filled with tears and the same stabbing pain that twisted in his gut. 'Please,' she cried. 'We can work this out. I can make this up to you.'

He didn't turn around. He didn't want to see her. 'I don't think so, Jane.'

'I love you.'

Her words were one more knife to his back, and the anger he'd been holding back finally broke free. He thought he would come apart with it. 'Then I would hate to see what you do to people you don't love.' He opened the door. 'Stay the hell away from me, and stay away from my sister.'

He moved down the hall. The busy pattern of the carpet was a blur. Jane was Honey Pie. His Jane. Even though he knew it was true, he was having a real hard time swallowing it all at once.

He walked into his room and leaned back against the closed door. The whole time he'd thought she was a prude, she wrote porn. The whole time he'd thought she was uptight, she knew more about sex than he did. The whole time they'd been together, he'd trusted her and she was taking notes.

She'd said she loved him. He didn't believe her for a second. He'd trusted her and she'd stabbed him in the back. She'd used him to write her porn article. She'd known how he'd feel about it, and she'd done it anyway.

The whole time he'd been careful not to make her feel like a groupie, she was actually . . . What was Honey Pie? A nymphomaniac?

Was Jane a nymphomaniac? No. Was she? He didn't know. He didn't know a thing about her.

The only thing he knew for certain was that he was a damn fool.

On the Limp: Injured

She'd been a fool. Several times over. First for falling in love with Luc, even as she'd known he'd break her heart. Then for looking him in the face and telling him that she was Honey Pie. He *hadn't* known. Chances were that he never would have known.

She knew, and it had burned like a charcoal briquet right beneath her sternum. In the end she'd told him to relieve his mind. He'd been so freaked out thinking that someone was lurking in the shadows... and she supposed someone was. Her. And she'd told him to relieve her own conscience. So why didn't she feel better?

Jane tossed her suitcase on the floor and burst into tears. She'd spent roughly seven hours in taxis or airports or on planes trying to get home. Trying to keep it together. She couldn't anymore. The pain of losing Luc racked her body and huge sobs tore at her lungs. She'd known losing him would hurt, but she'd never imagined so much pain was even possible.

Moonlight poured through the window of the small bedroom in her apartment, and she shut the curtain. Shutting herself up in darkness. She'd taken the first available flight out of Phoenix that afternoon. She'd had a two-hour layover in San Francisco before continuing on to Seattle. She was a physical and emotional wreck. She'd had to leave. She hadn't had a choice. She could not have walked into the locker room the next night and seen Luc's face. She would have fallen apart. Right there in front of everyone.

Before she left, she'd called Darby and told him she had a family emergency. She was needed at home, and she would catch up with the team once they returned to Seattle. Even though there was nothing in it for Darby, he'd helped arrange her flight, and she realized that he was more than just a cocky wheeler-dealer. There was a heart beneath those thousand-dollar suits and bad ties. And just maybe he would be good for Caroline.

She'd called Kirk Thornton, too. He hadn't been as understanding as Darby. He'd asked the nature of the emergency and she'd been forced to lie. She'd told him that her father had a heart attack. When it was actually her whose heart was breaking.

She fell onto her bed and closed her eyes. She couldn't stop thinking about Luc or remembering his face when she'd walked into the sports bar. He'd looked stunned, as if someone had hit him with a brick. She could recall every excruciating detail. The worst was his concern for her. And when he'd finally accepted that she was Honey Pie, his concern had turned to contempt. In that moment, she'd known she'd lost him forever.

Jane rolled onto her side and touched the pillow next

to her. Luc had been the last person to lay his head on that pillow. She ran her hand over the soft cotton case, then she held it to her nose. She could almost smell him.

Regret and anger mixed with the pain in her soul, and she wished she hadn't told him that she loved him. She wished he didn't know. Mostly, she wished he'd cared. But he hadn't.

Then I would hate to see what you do to people you don't love, he'd said.

Tossing the pillow aside, she sat up in bed and wiped the tears from her cheeks. She changed into a large T-shirt, then moved through her dark apartment to the kitchen. She opened the refrigerator and looked inside. It had been a while since she'd cleaned it out. She grabbed an old jar with one pickle chip floating on top and set it on the counter. She reached for an empty bottle of mustard and a half gallon of milk a week past its pull date and put them by the pickle jar. Her chest ached and her head felt like it was stuffed with cotton. She would love to fall asleep until the pain went away, but even if that were possible, when she woke, she would face it again.

The telephone rang, and when it stopped, she took the receiver off the hook. She got her garbage can and some Formula 409 from beneath the sink and set them next to her within the light from the refrigerator. She cleaned to keep busy. To keep from completely going insane. It didn't help because she relived every wonderful and exciting and horrible moment she'd spent with Luc Martineau. She remembered the way he threw a dart as if he could muscle a bull's-eye. The way he rode his motorcycle and how it had felt to ride behind him. She recalled the exact color of his eyes and hair. The sound of his voice and the scent of his skin. The touch of his hands and body pressed to her. The taste of him in her mouth. They way he looked at her during sex.

She loved everything about Luc. But he didn't love her. She'd known it would end. Eventually. The *Honey Pie* column had just prompted the inevitable. Even if she'd never sent it in, even if she'd never even written it, a relationship between her and Luc wouldn't have worked out, despite her hope to the contrary. Ken hooked up with Barbie. Mick dated supermodels, and Brad married Jennifer. Period. That was life. The breakup was not her fault. He would have left. It was probably a good thing he'd left now, she told herself, instead of in a few more months when she would have discovered even more to love about him. When it would have hurt worse. Although she couldn't imagine anything hurting worse. She felt as if a part of her had died.

Jane set her 409 on the counter and glanced across her apartment at her briefcase tossed on the coffee table.

There are some things in that Honey Pie piece-of-shit article that are just too close to be a coincidence, he'd said.

She'd always figured he'd recognize himself in the column, but she hadn't figured he'd recognize her. She moved to the couch and sat. *Things that were written about you and me that actually happened*. She pulled out her laptop and turned it on. She brought up her *Honey Pie* folder and clicked on the March file. Until now, she'd been reluctant to read it. Afraid it was horrible and not flattering and not as good as she'd originally thought or intended. As she read, she was struck by how obvious she'd made it that it *was* her. It would have been more surprising if he hadn't suspected anything. The more she read, the more she wondered if she'd left clues on purpose. It was almost as if she were jumping up and down from the pages and waving her arms and yelling, *It's me, Luc. It's Jane. I wrote this.*

Had she wanted him to figure out that she'd written the column? No. Of course not. That would be stupid. That would mean she'd purposely sabotaged the relationship.

She sat back and looked across the room at the fireplace mantel. At the photo of her and Caroline. At the crystal shark Luc had given her. When had she fallen in love with him? Was it the night of the banquet? The first night he'd kissed her? Or the day he'd bought her the hockey book all tied up in a pink bow? Perhaps she'd fallen a little in love with him all of those times.

She supposed the time didn't matter as much as the bigger question. Was what Caroline always said about her true? Did she enter relationships with one foot out the door? With an eye toward the exit sign? Had she purposely written the article in such an obvious way to get out of her relationship with Luc before she fell too deep? If that was the case, she'd gotten out too late. She'd fallen deeper and harder than ever before. She hadn't even known it was possible to fall so hard.

Her doorbell rang and she rose from the couch. It was past two a.m., and she couldn't imagine who'd be standing on her porch. Her heart pinched even as she told herself that it wasn't Luc, racing across the country after her like Dustin Hoffman in *The Graduate*.

It was Caroline.

'I called all the hospitals,' her friend said as she hugged Jane tight against her chest. 'No one would give me any information.'

'About what?' Jane extracted herself from Caroline's grasp and took a step back.

'Your father.' Caroline lowered her chin and peered into Jane's eyes. 'His heart attack.'

Jane shook her head and rubbed her chilled arms through her long T-shirt. 'My dad didn't have a heart attack.'

'Darby called me and told me that he did!'

Oh, no. 'That's what I told the paper, but I just needed to come home and I needed a good excuse.'

'Mr. Alcott isn't dying?'

'No.'

'I'm glad to hear it, of course.' Caroline sat hard on the sofa. 'But I ordered flowers.'

Jane sat next to her. 'Sorry. Can you cancel them?'

'I don't know.' Caroline turned and looked at her. 'Why the lie? Why did you have to come home? And why have you been crying?'

'Have you read *Honey Pie* this month?'

Caroline usually read all the columns. 'Of course.'

'It was Luc.'

'I gathered that. Was he flattered?'

'Not at all,' Jane answered, and then she told her why. Through tears that wouldn't stop, she told her friend everything. When she was finished, a frown pulled at Caroline's brows.

'You already know what I'm going to say.'

Yes, Jane knew. And for the first time she actually listened. Jane had always been the smart one. Caroline the pretty one. Tonight Caroline was the pretty *and* smart one.

'Can you fix it?' Caroline asked.

Jane recalled the look in Luc's eyes and him telling her to stay away from him and Marie. He'd meant it. 'No. He would never listen to me now.' She leaned back against the sofa and looked up at the ceiling. 'Men suck.' Jane rolled her head and looked at her friend. 'Let's make a pact to swear off men for a while.'

Caroline bit her lip. 'I can't. I'm sort of dating Darby now.'

Jane sat up straight. 'Really? I didn't know things had gotten that serious.'

'Well, he isn't my usual type. But he's nice to me and I like him. I like talking to him and I like the way he looks at me. And, well, let's face it, he needs me.'

Yes, he certainly did. Jane figured Darby could probably fill Caroline up with a lifetime of need.

The next morning, Jane received flowers from the Chinooks organization expressing their condolences. At noon, flowers from the *Times*, and at one, Darby sent his own arrangement. At three, Caroline's were delivered. They were all gorgeous and smelled wonderful and filled her with guilt. This was pure karmic retribution, and she promised God that she would never lie again if He would make the flowers stop.

On television that night, she watched the Chinooks play the Coyotes. Through the wire of his mask, Luc's blue eyes looked out at her, as hard and as cold as the ice he played on. When he wasn't cursing the air blue in front of his net, his lips were compressed into a grim line.

He looked up and the camera caught the anger in his eyes. He wasn't in his zone. His personal life was affecting his game, and if Jane had harbored any hidden hope that she could fix the relationship, that hope died.

It was truly over.

Luc drew three penalties as he let his rage loose on anyone dumb enough to step inside his crease.

'What's the matter, Martineau?' a Coyote forward asked after the first penalty. 'Got your period?'

'Kiss my hairy beanbag,' he answered, hooked his stick in the guy's skates, and pulled him off his feet.

'You're an asshole, Martineau,' the guy said as he looked up from his position on the ice. Whistles blew and Bruce Fish was sent to the penalty box instead of Luc.

Luc picked up his water bottle and sprayed his face. Mark Bressler joined him at the net.

'Having an anger management problem?' the captain asked.

'What the fuck do you think?' Water dripped from his face and mask. Jane wasn't in the press box. She wasn't even in the same state, but he couldn't get her out of his head.

'That's what the fuck I think.' Bressler punched his shoulder with his big glove. 'Try not to draw any more penalties and we just might win this thing.'

He was right. Luc needed to concentrate more on the game than on who was or wasn't in the press box. 'No more dumb penalties,' he agreed. But in the next frame, he whacked an opponent in the shin and the guy milked it for all it was worth.

'That didn't hurt, you pussy,' Luc said as he looked down at the guy holding his shin and writhing in pain. 'Get back up and I'll show you hurt.'

The whistles blew and Bressler skated by, shaking his head.

After the game, the locker room was more subdued than usual. They'd put up two goals late in the third period, but it hadn't been enough. They'd lost three–five. Phoenix sports reporters combed the room searching for sound bites, but no one was talking much.

Jane's father had suffered a heart attack, and the players felt her absence. Luc didn't believe the heart attack story, and was surprised that she'd turned tail and run. That wasn't like the Jane he knew. Then again, he didn't really know her at all. The real Jane had lied to him and used him and made a fool out of him. She knew things about him that he did not want to read in the newspapers. She knew that he iced down his knees and that everything wasn't one hundred percent.

He was an idiot. How in the hell had he let a short reporter with curly hair and a smart mouth into his life? He hadn't even liked her at first. How had he fallen so hard for her? She'd turned his life upside down and now he had to figure a way to get her out of his head. To get his focus back. He could do it. He'd battled back before, and he'd battled bigger demons than Jane Alcott. He figured all he needed was determination and a little time. Darby had told the team she wouldn't be back to work until next week.

One week. Now that she was out of his life physically, it shouldn't take that much time to get her the hell out of his head and get mentally back into the game.

And a week later, he was right. Partly, anyhow. He was back in his zone. Back to playing with skill instead of brute strength fueled by emotion, but he'd failed to get Jane out of his head completely.

The day he returned to Seattle, he felt bruised inside and out. He just wanted to sit on his couch, relax, and watch mindless television until Marie came home from school. Maybe they'd order out and have a nice relaxing dinner.

He should have known better. Like always with his sister, one minute things were fine, and the next everything went straight to hell. One minute she was filling him in on her day at school, then she took off her big bulky sweatshirt. Luc's jaw dropped when he got a good look at her tight T-shirt and her breasts. They were a lot bigger than when he'd left on his trip a week ago. Not that he stared, but he couldn't help but notice the difference.

'What are you wearing?'

'My BEBE shirt.'

'Your boobs are a lot bigger than they were last week. Are you wearing a padded bra?'

She folded her arms over her chest like he was a pervert. 'It's a water bra.'

'You can't wear that outside the apartment.' He couldn't let her outside with her breasts pushed up and out like that.

'I wore it to school all last week.'

Holy shit, he'd bet just about anything that the guys at her school had stared at her chest too. All week. While he'd been on the road. Christ, his life was a mess. A whole churning cauldron of crapola. 'I bet the guys at your school had a real good time staring at your hooters. And you can bet they weren't thinking very nice things about you.'

'Hooters,' she gasped. 'That's disgusting. You're so mean to me. You always say mean things.'

Hooters wasn't a bad word. Was it? 'I'm telling you how guys think. If you show up in a big padded bra, with your *breasts* falling out, they'll think you're smutty.'

She looked at him as if he were a child molester instead of her brother who wanted to protect her from the little perverts at her school. 'You're sick.'

Sick? 'No, I'm not. I'm just trying to tell you the truth.'

'You're not my mom or my dad. You can't tell me what to do.'

'You're right. I'm not Dad and I'm not your mother. I may not be the best brother either, but I am all you've got.'

Tears leaked from her eyes and messed up her makeover. 'I hate you, Luc.'

'No, you don't. You're just throwing a fit because I won't let you walk around in a padded bra.'

'I bet you like women who walk around in padded bras.'

Actually, he'd grown an affection for, and an obsession with, small breasts.

'You're a hypocrite, Luc. I'll bet your girlfriends wear padded bras.'

Out of all the women he'd known, the one woman who had fascinated him the most didn't wear a bra. He wondered what that said about him. He tried not to care, but he did. His cauldron of crapola churned a bit more.

'Marie, you're sixteen,' he reasoned. 'You can't walk around in a bra that turns boys on. You'll have to wear something else. Maybe a bra that has locking hooks.' That last he'd thrown in to be funny. As always, she failed to share his humor. His sister burst into tears.

'I want to go to boarding school,' she wailed and ran to her bedroom.

Her mention of boarding school set him back on his heels. He hadn't thought of boarding school for a while. If he sent her to boarding school, he wouldn't have to worry about her wearing padded bras when he was out of town. His life would be simpler. But suddenly the thought of her going away held not the slightest appeal. She was a pain and moody, but she was his sister. He was getting used to having her around, and the thought of boarding school no longer seemed like any kind of solution.

He followed her to her room and leaned a shoulder into the doorframe. She lay on her bed staring up at the ceiling, her arms spread out like she was a martyr on the cross.

'Do you really want to go to boarding school?' he asked.

'I know you don't want me here.'

'I've never said that.' They'd had this conversation before. 'And it's not true.'

'You want to get rid of me,' she sobbed. 'So I'll go away to school.'

He knew what she needed to hear and what he needed to say. For her as much as for him. He'd been indecisive long enough. 'Too late.' He folded his arms across his chest. 'You're not going anywhere. You live here with me. If you don't like it, that's too damn bad.'

She looked over at him then. 'Even if I want to go?'

'Yeah,' he said and was surprised at how much he meant it. 'Even if you want to go, you're stuck here. You're my sister and I want you to live with me.' He shrugged. 'You're a pain in the keister, but I like having you around bugging me.'

She was quiet a minute, then whispered, 'Okay. I'll stay.'

'Okay, then.' He pushed away from the doorframe and moved into the living room. He looked out the tall windows toward the bay. His relationship with his sister wasn't the best. Their living arrangement was less than ideal; he was gone almost as much as he was in town. But he wanted to know her before she left for college and grew into an adult.

Over the past sixteen years, he should have seen her more. He certainly could have. He had no excuses. No good ones, anyway. He'd been so wrapped up in his own life, he hadn't thought about her all that much. And that made him ashamed for all the times he'd been in LA and had never made a real effort to see her. To know her. He'd always known that made him a selfish bastard. He just hadn't ever really thought there was anything wrong with being selfish – until now.

He heard her soft footsteps and he turned around. With her cheeks still wet and mascara running down her face, she wrapped her arms around him and laid her head on his chest. 'I like living here bugging you.'

'Good.' He hugged her. 'I know I can never take the place of your mother or dad, but I'll try to make you happy.'

'I was very happy today.'

'You still can't wear that bra.'

She was quiet a moment, then gave a long-suffering sigh. 'Fine.'

They looked out the windows together for a long time. She talked about her mother, and she told him the reason she kept the dried flowers on her dresser. He guessed he understood, although he did think it was creepy. She told him she'd talked about it with Jane too, and that Jane had told her she would put them away someday when she was ready.

Jane. What was he going to do about Jane? All he'd wanted was a peaceful life. That's it, but he hadn't had a peaceful moment since he'd met Jane. No, that wasn't true. When she'd been with him for those few short weeks, his life had been better than he could ever remember. Being with her was like being home for the first time since he'd moved to Seattle. But that had been an illusion.

She said she loved him. He knew better than to believe it, but deep down in a place he couldn't ignore, he wanted that lie to be true. He was a sucker and a chump. He would see her tomorrow night for the first time in a week, but he hoped that, like all pain, after the initial sting he'd become numb and wouldn't feel it anymore.

That's what he hoped, but that wasn't what happened when she walked into the locker room the next night. Luc felt her presence even before he glanced up and saw her. The impact of seeing her slammed in his chest and left him winded. When she spoke, her voice poured through him, and against his iron will, he soaked her up like a dry sponge. He was in love with her. There was no denying it to himself any longer. He'd fallen in love with Jane, and he didn't have a clue what to do about it. As he sat there with his feet jammed into his untied skates and the laces in his hands, he watched her walk toward him, and with each step his heart felt like it was pounding a hole in his chest.

Dressed in black, with her smooth white skin, she

looked the same as always. Her dark hair curled about her face, and he forced himself to lace his skates, when what he really wanted to do was shake her, then hold her tight until he absorbed all of her.

The hardest thing Jane had ever done was walk across the locker room and face Luc. When she approached, he looked down at his laces. For several long seconds she watched him lace his skates, and when he wouldn't look up at her, she spoke to the top of his head. 'Big dumb dodo.' She balled her hands into fists to keep from reaching out and touching his hair. 'I want you to know,' she said, 'that I have no intention of writing anything about you ever again.'

Finally he looked up. His brows were drawn over the turmoil in his blue eyes. 'Do you expect me to believe you?'

She shook her head. Her heart cried for him. For her. For what they might have had together. 'No. I don't, but I thought I'd tell you anyway.' She looked at him one last time, then walked away. She joined Darby and Caroline in the press box and took out her laptop to take notes.

'How's your father?' Darby asked, heaping more guilt on her head.

'He's feeling much better. He's at home now.'

'His recovery has been amazing,' Caroline added with a knowing smile.

After the first period, the Chinooks scored a goal against the Ottawa Senators, but the Senators rallied in the second frame and put up a goal of their own. When the final buzzer sounded, the Chinooks won by two points.

As Jane moved to the locker room once again, she wondered how much longer she could take this. Seeing Luc constantly was more than her heart could take. She didn't know how much longer she could continue covering the Chinooks, even though it meant giving up the best job she'd ever had and a chance for a better career.

She took a deep breath and entered the locker room. Luc sat in front of his stall as usual. He was bare from the waist up. His arms were folded across his chest, and he watched her as if he were trying to figure out a puzzle. She asked as few questions of the players as possible and beat a hasty exit before she broke into tears in front of the team. They'd assume she was crying because of her sick father and would probably send her more flowers.

She practically ran from the room, but when she was halfway to the exit, she stopped. If ever there was something she needed to stick around and fight for, Luc was that something. Even if he told her he hated her, at least she would know.

She turned and leaned a shoulder into the cinder block wall, in the same place Luc had once waited for her. He was the first to enter the tunnel, and his gaze locked with hers as he walked toward her, looking obscenely handsome in his suit and red tie. With her heart in her throat, she straightened and stepped in front of him. 'Do you have a minute?'

'Why?'

'I wanted to talk to you. I have something I need to say, and think it's important.'

He looked behind him at the empty tunnel, opened the janitor's closet they'd been in before, and shoved her inside. He flipped on the light as the door shut behind them, sealing them together in the same place where he'd once kissed her passionately. As she gazed into his face, he neither smiled nor frowned, and his eyes looked tired but gave nothing away. Nothing of the emotion she'd seen earlier in the locker room.

'I thought you needed to say something.'

She nodded and leaned back against the closed door. The scent of his skin filled her with a visceral memory and deep longing. Now that the time had come, she didn't know where to begin. So she just talked. 'I want to tell you again how sorry I am for the *Honey Pie* column. I know you probably don't believe me, and I don't blame you.' She shook her head. 'At the time I wrote it, I was falling in love with you, and I just sat down and poured out my fantasy about you. I wasn't even sure if I was going to send it in. I just wrote, and when I was through, I knew it was the best thing I'd ever written.' She pushed away from the door and walked past him in the small closet. She couldn't look at him and tell him everything that needed to be said. 'When I finished it, I knew I shouldn't send it in, because I knew you wouldn't like it. I knew how you felt about untrue things written about you. You'd made that really clear.' With her back to him, she wrapped her hand around a part of the metal shelving. 'I sent it anyway.'

'Why?'

Why? This was the hard part. 'Because I loved you and you didn't love me. I'm not the kind of woman you date. I'm short and flat-chested and I can hardly dress myself. I didn't think you'd ever care for me the way I care for you.'

'So you did it to get back at me?'

She looked over her shoulder and forced herself to turn and face him. To face the contempt she might once again see in his eyes. 'No. If I'd wanted just to get back at you for not loving me, I would have kept myself anonymous.' She folded her arms across her chest as if to keep her pain from spilling out on the floor. 'I did it to end the relationship before it began. So I could blame the article. So that I wouldn't get in too deep.'

He shook his head. 'That doesn't make sense.'

'No. I'm sure it doesn't to you, but it does to me.'

'That's the most ass-backward excuse I've ever heard.'

Her heart sank. He didn't believe her. 'I've been thinking a lot this past week, and I've realized that in every relationship with a man that I've had, I've always entered an escape hatch just in case I might get hurt. The *Honey Pie* column was my escape hatch. Problem was, I didn't get out fast enough.' She took a deep breath and slowly let it out. 'I love you, Luc. I fell in love with you, and I was so afraid that you would never love me. Instead of thinking a relationship with you was doomed to end, I should have fought to keep it together. I should have . . . I don't exactly know what. But I do know it ended badly. I take the blame for that, and I'm sorry.' When he didn't say anything, her heart plummeted further. There was nothing left to say except, 'I was hoping we could still be friends.'

He raised a dubious brow. 'You want to be friends?'

'Yes.'

'No.'

She'd never thought one little word could hurt so much.

'I don't want to be your friend, Jane.'

'I understand.' She put her head down and moved past him to the door. She hadn't thought she had any more tears to shed. She thought she'd cried them all, but she was wrong. She didn't care if the rest of the Chinooks were in the tunnel; she had to get out of there before she fell apart. She twisted the door handle and pulled, but nothing happened. She pulled harder, but the door didn't budge. She turned the lock, but it still didn't open. She looked up and saw Luc's hands above her head holding the door shut.

'What are you doing?' she asked as she turned to face him. He stood so close her nose was inches from his chest and she could smell the clean cotton scent of his dress shirt mixed with his deodorant.

'Don't play games, Jane.'

'I'm not.'

'Then why do you tell me you love me in one breath, and then in the next tell me you just want to be friends?' He placed his fingers beneath her chin and lifted her gaze to his. 'I have friends. I want more from you than that. I'm a selfish guy, Jane. If I can't be your lover, if I can't have all of you, then I don't want anything.' He lowered his face to hers and kissed her, a soft press of his lips to hers, and the tears she'd been trying to hold back filled her eyes. Her hands grasped the front of his shirt and she held on tight. She would be his lover, and this time she wouldn't invent reasons to get out. She wanted this too much.

He slid his mouth across her cheek and he whispered in her ear, 'I love you, Jane. And I've missed you. My life has been total shit without you.'

She pulled back and looked into his face. 'Say it again.'

He raised his hands to her face and brushed his thumbs across her cheeks. 'I love you, and I want to be with you because you make my life better.' He pushed her hair behind her ear. 'You asked me once what I see when I look into my future.' He slid his palm down her shoulder and took her hand. 'I see you,' he said and kissed her knuckles.

'You're not mad at me?' she asked.

He shook his head and his lips brushed the backs of her fingers. 'I thought I was. I thought I'd be mad at you forever, but I'm not. I don't really understand your reasons for sending that column in, but I just don't care anymore. I think I was more pissed off about feeling like a fool than about the actual column.' He placed her palm on his chest. 'When I saw you waiting for me, my anger evaporated and I knew I'd be a bigger fool if I let you go. I want to spend the rest of my life getting to know your secrets.'

'I don't have any more secrets.'

'Are you sure there isn't at least one?' He wrapped an arm around her back and kissed her neck.

'Like what?'

'Like you're a nymphomaniac?'

'Are you serious?'

'Well . . . yes.'

Jane shook her head and managed a weak, 'No,' before she burst out laughing.

'Shh.' Luc pulled back and looked into her face. 'Someone will hear you and bust in on us.'

She couldn't stop laughing and so he silenced her with his mouth. His lips were warm and welcoming and she slid into the kiss with the abandon of a true nympho. Because sometimes in life, Ken didn't always choose Barbie. For that, he had to be rewarded.

Epilogue:

She Shoots! She Scores!

Luc stepped off the elevator to the observation deck of the Space Needle and looked to his left. A woman in a red dress looked out at the glittering skyline of downtown Seattle. Her hair fell to her shoulders in soft dark curls, and a warm August breeze tossed a few strands about her face. They'd just finished having dinner in the restaurant below, and as he waited for the bill, she slipped away to the upper deck.

As she watched him walk toward her, the corners of her red mouth turned up in a seductive smile.

'Nice night for watching stars,' he said.

She bit her bottom lip, then spoke just above a whisper, 'Do you like to watch?'

'I'm more of a doer.' He wrapped his arms around her and pulled her back against his chest. 'And right now, I want to do my wife.'

'That's not in the script,' Jane said as she rested against him.

They'd been married for five weeks now. Five weeks

of waking with her every morning. Of looking at her across their dinner table, and then loading the dishwasher together. Of watching her brush her teeth and pull on her socks. Never in a million years would he have ever thought those mundane, ordinary things could be so sexy.

Most of all, he liked to watch her work. To create all those erotic stories in her head. To look beyond that natural girl face, and see the real woman.

Since their engagement, she no longer wrote about being single in Seattle. And Chris Evans was back from his medical leave, working his sports beat. The *Times* had let Jane go completely, and now she was the newest sports reporter for their rival, the *Seattle Post-Intelligencer*.

They'd had to plan the wedding around the Stanley Cup playoffs, and since Luc had been out of town about half the time, Jane and Marie and Caroline had done the planning mostly on their own. Which had been just fine with him. All he'd had to do was show up in a tux and say, 'I do.' That part had been easy. Watching her dance with every damn Chinook at the reception had been difficult.

A few months before the wedding, the Chinooks had made it to the finals, but they got beat out for the Cup by the Colorado Avalanche in the third round. Luc lowered his face and buried his nose in Jane's hair. There was always next year.

'Do you want to go somewhere else?' she asked.

They'd spent a lot of time exploring Seattle together. Him and Jane and Marie. Jane knew all the good spots and the places to avoid. 'I want to go home,' he said. Marie was spending the night with Hanna, and Luc wanted to take advantage of some time alone with his wife. 'What do you say?'

She turned and wrapped her arms around him. 'Home is my favorite place.'

Home was his favorite place too. But home for him was anywhere Jane happened to be. Never in his life had he loved someone as much as he loved her. So much that it scared him sometimes.

He pulled her against him and looked out over the city. He was in love with his wife. Yeah, he knew what that said about him. That he was a goner. Leg-shackled for life. Whipped by a short woman with a big attitude.

Yep, that's what it said about him, and he didn't care.

Pick up a *little black dress* – it's a girl thing.

978 0 7553 3746 0

IT MUST BE LOVE
Rachel Gibson
PB £4.99

Gabrielle Breedlove is the sexiest suspect that undercover cop Joe Shanahan has ever had the pleasure of tailing. But when he's assigned to pose as her boyfriend things start to get complicated.

She thinks he's stalking her. He thinks she's a crook. Surely, it must be love?

ONE NIGHT STAND
Julie Cohen
PB £4.99

When popular novelist Estelle Connor finds herself pregnant after an uncharacteristic one-night stand, she enlists the help of sexy neighbour Hugh to help look for the father. But will she find what she really needs?

One of the freshest and funniest voices in romantic fiction

978 0 7553 3483 4

Pick up a *little black dress* – it's a girl thing.

THE TRUE NAOMI STORY
A.M. Goldsher
PB £4.99

Naomi Braver is catapulted from waiting tables to being the new rock sensation overnight. But stardom isn't all it's cracked up to be . . . Can Naomi master the game of fame before it's too late?

A rock'n'roll romance about one girl's journey to stardom

978 0 7553 3992 1

FORGET ABOUT IT
Caprice Crane
PB £4.99

When Jordan Landeua is hit by a car, she seizes the opportunity to start over and fakes amnesia. But just as she's said goodbye to Jordan the pushover, the unthinkable happens and she has to start over for real. Will she remember in time what truly makes her happy?

978 0 7553 4204 4

Pick up a *little black dress* – it's a girl thing.

TANGLED UP IN YOU
Rachel Gibson
PB £4.99

Sex, lies and tequila slammers

When Maddie Dupree arrives at Hennessy's bar looking for the truth about her past she doesn't want to be distracted by head-turning, heart-stopping owner Mick Hennessy. Especially as he doesn't know why she's really in town . . .

978 0 7553 3959 4

SPIRIT WILLING, FLESH WEAK
Julie Cohen
PB £4.99

Welcome to the world of Julie Cohen, one of the freshest, funniest voices in romantic fiction!

When fake psychic Rosie meets a gorgeous investigative journalist, she thinks she can trust him not to blow her cover – but is she right?

978 0 7553 3481 0

You can buy any of these other
Little Black Dress titles from your
bookshop or *direct from the publisher*.

FREE P&P AND UK DELIVERY
(Overseas and Ireland £3.50 per book)

TO ORDER SIMPLY CALL THIS NUMBER

01235 400 414

or visit our website: www.headline.co.uk

Prices and availability subject to change without notice.